DEATH BOOKS
A RETURN

ALSO BY MARION MOORE HILL:

The Deadly Past Mystery Series:
Deadly Will

The Scrappy Librarian Series:
Bookmarked for Murder

DEATH BOOKS A RETURN

MARION MOORE HILL

PEMBERLEY PRESS
CORONA DEL MAR

Published by
PEMBERLEY PRESS
P O Box 1027
Corona del Mar, CA 92625
www.pemberleypress.com

A member of The Authors Studio
www.theauthorsstudio.org

The Scrappy Librarian Mystery Series

Cover art and design by Andree Valley

ISBN13 978-0-9771913-6-9
LCCN 2008009326

Library of Congress Cataloging-in-Publication Data

Hill, Marion Moore, 1937-
Death books a return / Marion Moore Hill.
p. cm. -- (The scrappy librarian mystery series)
ISBN 978-0-9771913-6-9 (pbk. : alk. paper) 1. Librarians--Fiction. 2. Race relations--Fiction. 3. Oklahoma--Fiction. I. Title.
PS3608.I4348D45 2006
813'.6--dc22

2008009326

The Scrappy Librarian series is dedicated to librarians everywhere: those gentle souls who inspire children's love of books, those tenacious bloodhounds who track down researchers' sources, and those heroic opponents of limits on what we all can know.

One

Juanita rapped a fourth time on the cloudy door pane. No response this time either. No light appeared behind the curtained windows of the shabby frame house, no sound came from within. Where *was* Samuel Davis? He had made this appointment reluctantly. Had he decided not to keep it?

Shifting her bag to ease her shoulder, she glanced around nervously. A street lamp came on in the early dusk just as a young black man in jeans and no shirt bicycled into its glow. He pedaled slowly past the yard, eyeing Juanita curiously.

She peered at her watch again. She was right on time. Was Davis inside the house, hiding?

What now?

Some people must know the truth about that old atrocity. Others must strongly suspect, yet it had never come out. Someone—maybe someones—must badly want the past to stay buried. So why should she think she could ferret it out?

Because snooping's your specialty, her wise-guy conscience nagged. And because you ought to occasionally use your powers for good.

Further knocking seemed useless. Juanita closed the screen

door, sidestepped a hole in the porch floor, and climbed back down the uneven wooden steps.

As she walked towards her car, chunky heels clomping on wooden planks laid across the drainage ditch that fronted the lot, another possibility occurred. Davis was getting on in years. Maybe he had fallen and was too weak to cry for help. Too, she hated leaving without satisfying her curiosity.

A yellow tabby stretched languidly on a park bench under a tree near the front of Davis's lawn. A breeze ruffled Juanita's short dark hair.

Reaching a decision, she reversed her course and detoured around the corner of the house. A squeaky, grating sound from behind the dwelling sent a shiver through her. She paused, realized she was holding her breath.

"Silly," she scolded herself, and continued her stroll.

Behind the house, rays from a pole light in the yard next door pierced the encroaching gloom. A door on a decrepit tool shed swung lazily on creaking hinges—the squeaking sound she'd heard. Beside the ragged remains of a vegetable garden, a worn pair of overalls drooped from a clothesline.

Juanita approached the back door, pausing as something metallic glinted on the ground near the stoop. An aluminum TV-dinner pan, evidently now a pet dish. She lifted a tentative fist to beat on the door.

She lowered it again. In Bryson's Corner, Oklahoma, still a mostly black town decades after school integration and fair-housing legislation, her fair complexion stood out like a penguin in the tropics. Someone might find her presence back here suspicious. Juanita retraced her steps around the residence.

The neighboring house beckoned, its window panes and open front door spilling brightness into the night.

"I can at least ask about Davis," she muttered, hurrying towards the beacon. She climbed solid homemade steps onto a wide porch edged with flower boxes of spicy sweet williams and presided over by a white bench swing decorated with dusky rose accents. Through the screen door, she glimpsed overstuffed chairs covered in splashy red-and-yellow fabric that suggested sun-drenched climes.

Reassured by the welcoming air of the house, Juanita felt the lump of tension in her throat dissolve. She knocked and waited a moment, gazing approvingly around the yard. Hearing a step inside, she turned expectantly, lips parted to ask a question.

The screen door jerked open. A wave of cold liquid sloshed Juanita in the face. She gasped, dropped her purse, and clutched the door frame.

"And don't come back!" cried an indignant male voice.

Spluttering, Juanita eased open a smarting eye. The blurry figure of a thin African-American man stood there. Speechless with surprise, she brushed her sight clear. Wide dark eyes stared from his walnut-hued face, topped by a graying frizz. His arms cradled an empty pitcher.

"Uh-oh." He gulped. Banging the screen door, he back-pedaled and fled.

Juanita licked her lips. Grape flavor, sticky.

What had she walked into? She tugged at the new shirtwaist now glued to her stomach. In the light pouring from the living room, she saw the pristine ivory of her dress was now splotched a deep reddish violet.

"Hey!" she called through the screen. "What was that about?"

A raised female voice inside demanded, "What happened to that juice I poured up, Daddy? The jug's empty. You couldn't've drunk it all."

Low-pitched tones replied. A back door slammed.

"Lord, what've you done now?" the feminine voice said. A plump woman entered the living room and marched across to the front entry. As she peered at Juanita through the screen, her vexed frown vanished. She suppressed a chuckle.

Juanita pushed dripping hair off her forehead and straightened her shoulders, trying to regain a shred of dignity.

The woman composed her features and opened the door. She was about Juanita's age, with skin dark and rich as topsoil and shining black hair in neat corn-rows. A Wyndham Community College T-shirt snugged her heavy upper body.

"Sorry about that, ma'am," she said. "Daddy thought you were a pesky salesman come back. He was trying to teach the fellow a lesson."

Juanita managed a shaky smile. "Actually, I came to ask if you know where your neighbor might be. Mr. Davis?"

The brown eyes narrowed. "Why?"

"I had an appointment with him tonight. But no one answers at his place, and it's all dark."

"Uncle Sa—Mr. Davis—is in the hospital." The woman hesitated. "I'll get something to wipe that mess off you." She left, and returned with a roll of paper towels, ripped off a few, and handed them out.

Juanita blotted her face, hair, and clothing. "Hospital? I hope it's nothing serious. I'm Juanita Wills, by the way—librarian at Wyndham Public Library."

"Althea McCoy." She eyed Juanita thoughtfully. "You drove all the way out here from Wyndham?"

"Yes, and I'd better get home and try to clean this dress."

Althea tossed the roll of towels from hand to hand. "Is it washable?"

"Yes."

"Time you get home, the stuff'll be about dry—might not come out then." Althea sighed. "You better come in and let me wash it for you."

"Oh, I couldn't put you to that trouble."

Althea lifted her chin. "I do know what to do with stains. You ought to see what Daddy brings in sometimes."

"I don't want to be a bother. Really."

"It's his fault you're in that fix. Come on in."

Envisioning the beautiful fabric upholstery in her new car stained with sticky grape juice, Juanita grabbed her bag and followed. Althea led her to a neat yellow-and-white bathroom and handed her a soft blue robe.

"You're about my size, so this ought to fit. Toss your things in the hall. Clean towels're in that cabinet."

Juanita removed her sticky dress as directed but kept her purple-specked underwear on. She scrubbed blotches from her arms and face, rinsed gumminess from her hair, wrapped the housecoat around her sturdy body, and joined her hostess in the kitchen.

A pot of fragrant stew simmered on a range, and a coffeemaker on a counter brewed accompaniment. Althea stood at the sink, spraying something on the soiled dress. She looked up, frowning, as Juanita entered.

"Take a seat. I see you got most of it off you."

Feeling awkward, Juanita sat at a chrome-and-Formica table laid with two place-settings.

"This is kind. I'm sorry to interrupt your supper preparations."

"Mm," Althea said noncommittally. She held up the dress and studied it, then sprayed a few lingering spots.

Silence yawned between them. Althea put a stopper in the sink and ran water. Examining the dress again, she nodded her satisfaction.

"Glad the summer's about over," Juanita ventured. "It's been a bad one."

"Mm." Althea swished detergent into the water and dunked the dress.

"My tomatoes dried up in the heat. You do any gardening?"

"Not me. Daddy and Uncle Sam—Mr. Davis—do a little together." Althea emptied the sink, filled it, and rinsed the dress.

Juanita fidgeted. Her hostess didn't seem any more thrilled to have her than she was to be here. Finally, Althea heaved a relieved sigh and squeezed water from the garment.

"That got it. I'll put this in the dryer. Want some coffee?" She head-gestured towards the pot. "I'm having some."

"Okay, then. Thanks."

After Althea started the dryer, she and Juanita carried full cups to the living room. Juanita sat in a deep-gold recliner and gazed about.

"Pleasant room. What an interesting wood sculpture."

"A friend bought it in Nigeria."

"Powerful."

Juanita studied her hostess. Resolute chin, keen eyes, laugh lines around the mouth. The hands of a doer, capable and strong. A stack of textbooks sat on an end table beside Althea.

"Are you a WCC student?" Juanita asked.

Althea pulled at the logo on her top. "I was. Now I go to T.U. at night, work days."

"I never attended Tulsa University, but I hear it's good. What's your major?"

"English."

"That was mine, too. Good coffee."

"Thanks."

"You work in Tulsa?"

"Yes. Pierce and Hammersmith. I'm a legal secretary."

Minutes passed, a wall clock ticking loudly in the quiet.

For something to say, Juanita asked what classes Althea was taking.

"Chemistry, which I don't enjoy, and Victorian lit, which I do."

"I like that period of literature, too."

They found similar tastes in books and authors, and Juanita impulsively asked Althea to join the Wyndham Literary Society. "'Books,' we call it for short. We used to meet weekly, then went to twice a month, now once a month—people are so busy. Our moderator's out of town now, but I can let you know when we'll meet again."

"Thanks, but between work and classes I'm snowed. Got to get busy on a term paper about Dickens's travels in America. This prof's tough."

"I'm researching a history, myself. Of Wyndham. That's why I need to see Mr. Davis."

"He's never lived there."

"I was told he might have information about an old murder . . . of Luther Dunlap, a young man from Bryson's Corner who was . . . killed in Wyndham." As Juanita recalled the few details she knew about the horror that had occurred in *her* generally peaceful town, a shiver of shame and revulsion went though her.

"It happened back in the late fifties. I just recently learned about it myself. You know anything about that?"

A shadow crossed Althea's face. "No."

"I understand Wyndham boys were thought to be involved, but no one's ever stood trial."

Althea picked up her cup, and Juanita noticed the brown hand shook slightly. "More coffee?"

"Better not, though it's delicious."

The dryer buzzed. Althea carried their cups to the kitchen and brought the clean garment back. Juanita went to change in the bathroom.

"I'll be going now," she said on returning. "Thanks for saving my dress."

Her hostess smiled. "You were a sight. Daddy owes you an apology himself, but he seems to've lit out for other parts."

Something clicked for Juanita. "McCoy—is your dad Garvin McCoy?"

The frown returned. "Yes. Why?"

"He was mentioned as another possible source on that old case."

Althea bit her lip. "Daddy can't help you with that. Anyway, why're you so interested? It's not like anyone could do anything about it now."

"Probably not. But this case intrigues me—partly because almost everyone I've asked about it clams up or changes the subject. Anyway, I'm trying to record the history of Wyndham, and that means telling it all, not just the parts that make the town look good. Wyndhamites need to know this chapter of their story, too."

Juanita picked up her purse. "Mr. Davis's illness must've come on suddenly. I talked to him by phone just yesterday."

Althea hesitated. "I guess it did." She pressed her lips together, then added in a worried tone, "His neighbor on the other side, Mrs. Umstead, said he called her soon after lunch, needed to get to the hospital but was too giddy to drive. Daddy'd gone fishing, or he'd have asked him."

"Hmm. Is Mr. Davis subject to such 'spells'?"

"No. For his age, he's healthy as a mule. But Mrs. Umstead said he complained of headache and stomach pain all the way into Wyndham."

"That doesn't sound good. I do hope he'll be okay. Well, thanks a—" Juanita turned to go, then stopped. "You know, we've got something at the library that might help with your paper. The son of a woman named Maizie Stevens left us her books when she died—they're worthless except for some journals kept by people in her family. One, I remember, tells about the diarist's seeing Dickens in person. In Cincinnati, I believe. The Stevens Collection isn't open to the public, but I could let you use the diaries."

Twisting a sparkly bracelet on her arm, Althea considered. Slowly, she shook her head. "I . . . I guess not. Thanks, anyway."

"Just a thought. I appreciate your help tonight."

"Take it easy now."

Walking to her car, Juanita thought about the conversation. Once they'd gotten past the awkwardness of the situation, a camaraderie had developed over books and classes. But the subject of Luther Dunlap had made Althea wary. That might simply be because the killing of a black man was a painful subject. Or was there more to it?

Juanita crawled into her late-model blue Civic and started it. As she reversed to turn in the narrow street, her car lights picked out a man seated on the bench in front of Samuel Davis's house. He seemed to be watching her, his skin gleaming with a chocolaty sheen in the glow from her headlamps. She spun the wheel, shifted, and drove off. In her mirror, she saw the man rise and meander towards the McCoy home.

Garvin McCoy, she guessed. Returning home, now that she was leaving.

Two

"Give her a break, Mavis," Calvin Meador said late the next morning, as he lackadaisically scanned a stack of returned books. His latest enthusiasm, physical fitness, had slimmed his once-heavy body, though his face retained a doughy look. From Juanita's perspective, his newly svelte form had also made him a more social being. "She's your sister, after all."

"Not by my choice." Mavis Ralston slapped a magazine onto a pile on the checkout counter, her bony body rigid with self-righteousness.

"You and your sister don't get along?" Juanita glanced up from a brochure on new software for libraries, determined not to let Mavis make her feel guilty. Again. The feverish pace Mavis kept had a way of making her feel she should be constantly rushing hither and yon.

"Mmph."

They all sat on stools within the oval checkout counter, looking out over the huge reading room. Immediately in front of the counter was a series of reading alcoves formed by bookcase half-walls, a library table and chairs centering each. In one corner of the room, a wall rack held magazines, and a cluster of overstuffed chairs encouraged browsing. Rows of floor-to-ceiling bookcases occupied the rest of the space.

Behind the counter was Juanita's office. On one side of it sat a bank of computers for public use; on the other, a hall led past a small meeting room to a rear entry. Wings off the reading room housed open-stack shelves and a reference room.

"How long since you've seen each other?" Juanita asked.

"Twenty years, give or take."

"Then it's wonderful you're together again after so long."

Mavis pressed her lips together in a grim line.

"Where's she living now?" Meador asked.

"Did she say? Just showed up out of the blue, expecting to be taken care of."

"What's wrong with her?"

"Old age, hard living."

"Is Martha much older than you?" Juanita put in.

"Ten years."

"She must've been more like a mother to you than a sister."

Mavis glared at her.

"So what kind of care does she need?" Meador asked.

"You two sure are nosy."

"Good grief, Mavis!" he said. "You complain about your sister, then when we get interested and ask questions, you get your back up."

"I said Martha'd suddenly arrived yesterday. Didn't promise to tell you her life story."

"Pardon us for caring," Meador said.

"You're pardoned," Mavis responded.

"Fine. Forget it."

"I will."

Twenty-something Meador was a likable slough-off, fifty-plus Mavis a hard worker, but disagreeable as a cornered cougar. She and her husband Tully had recently moved into Juanita's neighborhood. Juanita hoped they wouldn't see more of each other as a result.

Having learned the wisdom of ignoring her staff at times, Juanita tuned out the rest of their competition for the last word and indulged in her favorite daydream, devising interesting ways to murder Mavis. This time, she imagined layering her with *papier maché*, sealing the stern mouth first, the snapping eyes last.

The ringing phone broke into her reverie. Juanita answered.

"Hi, babe," Detective Lieutenant Wayne Cleary's deep voice said. "How about dinner and a movie Saturday?"

"Great! I haven't seen you all week."

"Yeah, I've missed you too. Between overtime at work and that class I was taking in the City, I haven't had a minute." As every Okie knew, "the City" referred to was Oklahoma City. "But things should slow down, now we've wrapped up that big burglary."

"Did Ruth crack it for you?" Juanita couldn't resist teasing.

Wayne groaned. "Too bad she's such a nice lady. Never complains about having to stay late or do crappy jobs. Brings us cookies and cake she's baked. Heck of a cook, too."

"Bu-u-ut—"

"But we can't break her of feeding us weird theories about our cases. You know that body that turned up out on the Felcher place—"

"The undeveloped land Wyndham annexed with that subdivision to the north?"

"Yep. Guy fell in a ravine and hit his head. Forensics said he'd been dead a few days, no sign of foul play. But Ruth the Sleuth figured it for a homicide that happened months or even years ago."

"How come?"

"She'd read some pop-forensics article about *adipocere* and decided the body was unusually well preserved because of that."

"Adi-what?"

"*Adipocere*. It can occur when a corpse lies in water or damp conditions a long time. The natural body fats solidify and adhere to the bone. It can make limbs, chest walls, even faces, retain their shape for months or years."

"That's one off-the-wall theory."

"One worthy even of you."

Juanita said stiffly, "I've just recalled a prior engagement for Saturday."

"Just kidding, babe. You've never come up with anything so ridiculous. I pointed out to Ruth that, dry as the past year's been, that ravine probably hadn't seen a teacupful of water in months—one of many reasons her theory didn't work."

"And she accepted that?"

"Yep. One thing about Ruth, you show her an error in her logic and she'll admit she's wrong. But she loves learning odd facts about crimes. She's reading up on poisons now. We should be hearing about curare and deadly nightshade any day now."

"Sounds like a hypochondriac reading a medical book and deciding he has every disease."

"Yeah. But Ruth's trying to help, so I can't get too pissed off."

"Hope you'll be so understanding the next time *I* make a suggestion about one of your cases."

"You're a different matter. Ruth never risks her life by getting in the middle of an investigation."

Sensing that the conversation was veering towards an old argument, Juanita said, "I'd better get to work. See you Saturday."

"Pick you up at 5:30."

Ringing off, Juanita saw the massive front door open, to admit a well-built, sandy-haired Doug Darrow. He approached the counter and slid two books into its "Returns" slot. They thumped onto the shelf below.

"'Lo, everyone," he said. "How's the research coming, Juanita?" A high school history teacher, Doug often dropped by the library on his lunch hour. He had introduced Juanita to Robert Norwood, the math teacher and coach who had put her in touch with Samuel Davis.

"Hi, Doug," Juanita and Meador chorused.

"It's going slowly," Juanita went on. "I was supposed to interview Samuel Davis last night, but he was taken to the hospital earlier yesterday."

"Yeah, Robert told me this morning. Said he's in a coma."

"Oh. It's serious, then."

"Sounds that way. The son's on his way here from Florida. Robert's worried he may not make it in time."

"How awful."

"Yeah. Robert says Davis always seemed healthy, except for the usual aches and pains of someone his age. What about the other name Robert gave you—McCoy, wasn't it?"

"I saw Garvin McCoy briefly last evening. He doused me with grape juice and scrammed." Juanita recounted the incident.

Doug and Meador guffawed. Mavis smirked.

"Mr. McCoy's daughter was nice enough to clean my dress, but her dad didn't come back the whole time I was there."

"Too embarrassed," Doug said. "Maybe if you go back . . ."

"Possibly," Juanita hedged.

"Robert said Davis was plenty reluctant to talk to a white woman—or anybody—about that old killing. He finally agreed for Robert's sake, though Davis warned him he probably couldn't help you."

"I appreciate Robert's pleading my case. Especially since he didn't really know me, himself."

"*I* vouched for you, remember."

"Yet Robert still agreed to meet me." She grinned.

"You do realize I did you a favor? That's not entirely clear."

"Okay. Seriously, I appreciate your help, Doug. Oh, that biography of General Sherman came in. It should be ready to check out tomorrow."

"Great. You call the hospital to see how Davis is doing?"

"They wouldn't tell me anything over the phone. I'm not

family."

"I don't think he has any relatives around here. When I get back to school, I'll ask Robert how he's doing and call you."

"Thanks, Doug. I owe you one."

"You owe me 153 at last count. But as you know, I'm entirely smitten by you. If you weren't seeing a cop the size of Madagascar—" Doug grinned the lazy smile that made Wyndham female hearts flutter.

"Begone, liar. Appearances to the contrary, I'm busy."

Juanita didn't hear from Doug that afternoon. She spent a part of it downtown at the office of one of her least favorite people, Simon Simms, the dour accountant who chaired the library board.

When she arrived for her appointment, Simon's secretary said he was busy on a conference call but would be with her as soon as he finished. Juanita sat idly thumbing through a magazine and looking around the utilitarian outer office, where she had been numerous times before. Currently she was the only one seated in the line of straight-backed, leather-seated clients' chairs that extended along the street-side wall. Across the room, the secretary's desk sat like a guard-post at the entrance to the hallway that led to her employer's office. Several filing cabinets, a couple of potted ferns, and a coffee table holding magazines completed the simple décor.

A sign on the secretary's desk identified her as Phyllida Campbell. Sitting ramrod-straight in a navy shirtwaist and tiny gold earrings, wearing glasses with plain black frames, she looked as no-nonsense as Simon himself. The phone on her desk rang and she answered, then told Juanita that Mr. Simms would see her now.

Carrying her purse and briefcase, Juanita went along the hall to Simon's office. Like the reception room, it was devoid of frills. Simon sat at a gray metal desk, empty save for a stapler, a pen set, a blotter, and three file folders. Behind him, a plain wooden bookshelf held tax manuals and other references. The few chairs in the room, including his, appeared to have been chosen for functionality rather than style or comfort.

Man and surroundings seemed well suited, Juanita thought. Simms's bony fingers tugged his unfashionably thin tie into place against a white short-sleeved shirt. His gray hair, curling at the neck, lay thin and straight across the crown. He peered over half-glasses at Juanita, seated in front of his desk.

She took a sheaf of papers from her briefcase and laid before him pages of information he had requested, to help him fend off a move by one Wyndham City Councilman to cut the library's share of the town's next budget. Accordingly, she had compiled comparison figures for the past five years on such items as total books, videotapes, audio books, and DVDs owned by the library, circulation figures of various genres and media, numbers of children in summer story-time, and frequency with which community groups used library facilities. The accountant studied the various sheets, asked a few questions, and finally nodded his satisfaction.

"This is excellent, Juanita. We can show a clear increase not only in the library's holdings and circulation, but also in the growing importance of the library to families and the community. If this doesn't convince the budget-slashers to back off, nothing will."

"Hope so, Simon. I try to spend whatever money the library gets wisely, but we couldn't stand much of a cut. Not without reducing services, maybe being open fewer hours."

"I don't think you need worry too much, Juanita. I can be very persuasive when I have figures to support whatever position I'm arguing. And you've given me those."

"Great! It seems libraries are one of the first places cut when retrenchment happens. Thanks for standing up for us, Simon."

He waved away her appreciation. "No need to thank me. Libraries are one of the things a city needs to have, to be really civilized."

"I agree. Glad to hear you say that." Juanita closed and fastened her briefcase and stood.

"Good day, Miss Wills. Thanks for getting the information together and bringing it down." He reached for the top folder on the stack before him.

Turning to leave, Juanita paused. "Simon, could I ask you about something totally unrelated to what we've been discussing?"

He looked up and frowned. "If it won't take long. I have a full schedule today."

Resuming her seat, she asked if he'd grown up in Wyndham.

"Yes. Why?"

"I'm researching a history of the town and want it to tell the truth, warts and all. I hope it'll generally show Wyndham in a good light—I am fond of this place—but whatever I ultimately write, I want it to be accurate."

"I'm all in favor of accuracy."

"I would hope so, since you're an accountant."

He didn't return her grin. From years of knowing him superficially, Juanita doubted he even recognized irony.

"So, Simon, what do you recall about the murder of Luther Dunlap?"

His eyes widened almost imperceptibly. "Umm. You're not much for preliminaries, are you?"

"Guess I'm not the most tactful person ever. But what can you tell me about that death?"

"Not much, I'm afraid. It was a long time ago."

"Everyone says that. But people often remember events from their early years better than recent ones. Particularly if the incident was frightening or scandalous."

"Perhaps I should recall more than I do. But I'm sure you know the basics, from what the newspaper printed at the time, and I really can't tell you anything more."

"You sure, Simon? Just hearing you tell about it from your perspective would probably be useful. Your account of it might include some helpful detail I didn't know."

He passed a hand over his balding crown, his fingers trembling. Odd, she thought. If that was an age-related tremor, she'd never noticed it before.

"I really can't help you, Juanita. And as I mentioned, this is a busy day for me."

Juanita thanked him again for his advocacy with the City Council and took her leave. As she strolled through the outer office, seeing the empty row of clients' chairs, she wondered what would keep an accountant so busy in the fall, well before the dreaded April 15.

But Simms also did work for the city, and probably for corporate clients, and they undoubtedly had different needs throughout a calendar year than did individuals.

Still, she walked back to the library feeling frustrated and wondering if she'd ever learn the truth about that dark chapter in Wyndham's history.

Following work, she fed Rip, her timid collie-mongrel, named—in her own bit of irony—for Jack the Ripper, and made a roast-beef sandwich for herself. The dog ate and drank from plastic bowls in a corner of the kitchen, then lay under the dinette table, placidly watching her eat at the counter.

"You know, Rip, I'm sorry for Davis and his son, but I'm also bugged I didn't get to him a day earlier." Juanita had fallen into the habit of addressing the dog as she thought. "Now I may never get to talk to him."

A low scraping sound came from the front of the house. The dog's ears pricked, and he growled softly.

"Hush, Rip," Juanita said. "It won't be the postman or trash collector, so you needn't do your menacing act."

He followed her to the front door, staying well behind as she opened it. A skinny white-haired woman in a dowdy aqua housedress was bent over, placing something on the mat. She smiled vaguely up at Juanita.

"Gracie!" Juanita said. "I haven't seen you for ages. How've you been? Oh, you brought those wonderful bread-and-butter pickles. Come in." Taking the older woman's hand, she tried to lead her inside.

Grace resisted. "Can't stay. More jars in the car." Her sallow complexion, topped with too-bright rouge, reminded Juanita of waxed fruit.

"Where-all you delivering tonight? Just in this neighborhood?"

"Dunno. It's a nice night. I may take the rest over to Capshaw, or Buffalo Flats, or maybe Lydell." Grace straightened her tall, thin body from its usual stoop. "Made sure to bring you a jar first, though. I know how you like my pickles."

"Sure do. Thanks, Grace, I'll enjoy these." Clutching the Mason jar with the label that read "From the kitchen of Grace Hendershot," Juanita went back inside.

Grace was the town "character," an eccentric who had resumed her maiden name after a brief marriage, and who lived alone with no one to serve the kitchen goodies she loved preparing. She had found an outlet, however. Periodically, area residents would find samples of her preserves or baked treats on their porches or inside their screen doors.

The pickles Juanita ate with the rest of her sandwich proved as crisp and delicious as Grace's earlier batches, with just the right blend of sweet and sour. Juanita felt privileged to be a "regular."

Of course, Mavis said anyone was crazy to eat food left on a doorstep, even with a label identifying its source. Juanita might have agreed if Grace's person and auto weren't always immaculate and her reputation as a cook unsullied after years of such deliveries.

Juanita spent a contented evening reading a Barbara Kingsolver novel and enjoying the guilty pleasure of being home on a Thursday evening. For months, until last spring, she had driven a collection van each Thursday for Wyndham Relief Agency. But after a fright in connection with that van, she had resigned, allowing her to rotate Thursday evenings off with Mavis and Meador. Tonight was her assistants' turn to stay late at the library.

As Juanita prepared for bed, the phone rang. It was Doug Darrow.

"Sorry not to call earlier, Juanita. Robert had left school before I got back from lunch, and I didn't get to talk to him till he phoned a few minutes ago." Doug paused, then went on somberly.

"Davis died around noon today."

"Oh, no!" Juanita gasped. "Did his son arrive in time to see him first?"

"Half an hour too late. Robert said the son—Bill—chewed Davis's doctor out like you wouldn't believe, insisting his dad was never sick and must've gotten incompetent care. Robert told Bill that Samuel had been feeling tired lately, but Bill demanded an autopsy and the doctor went along. Robert figures Bill's pitching a fit because he feels guilty he didn't come home more often. I think Bill has a malpractice suit in mind, myself."

"This is terrible news, Doug. But thanks for letting me know."

"No problem. 'Night, Juanita."

Three

Discouragement sat like a leaden yoke on Juanita's shoulders for several weeks after the death of Samuel Davis. She stayed busy at work, hosted a gourmet-club dinner, occasionally saw Wayne, and dealt with a lingering attack of bronchitis. But she couldn't seem to proceed with her history project. The enigma of Luther Dunlap's fate, along with the mind-picture evoked by the few horrible details she knew of it, never fully left her thoughts, however.

"This isn't like me," she muttered one afternoon, sitting in her office trying to type a book order. "Why can't I get on with that research or else put it out of my mind, one or the other?"

Meador strolled in carrying a lime-green Post-it© note, marched past her desk to a wall dotted with similar scraps of paper, and, with a flourish, added it to the others.

"What's the subject this time?" Juanita asked, wondering if he'd ever learn.

A few months ago, her assistants had carried on a war of quotations, Meador posting one about a chosen subject, Mavis countering with an opposing view. Each had tried to best the other, the advantage often shifting, some topics occupying them for weeks. Then one day Mavis had brought things to a halt, posting what had proved to be her final quote:

> Answer not a fool according to his
> folly, lest thou also be like unto him.
> —*Proverbs* 26:5

Since then, Meador had periodically tried to renew combat but had met only stonewalling. Juanita suspected Mavis missed the "war," too, though.

"Age versus youth," Meador replied now.

"You've done that one before."

"It's a perennial favorite. I keep finding good quotes." He swept out.

Juanita went to the wall and read:

> Nature abhors the old, and old age seems
> the only disease; all others run into this one.
> —Ralph Waldo Emerson, *Essays: First Series. Circles*

Digs at Mavis about her advanced years had worked before, but no response came from her this time.

Over her lunch hour, Juanita drove to a warehouse grocery to pick up dog food and paper towels. She was passing the produce section when she spotted Katherine Greer, a long-retired WCC teacher, sniffing a cantaloupe. A silver-headed cane protruded from a sparsely filled cart beside the frail, dignified woman.

"Oh, you're home," Juanita said with a grin. "How's your back?"

"Much better. It's a good thing my niece was handy when I took that tumble off her steps." Katherine tilted her snowy head, overhead light strobing from her thick lenses. "How's a week from next Tuesday for Books?"

"Fine for me. I need to re-read *To Kill a Mockingbird*. But as I recall, it goes fast."

"Good. I'll check with the others and get back to you."

"Fine." A thought struck. "Oh, while I'm talking to you, Katherine, do you by any chance recall the murder of Luther Dunlap? Back in the fifties?"

"Of course I remember it."

Hope mounting, Juanita briefly described her history project. "It has to be accurate, not a whitewash job. But the *Wyndham Daily News* articles from that time leave lots of questions unanswered. And people I've asked don't seem to want to talk about it."

"Many would prefer not to remember, I'm sure. But I agree you must tell the truth. Have you time to talk now? In the cafeteria?"

"Sure!"

Moving a trifle stiffly, Katherine returned three TV dinners to the freezer. Trying to contain her eagerness, Juanita pushed her elderly friend's cart holding cereal and canned goods to a cafe at the front of the grocery. Juanita parked the trolley near the one available booth, went through the line, and returned with a tray holding two cups of coffee, napkins, and a plate of cake doughnuts, two chocolate and two plain. She sat across from Katherine, who accepted coffee but declined the pastries.

"No, thank you, dear, I'm not a sweets lover. Let's see, that murder would have happened before you were born . . ."

"Guess I'll have to eat them all, then. They'll have to be my lunch." Juanita took a bite of chocolate cruller and chewed thoughtfully. "I never even heard much about the killing while growing up here." She sipped hot coffee. "One thing I do remember—if anyone mentioned Luther Dunlap, someone else would change the subject. When I ran across that old newspaper recently, I recalled the secrecy, and it whetted my appetite for a good story."

Katherine smiled. "Lieutenant Cleary says your meddling instinct stays in a perpetual state of 'whetness.'"

"The Punning Policeman and I have differing views of my investigative abilities." It was their old argument. Wayne said he had to manage his own investigations and protect her, his sweetie. She said he didn't sufficiently appreciate her help.

She took pen and notepad from her shoulder bag. "Can you tell me what happened back then, Katherine? Who was thought to've been involved?"

"Hm-m-m, I would have been teaching at the junior college and working on my master's at T.U. then. I recall several stories circulated about the possible motive. One, that Mr. Dunlap had stolen a deer a Wyndham boy had shot and was killed in retaliation. 'Lifted that carcass right off his hood,' someone said—as if its being on an automobile somehow made the offense worse."

"You ever hear a name for the Wyndham guy?"

Katherine frowned. "I did . . . Oh yes!—Ward Nutchell." She spelled the last name. "He lived in east Wyndham. I never knew him, but a couple of my students who had grown up in the neighborhood characterized him as 'meaner'n a snake.'"

"Would you know if Nutchell still lives around here?"

"I heard he went into the army without finishing high school. Goodness, this is taxing my old brain."

"I'd be happy to have what you'll keep *after* taxes."

Katherine smiled at the compliment. "Another story said Mr. Dunlap and a white boy were rivals for the same girl. In the fifties, of course, interracial dating was a much bigger deal than it is now.

"Still another version had it that a white boy had injured Mr. Dunlap's dog and gotten his gas tank sugared in revenge, and the dispute escalated from there. But you know how rumors abound in a small town."

"True." Finding a willing source renewed Juanita's excitement about the old case, even as hearing new details renewed the shock she'd felt on learning of the brutality. She forced herself to concentrate, her pen flying to record Katherine's information. "So whichever you believe, it sounds as if the problem was between Dunlap and one other fellow. But the newspaper story implied a gang of teenagers was involved."

"It's hard to know at this point. But adolescents are clannish, you know. If a boy's friends decided he'd been treated badly, they might've gone after the person they blamed in a body. Especially, I'm afraid, if he was of another race.

"Oh, there was a fourth possibility. A big inter-school track meet had been held in Wyndham the week before Mr. Dun—"

She broke off as someone paused beside their booth—a stocky, white-haired man with arresting dark eyes and a bulbous nose. He wore a blue Western-style shirt, new jeans, and black cowboy boots.

"Miss Greer, wonderful to see you again." He took her wrinkled hand and patted it. "And Miss Wills, isn't it?" He smiled genially and offered a big paw, which Juanita shook. "We met at the Chamber of Commerce barbecue a few months ago. Claude Gilroy, if you don't recall." His eyes held hers as if underscoring the importance of the encounter.

"Of course. I'm surprised you remember me, though, considering the number of people you must meet." Juanita found it disarming that State Representative Gilroy didn't automatically expect to be recognized in his own district, especially in his home town.

He chuckled. "I make a point of memorizing lovely ladies' names. Besides, you were talking to people that day about some event in the past—for a book you were writing on Wyndham—and that roused my interest. I've a fondness for local history, myself."

"Unfortunately, my research is moving slowly."

"Sounds like a worthy project, though. You're at the Wyndham library, are you not?"

"Yes. You *do* have a good memory."

"It's a useful skill to cultivate when you're in public life.

Something else made me remember you, though. There was a young man with you that day—Merritt—Melcher—"

"Meador."

Gilroy cupped a hand around one ear. "Major?"

Juanita repeated, more loudly.

"Oh, yes. Meador. He expressed an interest in volunteering at my headquarters here, but my staff tell me he hasn't been in. Do you know if he's still interested?"

"Hard to tell with him. Meador's enthusiasms heat up fast but can cool just as quickly."

"Tell him we can always use a capable young fellow like him."

"I'll pass it on."

"Good. Miss Greer, did you think when I was a lowly student that you'd see me in the state legislature some day?"

She smiled. "Actually, I'm not surprised. You were active in student government and were always selling something, yearbook and newspaper ads, magazine subscriptions. I assumed you'd be either a salesman or a politician, and you became both. How's the insurance business, now that you're in Oklahoma City so much?"

"Doing well. I have good people working for me. Well, I must run. Marvelous seeing you both." Gilroy's boots clattered as he strode through the café, pausing to shake hands and slap shoulders.

"He seems to be in campaign mode," Juanita murmured. "But he got reelected last year with only token opposition. I guess glad-handing comes automatically to politicians."

"I hear he's planning a race for the U.S. Senate. Mr. Cunningham's in ill health, you know, and expected to retire. Mr. Gilroy's problem will be name recognition beyond his district. I understand he's making speeches across the state but also making sure his base here is secure. Now, where were we?"

"The track meet?"

"Ah, yes. Black schools weren't typically included in such events in those days. Wyndham's school superintendent left soon after the match, and I've always thought he was forced out for that courageous choice. He died a few years ago. A good man."

Juanita closed her eyes a moment in silent acknowledgment of someone who had tried to make a difference in racist times. Bryson's Corner athletes had participated as equals with Wyndham's, that one day. And Wyndhamites had had to interact with those they customarily treated as inferiors. Lost job or no, who was to say the superintendent had failed?

"I suppose Dunlap beat white competitors in a track event?"

"He won several events, I believe, including a fiercely contested 100-yard dash. Those victories caused quite an uproar in Wyndham and surrounding towns."

"I can imagine." Juanita thought for a moment. "Track. H-m-m. The newspaper said Dunlap's body was found on the *track* at the Wyndham High athletic field."

"I'd forgotten that. Do you suppose that was his killers' way of warning other blacks not to get 'uppity'?"

"Maybe. You know any other people connected to that case?"

Katherine tapped a withered finger on her chin. "No boys' names. I did hear about one girl rumored to have been part of the love triangle—now, who was she? I can see her face, pretty little thing. Her mother drove in from Bryson's Corner to do housework for Wyndham women. The daughter came along to help when she wasn't in school. Brown, that was it. Leona Brown."

"You know if she's still around?"

"No, I haven't heard of her in years."

"Okay. I guess that's all I can think of now. Thanks a heap, Katherine."

"I look forward to your book's publication."

"That may never happen. My best potential source died a few weeks ago, and others don't seem to want to help, black or white."

"It's probably still a sore subject to some. And black people may fear you wouldn't be accurate."

"When you think about it, why *should* they trust a white person to tell this story? But the more I learn, the surer I am that someone needs to."

"I agree. I'm ashamed people in Wyndham didn't demand years ago that the authorities find those killers. I was so busy myself, a young woman trying to establish herself—and then later—oh, I guess the real reason is, I hadn't the courage."

"It would've taken a lot more then, I'm sure. I hope my book will at least make people acknowledge what happened."

Katherine removed her thick glasses, and her bright blue eyes fixed Juanita with a kindly but firm gaze. "It may do a good deal more than that, Miss Wills. That young man's murderers may still be around here. Be careful, Miss Wills."

Juanita drew a quick breath. The elderly teacher had voiced a concern she hadn't allowed herself to think much about. Of course there'd be a trial, if evidence was found even now that pointed to Luther's killers. No statute of limitations existed on murder. And she couldn't write about that death without having concrete facts.

For a moment, she thought about giving up on the town history. People abandoned writing projects all the time. True, several townsfolk knew she was working on it. Some would be disappointed—probably including Katherine now—but Juanita had a right to make that choice.

Except it wouldn't be *her* choice. It would be taking the path of least resistance. If she opted out now, could she continue to respect herself? Juanita lifted her chin, her eyes meeting Katherine's sad blue ones.

"I'll be careful," she said. "And thanks, Katherine. Thanks very much."

That evening, while brushing Rip on her screened-in back

porch, Juanita told him what she had learned from Katherine. He loved being brushed, loved the attention, though he hated being bathed.

"You know, Rip, it never fails to amaze me that some people can behave the way they do. I mean, how can anyone convince himself that even an enemy *deserves* to be treated the way Dunlap's killers treated him?"

Eyes drowsily half-closed, the dog stood on a low table as if chiseled from stone.

"The truth has to come out, Rip. And even Wayne admits that asking questions is something I'm good at. But I am somewhat nervous about trying to expose men who've already killed once.

"Wish I knew how many of them there were, and who's still here."

An image rose in her mind of a dozen young men, big and strong, hands balled into fists or wielding chains or tire irons, faces contorted with rage, leaping towards her like a many-headed creature bent on her destruction.

Was that what Dunlap had seen near the end of his life?

Injustice and hatred, she thought, the world's twin evils, people despising other people simply because they looked, acted, or thought differently from themselves.

Thinking about the many inhumane ways humans had found to treat each other, Juanita laid down the brush and dropped dejectedly into a chair. Noticing his groom's desertion, Rip jumped off the table and laid a paw on her knee. She threw her arms around his neck and buried her face in his fur.

They remained that way a few minutes, Rip's tail wagging slowly, reassuringly. Finally, she released him, sat up, and took a deep breath. He wagged harder, his mouth opening in his version of a grin.

"Thanks, Rip. I'm so glad you're in my life."

She picked up the brush and pulled hair from its bristles. "Okay, here's the deal. I can't fix most of the world's injustices.

But I can at least try to find out who took Luther Dunlap's life. I will be careful, but I can't give up, Rip. Not yet, at least."

She stood and walked to the low table, snapping her fingers above it. Rip obediently jumped onto it and sat on his haunches, ready for more cosseting. Juanita brushed and brushed, until his coat took on a glossy sheen. He let out a contented sigh.

"You know, if you were a cat," Juanita said, "your purr would be lifting the rafters."

He opened an accusing eye.

Juanita chuckled. "Wrong comparison, huh?" She scratched under his chin. "I suppose if I keep at this research, someone will eventually tell me the whole story. At times I envy the simplicity of your life, Rip."

The dog closed both eyes. Looking a little smug, she thought.

Four

A speeding ambulance careened down the narrow street mere inches behind Juanita, the heat from its motor warming her backside. The siren shrilled, urged her to stop, give up. Her legs felt weighted, the asphalt underfoot as spongy as oatmeal. Spiky skyscrapers lined the lane, cutting off escape.

Somewhere, a dog yipped.

Juanita twisted to look at her pursuer, staggered, nearly fell. The white van had become an ice monster shooting knobby icicles, its orange stripes trailing like ribbons. She teetered, regained her footing, raced on.

Spying an opening between buildings, she summoned strength and hurled herself into it. The ambulance sped by, its shriek fading in the distance. Sobbing with relief, she sagged against the alley wall.

A siren wailed again, louder. A gramophone zoomed towards her, growing larger by the moment. Scrambling alongside, the RCA Victor dog of "His Master's Voice" ads fame yelped once, twice—

A yapping in her ear woke Juanita. Chilly, she pulled a quilt around her shoulders and dazedly opened her eyes. Rip whined, barked again, his nose nudging her hand. She had let him stay in last night, for company. Raising her head, she looked at the luminous clock face atop her nightstand—2:23.

Above Rip's excited appeals, the piercing wail of a siren sounded, slackened, then died. That part of the dream had been real.

An emergency vehicle must have stopped nearby.

Juanita jumped up, slid her feet into scuffs, and grabbed a housecoat. Running to the living room's bay window, she yanked the drape aside. A reddish glow lit the world beyond the panes. She struggled into her wrapper, gave Rip a farewell pat, wrenched open the front door and dashed out.

Russet haze filled the sky to the west. Juanita ran towards it, hugging herself in the night chill, houseshoes slapping the sidewalk. Two blocks along, she heard a shout. Just past a line of crepe-myrtle bushes, she saw a red pumper truck parked at the curb.

Firemen scurried about, unfurling a hose, raising a ladder against a frame house. Flames and smoke poured from the attic. Blazing tongues leapt from that dwelling and licked the side of the one next door.

Warm from the fire, Juanita unfolded her arms. Spectators in nightwear clustered in neighboring yards. To her surprise, one group consisted of Mavis Ralston, her husband Tully, and another woman cowering behind Mavis. All wore robes and pajamas. Countless tiny curlers dotted Mavis's head, gray tendrils of hair escaping.

Juanita shook herself, wondering if she was still dreaming. Then she recalled the Ralstons had moved into her neighborhood several weeks ago from an outlying part of Wyndham.

"Mavis!" Juanita called. "Is that *your* house that's on fire?"

Mavis turned, eyes glazed with worry, and pointed towards the less-involved of the two burning structures. She looked oddly tranquil, perhaps half in shock, Juanita thought.

"At least you and Tully got out. Your smoke detectors must've worked."

Mavis frowned, looking more like herself. "Tully hadn't got around to installing them yet." The complaint sounded more like Mavis.

"Martha smelled smoke," wheezed Tully Ralston. A slight man, he had a hangdog expression Juanita attributed to his having to live with Mavis.

"Don't hide back there, Martha," said his wife crossly. "This is Juanita Wills—her I told you about. My sister, Martha Jenkins." Mavis turned back to the fire, hands clasped anxiously at her breast.

Martha stepped into the light. Even thinner than her sister, she had warm brown eyes, a small, straight nose and graying chestnut curls. Attractive, in spite of time's ravages and an air of deep sadness, Juanita thought.

"Hello," Martha ventured, hesitantly extending a hand.

"Glad to meet you, Martha." Juanita shook the hand. "It's lucky you were awake to sound the alarm."

Martha gave a rueful shrug. "I did everything backwards, called 911 before getting everyone out. So scared I couldn't think straight."

"At least you're all okay. How about people in the other house?"

As she spoke, a beam fell in the attic of that dwelling. Juanita jumped. Mavis stood as if transfixed, watching a stream of water trained on her own house.

"Nobody lives there," Tully said. "Neighbor told me the woman moved to a nursing home a couple months ago."

"Good thing she wasn't here," Juanita said. "I wonder how the fire got started."

"Wiring, maybe," he suggested. "Old houses, you know."

Traffic had picked up in the area. Firefighting equipment blocked the thoroughfare, but enterprising sightseers had made a route through a vacant lot across the street, gawking out car windows that eased past. A light-colored sedan stopped a full minute before creeping on by. Martha ducked behind her sister again, as if embarrassed by all the attention.

A tan Camry Juanita recognized as Vivian Mathiesen's drove past and parked half a block away. The veteran *Wyndham Daily News* reporter, wearing a red jogging suit and carrying a camera bag, got out and approached. A few years older than Mavis, Vivian seemed to Juanita much younger. She waved at Juanita, set her bag down, took out a camera and focused it on a fireman silhouetted against the flames.

Mavis reached for Tully's hand, the simple gesture speaking her anguish. Tully awkwardly patted his wife's arm, as if unused to coping with a frightened Mavis. Juanita felt unaccustomed pity for her nemesis.

To break the tension, she said to Martha, "I hope the rest of your visit is better than this. You planning to be here much longer?"

Mavis's head swiveled towards her sister, as if she wondered the same thing.

"I . . . I'm . . . not sure," Martha said.

Silence fell over the spectators. For something else to say, Juanita asked, "Did you and Mavis grow up in Wyndham?"

Martha peered from behind her sister. "Yes . . . But I've . . . been away . . . for many years."

"Had a yen for the big city," said Mavis darkly. "Not enough high life in a small town for *her*."

No one could nurse a grievance like Mavis, even in the midst of anxiety, Juanita thought.

"Wyndham's not exciting," she said, "but I like the slow pace—as long as I can get to a city occasionally."

Martha didn't reply at first. Shy, Juanita decided. Something about this woman appealed to her, maybe just the fact she wasn't her sister.

"It's . . . changed since I left," Martha finally said. "And yet it . . . hasn't."

Another crash came from the empty house, sending sparks out an upper window. As one, the watchers flinched back.

An amiable-looking couple about the Ralstons' age joined them. Tully made introductions, explaining he had known Paula and Frank McMichaels since childhood and that they now lived a few houses away.

"Come stay with us tonight," Paula urged. "You won't want to be here, even once the fire's out. Not with that smoke smell."

Mavis glanced at Tully. "I guess that wouldn't be good for your asthma. Okay, thanks. We'll go in and get a few things when they say it's safe." She paused, glanced at Martha. "You have room for my sister too?"

"Sure," said Frank heartily. "The more the merrier."

Paula looked uncertain. "I'm afraid she'll have to sleep on the couch. It's not terribly comfortable."

"You can stay with me, Martha," Juanita heard herself say. "I have a spare room."

Martha's eyes widened. "How . . . kind. Especially when. . . you've just met me."

Mavis pursed her lips. "Don't put yourself out, Juanita. She'll be fine with the McMichaelses."

"Nonsense. I'll enjoy the company."

But Juanita wondered if she had spoken too hastily. What if, in spite of appearances, Martha turned out to have a disposition like her sister's?

Vivian moved among the bystanders with a notebook, asking questions, and soon reached Juanita's side.

"Lollygagging at this hour?" she asked with a grin.

"I'm entitled, when there's a fire in my neighborhood. You remember Mavis Ralston, who works at the library. And this is her husband Tully and her sister Martha."

"Why, hello, Martha," Vivian said. "Didn't know you were

back. You here for long?"

"A—a while, I guess."

"The Ralstons own that house," Juanita told Vivian, gesturing towards their residence.

"So the folks over there said. Haven't time to visit now, Martha, but call me at the paper and we'll get together." Vivian turned to address Mavis. "Who or what alerted you to the fire? Did you have smoke detectors?"

The homeowners answered her low-voiced queries. Juanita noticed the blazes in both houses had lessened substantially, the one at the Ralstons' now just smoke. She drew her robe closer against the returning chill. Spectators began to drift away. Soon, Vivian thanked the Ralstons, waved to Juanita and Martha, and moved on.

Given the "all-clear" by a fireman, the sisters went to get some belongings for an overnight stay. As they came out, Juanita heard Mavis tell her sister, with a head-gesture in Juanita's direction, "Watch yourself with that one. She's snoopy as they come."

Martha gave Juanita an apprehensive glance, but accompanied her to her house. She said little during their walk.

As they entered Juanita's living room, Rip came forward to greet his mistress. Seeing the stranger, he cowered back. His wariness seemed to melt something in Martha. She knelt down, crooned softly, scratched his head, and soon won him over. Juanita got her settled in the guest bedroom and offered a nightcap of decaffeinated coffee.

"Not that there's much of the night left," Juanita said. "But a warm drink may help us settle down and get to sleep."

Martha accepted, clearly more relaxed now. They sat at the kitchen table and sipped decaf, Rip lying at Juanita's feet.

"Mavis didn't say where you're from," Juanita hinted.

"Toronto—most recently."

"Really. Where else have you lived?"

"Several cities in Canada and Europe. And several states."

"You must've had a wealth of experiences."

Martha stared into her steaming cup. "They weren't . . . all happy."

"No one's are. Do you have a husband? Children?"

Martha hesitated, then shook her head. "No. No, I haven't."

The silence stretched to a minute, then two.

"Do you enjoy reading?" Juanita finally asked, wanting to continue the conversation.

Martha smiled. "Romances, mostly. But I read anything."

"Help yourself to my bookshelves. I'm not big on romances, myself, but the library has lots. You should come down."

Martha's eyes widened. "Maybe I will." She shifted positions. "It—it must be enjoyable—working in a library."

"I love it. Being around books, buying and looking after them, recommending them to people. It's not all fun, of course. What kind of work do you do?"

"A little of everything."

Juanita stifled a yawn. "Mavis said something about your needing care. Are you on a special diet? I can go to the grocery tomorrow—today—if I don't have what you need."

Martha frowned. "Care? I've no—oh, I did tell her I take medicine for my nerves." She chuckled. "Mavis must've convinced herself the reason I came back is that I'm dying."

"So why *did* you? Sorry, that sounds inhospitable. I'm just interested."

The gentle face blanched. "I . . . wanted to see my sister."

"But why now?"

"Oh . . . you know . . . we're both getting older."

"Mm. You two have siblings? I don't recall Mavis mentioning any. But then, she hadn't told me about you either."

"Just us."

"Were you and Mavis close, growing up?"

Martha nodded thoughtfully. "We were."

She appeared to struggle with some memory, then fell silent.

Watching her, Juanita felt compassion for this quiet woman who seemed broken by life.

"What was Mavis like as a kid?"

Martha roused. "Cheerful. Sparkly."

"Mavis?" Juanita choked. "Sorry, I know she's your sister. But what in the world changed her?"

"I'm not sure. She was only eight when I—" Martha abruptly rose, eyes brimming with sudden tears. "I've—talked too much. I'll find something to read and turn in. Thanks for the coffee."

Once Juanita got to bed, she didn't fall asleep for a while, thinking about once-sunny Mavis, who had somehow grown up hating the world.

Five

As Juanita and Martha breakfasted in the kitchen the next day, a Saturday, they listened to local news on the radio. The lead story reported autopsy results on Samuel Davis, an elderly Bryson's Corner man who had died several weeks earlier.

Cause of death, according to the autopsy, was an old-fashioned one: bread poisoning.

Bread poisoning? Juanita dropped the slice of toast she was buttering.

"An unnamed source close to the Wyndham Police Department," the disembodied voice said, "told this reporter that Davis died as a result of ingesting corn cockle, a noxious weed sometimes found in wheat fields."

He noted that Davis had been hospitalized the day before his death with a sudden onset of severe stomach pain, weakness, and nausea.

Juanita looked at her house guest. "Bread poisoning. Ever heard of such a thing?"

Martha shook her head.

"Corn cockle is a common weed that can be a danger to livestock," the report went on. "But accidental poisoning of humans is extremely rare these days, because of modern herbicides, good commercial seed screening, and the decline in home-grinding of flour."

He quoted the anonymous source as saying that a partly eaten loaf of homemade bread that had been found in Davis's refrigerator after the victim's death was thought to be the source of the poison.

"A card attached to the bread wrapper indicated it came from the kitchen of a local woman known to distribute foods randomly to houses in the Wyndham area."

"Grace Hendershot!" Juanita said, a hand flying to her face.

"The Wyndham Police Department declined to either confirm or deny this report," the voice continued. "But Detective Lieutenant Wayne Cleary warns that members of the public should never eat any food acquired from a suspicious or unknown source."

"Poor Gracie." Switching off the radio after the news concluded, Juanita spread blackberry jam on her toast, a seven-grain variety from a commercial bakery. "This will devastate her . . ."

"Grace Hendershot . . ." Martha mused. "Grace . . . she was . . ."

"The worst thing about this—well, the worst is Davis's death, of course . . ."

" . . . I've wondered . . ."

" . . . the next worst is that Mavis will say 'I told you so' *ad nauseum*."

" . . . such poise . . . even when kids teased her . . ."

" . . . Mavis has said for years Gracie's food isn't safe . . ."

" . . . may've known about . . ."

" . . . but I, for one, won't quit eating her pickles. More coffee, Martha? Excuse me, were you saying something about Grace?"

"Half a cup, please . . . . It was nothing important."

After breakfast Juanita phoned Robert Norwood, Doug's fellow teacher, to whom she had written earlier expressing sympathy over Davis's death. It was Norwood who had arranged the Davis interview for her. Juanita asked if he could meet her for a quick lunch.

"Possibly," he said without enthusiasm, "though I'd just planned to work around the yard. Any particular reason?"

"It's about the Wyndham history I'm working on."

"Oh, okay." His voice held quickening interest. "Where?"

"The drugstore? Quarter to twelve?"

"See you then."

The day was bright and fair, though a little warm for mid-October. Juanita walked the few blocks to the library, which stayed open till two on Saturdays, and handled some correspondence. She then left Meador overseeing a new part-timer at the circulation desk and hiked on downtown to the drugstore. She ordered a tuna sandwich and coffee and was seated in a booth at one end of the old-style soda fountain, sipping the coffee, when a powerfully built man strode in the front door. Tall, with just a hint of a potbelly, Robert moved with an athlete's grace. He took the seat opposite her and said a somber hello.

"I'm terribly sorry about Mr. Davis's death, Robert," Juanita said. "I know he was like a second father to you."

"Thanks. Those flowers you sent were really nice. I hope Samuel's son sent a thank-you card." As she nodded, he ran a hand over his close-cropped hair, his handsome face gloomy.

"Sorry I couldn't make it to the funeral. I'd signed up for a literacy-training class that day and didn't want to cancel at the last minute. As it turned out, I probably could've come—the instructor got sick halfway through and couldn't finish. She'd had recent surgery and evidently was trying to do too much too soon. They rescheduled the workshop."

Juanita moved her arm to let the elderly counter clerk place a sandwich in front of her.

"The news about the autopsy must've been difficult to hear," she went on. "What an awful accident."

Robert turned to give the server his order, then faced Juanita again. His left eyebrow rose.

"You do think it was accidental?" Juanita asked, pausing with the sandwich almost to her mouth.

"Hard to believe anybody'd deliver food to people's houses just at random."

"I know a woman who does. She enjoys cooking and likes giving away the finished product—doesn't much care who gets to eat it."

Robert sat up straight. "You know who the person is? You told the police yet?"

The elderly man brought Robert's Pepsi and sandwich, poured Juanita a refill, and returned behind the counter.

"Everybody in town knows Grace," Juanita said, "including the police. Anyway, the radio said a note was with the bread, telling who the baker was. Of course, we can't be sure how accurate that report was. 'Source close to the department,' indeed—that could be somebody who picks up trash at the police station."

Robert rubbed at his slim mustache, the gesture suggesting suppressed anger. "Why'd this nutcase have to take bread to *him*?"

"I don't know. But she isn't crazy—just odd—and she'd never poison anyone on purpose. She must've been crushed to learn her bread had caused a death." Juanita paused, her meal half finished.

His mouth worked with emotion. At last he cleared his throat and said, "Samuel was such a kind person. Good to the neighborhood kids. He'd play games with them, make toys for them."

In a kind of reverie, Robert went on. "He was especially partial to a Granger kid from down the street, carved lots of little boats and trains for him. Cory moved away years ago, never even came back to visit. You could tell that hurt Samuel." Robert rubbed his mustache again. "He was a buddy to all the kids. They called him Uncle Sam."

They sat silently a few minutes, each chewing reflectively.

"I'm sorry to intrude on your grief, Robert," Juanita said at last, "but I need to ask, do you still think I should look into that old murder case?"

"*Some*body should. And the police haven't . . . well, I know you're close to a cop . . ."

"I agree the truth needs to come out. But maybe I'm not the right one to see it does. After Mr. Davis died, I got discouraged, pretty much gave up. But I found a new source the other day, and she got me started again. Why don't you look into it, Robert? There must be people at Bryson's Corner who know things and who'd talk to you more readily than to me."

"I'm not a writer. You are. Doug told me about the essay prizes you won at school."

"That was a while back. I do like to write, though."

"Besides, you could be more objective. To be convincing, the evidence has to be presented factually, not emotionally." A slight smile lightened Robert's expression. "Doug says you're a notorious busybody, but fair, and that you have good instincts about what to do with secrets."

"I suppose that's his version of a compliment. Okay, I do want to do it, but I'll need help. You said Mr. Davis would probably be my best source, Garvin McCoy the next best. Can you think of any other possibilities?"

"Not offhand. I suggested Samuel because Dunlap had lived near him at Bryson's Corner, and Samuel hinted once that he knew something about that night. I figure Garvin does too, but getting the story out of *him* could be like trying to swim up a waterfall."

"Based on my brief meeting with Mr. McCoy, I doubt he'd talk to me anyhow." She related the grape-juice incident.

Robert chortled. "That's Garvin, full of piss and vinegar. He and Samuel were always fighting over some little thing. Wouldn't speak for days. Then one would set up a checkerboard on his front porch, and the other knew he was ready to be friends again."

"Did they both grow up in Bryson's Corner?"

"Yeah, and apparently went everywhere together in their youth. Except fishing—Garvin's into that, but Samuel always preferred hunting. Anyway, if Samuel knew about that old killing, I bet you anything Garvin does too."

"McCoy's daughter says he doesn't know anything."

"Thea may think he doesn't. Or *want* to think it."

"Suppose she's afraid I wouldn't accurately report what he'd tell me?"

"Maybe. Or she just doesn't want him getting involved. I don't know Thea well—she moved back to Bryson's Corner from Tulsa a few months ago after her marriage ended in divorce—but I know she's a real private person. Nice woman, but keeps herself to herself."

"That's my impression, too. So, can you think of anyone else who might have information?"

"Let me give it some thought. I'm not from Bryson's Corner myself, but I know a few folks in the town." He took a bite and chewed slowly. "I met Samuel through an uncle of mine who used to hunt with him. We hit it off and kept hanging out even after my uncle moved to Seattle. I'd've done anything for Samuel."

He stopped, put down his sandwich, and gave Juanita a speculative look. "You didn't happen to tell anybody you'd be meeting Samuel that night, did you?"

"No. Why?"

"'Cause if I had reason to think my arranging that interview led to his death . . ."

"You're suggesting he was poisoned deliberately?" Juanita realized as soon as she spoke that the same idea had been at the back of her own mind. "Oh, Robert, I don't think so. I hadn't mentioned Davis to a soul."

"Guess I'm paranoid. It's just that Dunlap's killers may still be around. 'Course Samuel probably wouldn't have told you anything anyway. He just agreed to see you as a favor to me."

"And I appreciate your calling in that favor."

In the silence, Juanita finished her coffee, eyes avoiding his. She *hadn't* mentioned the Davis interview to anyone beforehand, had she? No. But others had known generally that she was looking into the Dunlap death, she thought guiltily. When she had first gotten interested in the case, she had asked around, eager to find any source of information. Doug had known, for one, and had introduced her to Robert. She didn't remember who-all else she'd mentioned the case to.

Even more uncomfortably, she recalled that unnamed "source close to the police department" mentioned on the radio. Still, no one in the department—not even Wayne—had known of her appointment with Davis.

"I don't suppose you know a Leona Brown, Robert?" Juanita ventured. "She'd be about Davis's and McCoy's age. I don't know if she still lives at Bryson's Corner or not."

"Leona Brown. Can't place her. How's she involved?"

Juanita repeated the rumor Katherine had mentioned.

"A love triangle, huh? I'll ask around, see if I can find out anything about this Leona Brown."

"Thanks." She told him about the other possible motives she'd learned for Luther Dunlap's murder. "If you can find anyone else I could talk to, I'd be grateful. I may even take another crack at Garvin McCoy. Suppose it would help if you asked him for me? Or asked his daughter?"

Robert hesitated, finally shrugged and said, "I don't believe I'll be able to help you there. But remember, if I manage to set up anything with Leona Brown, or anyone at Bryson's Corner, it's got to be hush-hush. Just in case, you know."

"Absolutely. Thanks a million, Robert."

Early that evening Juanita and Wayne drove to Tulsa for dinner at Chez Tournedo, one of their favorite restaurants. They had invited Martha along, but she'd said she wanted to curl up with a romance novel Juanita had brought her from the library.

Wayne and Juanita sat at an outside table in the bistro's little courtyard, in one corner of a gray-stone, half-timbered shopping center called European Crossroads. Leaves on a silver maple above Wayne's head shimmered in the dying rays of sunlight. Juanita noticed how his tan suit and soft yellow shirt emphasized his gentle hazel eyes.

"This is great," he sighed, laying a huge hand over one of hers. "I don't get to see you near enough."

She smiled, resisting saying that she'd invited him over twice recently only to learn he'd volunteered for an extra shift or made a bowling date with buddies from work. Still, she liked her space too. Juanita briefly studied the menu, which she knew almost by heart, then clapped it shut.

"Sweetbreads as usual?" he asked.

"Sounds good."

"Mixed-greens salad, blue-cheese dressing on the side?"

"Of course."

"Raspberry souffle and decaf?"

"Yes. Am I too predictable?"

"Just predictable enough."

"And you're having pepper steak, garlic mashed potatoes, Caesar salad, and chocolate layer cake?"

"Yep."

"Wayne, we're in a rut."

"So? Ruts are okay sometimes."

Juanita mentioned hearing the radio report about the Davis autopsy.

"The media shouldn't report rumors," Wayne said.

"Your name was mentioned too."

"That right?"

"Yes. They quoted you as saying people shouldn't eat anything if they weren't sure of its source."

"Good advice, don't you think?"

"Sure. Then are you working the Davis poisoning?

"You know I can't talk about my cases with you, Juanita. Next subject?"

"Zheesh! A person can't even make conversation with you."

He grinned. "I shared information on an investigation with you last year, and you nearly got yourself shot as a result."

"To be accurate," she said stiffly, "someone almost shot me, but not at my instigation. At least tell me if Davis really was poisoned, accidentally or otherwise."

"No comment."

"Thanks a lot." Juanita decided to reveal a piece of information in hopes of loosening his tongue. "Wayne, I have a good reason for asking about Davis. I had an appointment to interview him the evening before he died. But when I arrived for it, I learned he'd been taken to the hospital that very afternoon."

"That so? What were you seeing him about?"

"The Luther Dunlap killing. That old unsolved case from the 1950s that I told you I was planning to write about."

Wayne's impassive expression gave nothing away.

Exasperated, Juanita said, "You know, Wayne, you could save me time and energy on this history I'm writing if you'd let me see the paperwork on that old murder."

"Private citizens have no business rummaging through police files, especially unsolved cases. New evidence could still surface. We don't need you muddying things up."

"What makes you think *I* couldn't crack it?"

"Get real, Juanita. Amateur detectives only solve crimes in those 'cozies' you read."

"Excuse me, I believe if you had listened to me last spring when I urged you to check out that mysterious farm . . . ."

He groaned. "We're not going to rehash all that again."

"I suppose it's a long shot, Wayne, but has it occurred to you that there might be a connection between Davis's death and

Dunlap's? At least tell me how they thought to check for corn cockle at the autopsy. That can't be a test that's typically run. Someone must've tipped the examiner off to look for it."

Wayne gave an exasperated sigh. "You're assuming that story about the autopsy findings was true, which I won't confirm or deny."

"If Grace Hendershot's bread was the murder weapon, she must be terribly upset about it."

Wayne narrowed his eyes. "The radio said Grace was responsible?"

"Not exactly—it gave no name—but who else gives out food that way?"

"No comment."

"The announcer quoted an 'unnamed source close to the police department.' That wouldn't have been you, would it?"

He glared at her. "Can you see me spilling information to the press but insisting it be off the record?"

"Then who do you think the anonymous tipster was?"

Wayne's jaw set in a grim line. "No comment on that."

She bit back another question. "I don't blame you for being angry if someone at the station leaked information, Wayne. But you know I'd never betray your confidence to the media. Wayne—sweetie—it would really help me to know who was interviewed right after that old murder and what they said."

"Sorry."

"You're not, but let's not fight about it. It's too nice an evening."

"My feeling, exactly."

Anyway, Juanita thought with satisfaction, the conversation had given her another idea. Wayne had said the decades-old killing might yet get unraveled. So that might mean he was, for some reason, looking into the old crime himself. If so, the Dunlap folder could be in the cabinet behind his desk at the police station, where he often kept files on cases he was working.

A cabinet that, judging from times she'd been there, wasn't always kept locked.

Six

Monday morning, Mavis crept about the library, hands busy as ever, mind seemingly half absent. Meador mostly stayed out of her way.

"I've never seen her like this," he said to Juanita as they sat at the circulation desk after lunch. "She's really in a funk."

"True." Juanita scrolled down a computer screen, checking availability of books by Martha's favorite authors. She glanced up, saw Mavis hadn't yet returned from the stacks, and went on. "I think it's smart of her to get all the wiring checked before they move back, but the electrician she called can't get to it for a while. Martha offered to help clean up after the smoke and water but was refused. She thinks Mavis just doesn't want her around."

"Knowing my esteemed colleague, I can believe that."

"Mavis is such a homebody, this is bound to bother her a lot."

Meador connected paper clips into a chain. Juanita clicked on a book listing and brought up another screen. He cleared his throat.

"Yes?" Juanita prompted, turning towards him.

"I stopped by the State Rep's office on my lunch hour. Gilroy happened to be there and was real friendly, asked what I did for fun. Told me he relaxes by riding his horse on a place he owns outside town. Seems to be a frustrated cowboy, likes Western wear, enjoys shooting snakes out on his farm with a revolver he carries. He showed me around his office, including a closet full of old radios. Gilroy's a radio nut, has an early one bigger'n my TV."

"Really."

"He even has a police scanner to monitor emergency calls, see if any property he insures gets vandalized."

"Mm." Juanita focused on the monitor again.

"He's speaking to several civic groups the next few weeks." Meador's tone became elaborately casual. "And he asked me to go along."

"You going to hand out campaign literature for him?"

"Dunno. He said he can see I have lots of potential and he wants me to get my feet wet in politics."

Juanita swiveled to face him. "He can tell you have 'lots of potential' from meeting you at the barbecue and showing you his office today?"

"Politicians are shrewd judges of character. They have to be." Meador's eyes glowed with satisfaction. "Anyway, he seems to like me."

"I never knew you had an interest in politics."

"Just think, a piddly town like Wyndham may send a man to the U.S. Senate. And I could help get him there."

"So Gilroy *is* planning to run."

"Not for sure. He's testing the waters now."

"The same ones you're supposed to get your feet wet in? Between you, you're a walking cliché. Shouldn't he be appearing in other districts, where he's not already known?"

"He will, but this is where he hopes to raise lots of early contributions."

"Ah, money—the mother's milk of maneuverers and

manipulators. You two must've had quite a chat."

Meador grinned. "I may just decide to run for something myself."

"That'll perk Mavis up. She'll announce against you, and I'll need full body armor when I stand between you."

"Ha, and ha. How're you and your house guest doing?"

"Fine. Martha's good-natured and pleasant to be around."

"Sure she's related to Mavis?"

"If temperament's genetic, she's not."

Later that day, Mavis showed signs of returning to her old self, snapping at Meador over a misshelved biography. He grinned at Juanita and said under his breath, "She's ba-a-ack."

Soon he had posted another quote on the office wall:

> Hope I die before I get old.
> This is my generation.
> —Peter Townshend, *My Generation*

"Ironic," Juanita said, as Meador started to leave.

"What is?"

"Pete Townshend. He penned those words years ago. And though he's not exactly ancient now, he's no kid. And I bet he's planning to live many more years yet."

"And your point is?"

"Only that things look different at sixtyish or seventyish than at twentyish or thirtyish. At least I'm guessing that's true, being only fortyish myself."

"Whatever."

Later that day, Katherine called to say she had checked with other Books members and set the next meeting date for a week from tomorrow.

That evening after supper, Juanita phoned Althea, whose greeting was courteous but carried an unspoken question. After opening pleasantries, Juanita came to the point.

"I called to let you know we're resuming our Books discussions. We'll meet Tuesday-week at 7:00 P.M. to discuss *To Kill a Mockingbird*. Please join us if you can. I'm sure you could contribute good insights."

"Particularly on *that* book?" Althea's voice had acquired an edge.

Juanita visualized the rich brown features arranged in a disapproving frown. "Why—oh, because of the racial issues in it? No, I just meant you're intelligent and love literature." Juanita waited through several moments of silence, then started to say goodbye.

When Althea finally spoke, she sounded slightly more friendly. "I can't make it this time. Maybe later." She hesitated. "Thanks for thinking of me."

"You're welcome. I'll keep you posted on future meetings."

Ringing off, Juanita looked up Grace Hendershot's address in the phone book. Since that news report about the Davis autopsy, Grace's odd ways had been the talk of Wyndham, and Juanita wondered how she was dealing with the notoriety. Phone calls to her had gone unanswered, so Juanita had decided on a different approach.

After work, she drove to the older section of south Wyndham where Grace's address was located. The modest one-story frame sat back from the street, its long yard given over to rosebushes, spindly and dull with their blooms gone.

As Juanita stood on the concrete stoop and knocked, she experienced a feeling of *déjà vu*, recalling the night weeks earlier that she had rapped on the Davis and McCoy doors in Bryson's Corner. She needed to go out there again. If only Robert would smooth the way with Leona Brown, maybe even the McCoys. But given what he'd said, she shouldn't count on the latter.

Robert had behaved oddly when Althea was mentioned, Juanita thought. Maybe there was bad blood between them.

At the third unanswered knock, she concluded Grace must have left town. But then a drape moved at one side of the picture window. Eyes peered out. Juanita smiled and waved. The curtain settled back, and the door opened.

"Juanita," Grace said warily. "This is a surprise." A pink zip-front housedress hung off her tall, gaunt frame. Her face, bare now of rouge, looked pasty and haggard, as if some sorrow weighed on her.

"I've tried to phone a few times but didn't get you," Juanita said cheerily. "Thought I'd run by, make sure you're okay."

Grace hesitated, looking as if she might start crying any minute. Then seeming to reach a decision, she opened the door wider. "Come in. I've not been answering the phone, so many reporters and curiosity-seekers." She pushed a stray white lock off her forehead and added, "But it is nice to see *you*."

Juanita took a seat on a floral-printed couch, thinking that her hostess must have been pretty before age and osteoporosis took their toll. The immaculate room seemed a springtime extension of the outside, roses of various hues, sizes, and styles blooming brightly on wallpaper, carpet, and upholstery.

"I see you like roses," Juanita commented.

Grace smiled, briefly girlish-looking. "They're so soft and beautiful. A beau of mine used to—" She nervously broke off, started to sit on a chair near the couch, then stood again. "Would you like some coffee and cake? I have decaf already made." She blushed. "But you won't want to eat anything *I* baked."

"Nonsense. I'd love some."

Mavis would be horrified at her taking such a risk, Juanita thought as Grace went to the kitchen. Particularly after all the talk about the "corn cockle caper," as some wags were callously calling the story about Davis's death.

Maybe not, though. Mavis might be plotting interesting ways to kill off her boss, too.

"Sorry about all the gossip," Juanita said, when Grace had

returned and placed a saucer of feathery chocolate angel food before her on the coffee table. "You had nothing to do with that death at Bryson's Corner, of course."

A grateful smile lit the wan face. "I wish everyone was so certain. Lieutenant Cleary's nice, but sure asks lots of questions, some over and over."

"The police have to investigate, even though it was clearly an accident. You'd never poison anyone on purpose."

"Thank you for saying that!" The worry lines in Grace's face eased. "Mr. Kauffman wouldn't either. When it got out that I buy wheat from him, people started claiming his grain's no good. And that's not fair."

"Have you always bought your wheat from him?"

Grace nodded. She opened a Thermos on the coffee table, lifted Juanita's cup, and started to pour.

"You don't like commercially made flour?"

This time, Grace didn't reply. She stared into space, the carafe poised above the cup. She must be bored with this subject after the grilling she has already gotten, Juanita thought. She tried again.

"I know you've already answered this for the police, Gracie, but how'd you happen to take bread to Mr. Davis that time? Was he one of your regulars?"

The Thermos jiggled. Coffee missed Juanita's cup and splashed onto the table. A tear spilled down her hostess's cheek.

After a moment, Grace said softly, "I've not even been to Bryson's Corner for several months."

"Couldn't you have forgotten? M-m-m, this cake's wonderful."

The thin shoulders straightened, as in defiance. "I might forget some houses but not whole *towns*."

"Do you suppose you could've left the bread at someone else's place, and that person gave it to Mr. Davis?"

Grace swallowed hard, seemed to be fighting tears. "Mr. Cleary asked that too. He wanted to know where-all I'd taken bread in the past few weeks."

"And where had you?"

"No place, not for months. Far as I recall. I've only delivered jellies and pickles—you remember, I brought you a jar a while back."

"Yes, I do. And they were great." Juanita sipped coffee. "Had you ground any flour lately?"

Grace shook her head. "My memory's not what it was, but . . ." The gravelly voice trailed off.

Juanita tried a new angle. "You grew up in Wyndham, didn't you? You still have family around here?"

Grace strangled on a gulp of coffee and coughed several times. "No," she said at last. "No family. None."

"You were married a while, I believe."

"Not long. He—" Grace sobbed once, and held her hand to her face.

Juanita reached across the space between them and laid a soothing hand on the other woman's knee. "I'm sorry to ask you all these questions, Grace, when you've been through so much already. I'd like to help you if I can. But if you'd rather not talk any more, I'll go."

Grace looked up. "No, don't leave." She wiped a palm over her damp eyes. "My husband wasn't—from here—went back where he came from."

Juanita sipped her coffee. "You attended school here, didn't you? You mentioned a beau earlier—a classmate, perhaps?"

Grace stiffened. "No, he wasn't that."

"Do you recall a Martha Jenkins? You might've even been in the same class."

"Jenkins? No."

"That's a married name. Now what was Mavis's maiden name? It'll come to me. Martha's back here visiting now—staying with me, in fact." Juanita explained about the fire at the Ralston home.

"Haney—that was it, Mavis Haney. Martha's been gone from here many years, moving around from place to place."

"Martha Haney . . . Martha—oh!" The watery eyes snapped shut, then wide open. "Martha Haney."

"You do remember her, then." Juanita savored her last bite of cake, then raised a new subject. "Grace, I know things are difficult for you right now. And I don't like bringing up sad things from the past, but you might be able to help me with something." She told briefly about her historical research. "Do you recall the murder of Luther Dunlap, back in the fifties? I believe you'd have been in high school then."

The slender shoulders sagged. A minute, then two passed, with Grace staring into space. When she stirred this time, she glanced about as if trying to recall where she was, then asked, "More cake?"

"It's delicious, but I mustn't. My annual physical's tomorrow, and the doctor will fuss about my weight as it is."

Grace turned to look full at Juanita. "You're not fat."

"I like myself fine this size, but Dr. Sweeney worries . . ."

Grace's eyes again took on a distant look. Her cup tilted in its saucer, and both seemed about to slide from her lap. Realizing she had drifted away once more, Juanita gently took the dishes and set them on the table.

"I should go—" she began.

Grace roused again. "No. Please. I like the company." The pale face took on an arch look, and Grace snickered. "Guess I'm having one of my 'spacey days.'" Seeing her guest's surprised look, she continued. "I know what people say. 'Poor Gracie, she has her spacey days—not right in the head, you see.' You'll have more decaf, at least?"

"Okay, then."

Juanita tried other questions, but they seemed to push Grace deeper into abstraction. Finally, she said a polite goodbye.

As she walked to her car, she pondered the interview. If Grace's memory was right—a big "if"—where *had* that bread in Davis's kitchen come from?

Perhaps the anonymous source of that radio report had been wrong, and Davis's death hadn't been caused by poison. Or perhaps he had ingested corn cockle another way. Had his death truly been accidental? Or planned?

Seven

Robert Norwood phoned Tuesday morning, saying he had been out to Bryson's Corner, located Leona Brown, and persuaded her to talk with Juanita.

"Terrific, Robert! Thank you!"

"I didn't mention the rumors about her and Dunlap," he went on. "I just said you needed to talk to anyone who was around in '59 about that old case. She's not in good health but said if you'll call the daughter she lives with and arrange a time, she'll see you." He told how to reach the daughter, a Mrs. Yvonne Cousins.

"I'm grateful, Robert. This could be an immense help."

"Also, I saw Garvin McCoy sitting out on Samuel's park bench, and—since Thea's car was gone—I stopped. He and I talked awhile, and I asked him about the Dunlap murder. He was cagey but didn't deny knowing something. The trick'll be getting any information he has *out* of him."

"Think it would be worth appealing to Althea for her help?"

Juanita heard a quick indrawn breath. "We'd better leave her out of this."

"Suppose it'd make her mad if I talked to him behind her back?"

"Possibly. Thea's a nice woman, but she watches over her dad like Cerberus guarding the gates of Hades."

"I didn't realize you were up on your Greek mythology."

"Because I'm a jock?" He chuckled. "Here I'd thought you weren't one to stereotype people. Seriously, Juanita, you may have to choose between angering Thea and losing the story." He paused. "The people who know what really happened are getting up in years. If you're going to find out the truth . . . ."

"I'd better get on with it?"

"Yeah. Anyway, Doug says you're congenitally unable to leave any secret alone."

"Doug's a wise-off. But I would hate to give up on this one, now that I'm finally making progress."

"Good. You talk to Leona, and I'll keep working on Garvin. But remember your promise to keep mum about these folks' cooperation. Just in case."

"Absolutely." Juanita hung up, spirits dampened by a feeling of foreboding brought on by Robert's last words.

As she had feared, her weight came in for criticism that afternoon. After giving Juanita her physical, Dr. Lauretta Sweeney sat at her desk in the examining room, frowning at a paper listing test results.

"This won't do, Juanita. Excess pounds carry health risks, and you need to lose at least forty, preferably fifty. Your blood pressure isn't dangerous now, but it's creeping upward, higher than someone your age ought to have." The doctor straightened her own compact body and swept a wing of salt-and-pepper hair off her cheek. "Heart problems or strokes could be in your future. Not to mention diabetes, which runs in your family—both sides."

"I've been a bad girl."

"Don't make light of this, Juanita. I'm prescribing a plan of diet and exercise, and I want your solemn word you'll follow it."

Juanita hesitated. "I already hike to work and back most days. I guess I could walk even more. But I have trouble sticking to a diet. I love to eat."

Dr. Sweeney's expression softened. "So do I. But there are things I value more. My family. My work." She folded her hands on the desktop. "My life."

"I'm not old yet. Can't I enjoy food a few more years before I have to count every calorie?"

"Juanita, you're too smart to think that way. We now know that poor eating habits, even in the teen years, have health consequences later in life. What you do now, matters. Are you going to take off weight and get fit?"

"I guess you won't let me leave till I promise."

"Damn straight."

Juanita sighed. "You've never steered me wrong before, Lauretta. Okay, you got me. I'll try."

"Don't try. Do it."

That evening after a light and somewhat unsatisfying dinner of broiled fish, green beans, and green salad, Juanita lolled on the living-room floor. One hand idly stroked Rip's fur, while she watched the night deepen through the bay window. Martha rose from her easy chair, stretched, and said, "Think I'll go rinse out a few things."

"Like to use the machine? I usually do laundry on weekends, but you're welcome to use it any time."

"No, thanks. I prefer washing my underthings by hand."

"Whatever. You know where the detergent is."

When Martha had left the room, Juanita went to the telephone and dialed. A female voice answered.

"Yvonne Cousins?" Juanita asked.

"Yes."

Juanita gave her name and said she was calling to arrange an interview with Leona Brown about events in Wyndham during the 1950s.

"Robert Norwood talked to your mother yesterday, and she agreed."

"Mama don't need nobody botherin' her about stuff happened long ago."

"I mainly need to ask her about a death that occurred back in 1959."

"Won't help you none. Mama don't dwell in the past like a lotta old folks."

"Could I speak to her, please?"

"She cain't come to the phone. She's asleep."

"Then would you ask her when she wakes up? Any evening except Thursday would work for me, or about any time during the weekend." Juanita left her number and cradled the receiver, doubting she would get a return call. "So much for that lead," she muttered. "Protective daughters—wonder if I'd have tried to control Mother's life if she'd lived, like Mrs. Cousins and Althea do with their elderly parents'?"

She glanced up, saw Martha had stepped back into the room. Her face looked colorless.

"I didn't . . . mean to intrude. I just . . . wanted to ask if you have any . . . um . . . plastic hangers that I could . . . dry things on."

"I think so. There are usually a few in here." Juanita rummaged in a coat closet near the entry door, found half a dozen hangers, and handed them to Martha, who took them with a shaking hand.

What was troubling this gentle woman? Juanita wondered.

Martha swallowed hard. "Juanita, I . . . wasn't trying to eavesdrop, but I did hear . . . part of your conversation. It sounds as if you're trying to do . . . a history of Wyndham."

"'Trying' is the operative word."

"That's . . . ambitious. Are you . . . finding out what you need?"

Juanita shrugged, wondering how much to say in view of

Robert's request that she keep quiet about the Bryson's Corner interviews. But surely Martha was safe to talk to. She might even prove to be a source of information. Juanita decided to trust her.

"There's an old, unsolved murder case I'm researching, and some people don't seem to want to talk about it." She sat on the couch and gestured for Martha to join her. "That only makes me more interested, of course. You'd have been here then, Martha. What do you recall about the Luther Dunlap killing?"

Martha half-collapsed onto the sofa beside Juanita, eyes closed, lips moving in silent conversation with herself. At last, she sat up straight and opened her eyes.

"It was a—horrid thing," she quavered. "It . . . taught me I . . . couldn't live in this town any more."

"It seems unbelievable, even years later," Juanita agreed sadly. "Martha, I hate to ask you to relive that time, but what's your best guess about why the murder happened?" Without mentioning Katherine Greer's name, Juanita listed possible motives she had heard mentioned. "Which do you think is the most likely?"

"Does . . . bigotry need a reason?"

"I guess not. But something usually triggers violence, even from a bigot."

Martha didn't reply for a long time, her face ashen.

"Juanita," she said at last, "I like you, and I'm . . . grateful you took me in—when my own sister didn't want me—but those days . . . are hard to talk about. Let me think about it."

"Of course." Juanita leaned over and laid an arm around Martha's shoulders. "I don't want to cause you distress. The story does cry out to be told, though. You may know something you don't even realize you know."

Martha stiffened. "I'm well aware of what I know—and what I don't."

Juanita decided on a change of subject. "What got Mavis so bent out of shape towards you, anyway? She's not the world's most charitable person, but, as you pointed out, you are her sister."

"Oh . . . that's all in the past, too."

"With such an age difference, she must've seemed more like a daughter or a niece than a sister."

"Yes, I suppose I mothered her." Martha's tone softened. "Our parents weren't good at showing affection. Especially Father." She appeared to struggle with some memory, then fell silent.

Maybe she'd open up later, Juanita thought, biting back another question. "Please don't mention my investigation to anyone, will you? I wouldn't want it to get out who has cooperated with me."

Slowly, Martha nodded.

Juanita removed her arm from the other woman's shoulder. "After you finish your washing, how about a stroll? It's a nice night, and I've been ordered to get more exercise. Also, I don't think you've left the house your whole time here."

Martha hesitated. "A . . . walk? Well . . ."

Rip pricked up his ears.

"We'll have to take the beast," Juanita said, "now that you've said his favorite word, 'w-a-l-k.'"

"O-o-okay."

"Better wear a sweater. The nights are getting chilly."

Martha finished her laundry, and they donned wraps and walking shoes. Juanita fastened Rip's leash, dodging his excitedly thrashing tail. As they stepped outside, his spurt of energy nearly yanked Juanita's arm from its socket. But soon he settled into a prancing gait, pulling her briskly along.

"Meet my trainer, Dr. Sweeney," Juanita puffed. "Naming this dog after Jack the Ripper may prove prophetic."

A nearly full moon had risen, revealing fuzzy-edged houses and trees. They had walked a couple of blocks when a light-colored auto drove slowly past, as if its occupant was hunting a house number. Rip watched alertly, apparently hoping it contained another dog for him to bark at. When the car sped up and turned a corner, taillights winking, he shifted his attention to a nearby tree.

"Beautiful night," said Juanita, gazing contentedly at the starry canopy overhead. "Guess I'll be seeing more evening skies now. That'll delight Rip. I've mostly let him exercise by running around the back yard, but he does adore being walked."

Looking fully recovered from her earlier distress, Martha smiled, teeth glinting in the moonlight. "I have to admit I've missed Wyndham. The stars seem brighter in small towns than in cities."

"It's not much of a commute from one end of town to the other."

"Doesn't take long to read the daily paper."

"It's not a true daily, in fact—comes out six days a week."

"Even I could tear the phone book in half."

"Not many zip codes or area codes to remember."

Martha laughed, a merry, infectious trill that suggested she had been a charming girl. Juanita wished she had known her then.

A short time after they returned home, the telephone rang. To Juanita's surprise, it was Yvonne Cousins.

"Mama says she'll talk to you."

"Wonderful."

They arranged that Juanita would drive out to Bryson's Corner the next evening. Mrs. Cousins gave directions to her home.

"Don't wear Mama out, hear? Or you'll have to leave."

"I understand. And thanks. Thanks very much."

"Ain't no doings of mine."

Eight

The next evening Juanita settled herself on Yvonne Cousins's green-striped couch and opened a steno pad. In a straight-backed chair nearby, her tiny subject sat erect, wrinkled hands folded serenely in lap, hair swept back in a tight knot. Across the room, her daughter, a solidly built woman who looked to be in her late forties, slumped sullenly in an easy chair.

"I appreciate your seeing me, Miz Brown," Juanita said, a trifle nervously. "Your recollections of events during 1959 could help me a lot."

Leona Brown graciously inclined her head. "I'm called Mrs. Brown, although I've never married. Mr. Norwood assured me you will correctly report what I say. I hadn't met him myself until yesterday, but the mutual friend who introduced us guaranteed his integrity."

Her daughter's fingertips drummed the arm of her chair, a reminder of her disapproving presence.

"I don't want to tire you," Juanita said hastily, thinking that mother and daughter could hardly be more different, certainly in their speech. "We can stop whenever you say. And if we aren't finished, perhaps I could come back another time."

"I'm not so fragile as my daughter fears," Mrs. Brown said, full lips smiling. "Pose your questions."

"Thanks. I need to know what you recall about the murder of Luther Dunlap. Even small details might help."

The ebony hands clasped each other tightly. Their owner didn't speak for a moment. "I didn't witness the slaying myself. As you probably know, colored people were not supposed to be in Wyndham after sundown at that time."

"Lose the 'colored' crap, Mama," growled her daughter. "Say 'African-American' or 'black.'"

"In those days, dear," Mrs. Brown said quietly, "'colored' was the term used—or something worse. I'm trying to give Miss Wills a sense of the way things were."

"No need to talk to her a-tall," Mrs. Cousins muttered.

"Please be courteous to our visitor, dear. Continue, Miss Wills."

"Do you think Mr. Dunlap was killed because he challenged the accepted practice? You know, deliberately stayed in town after nightfall. Could that have brought on the attack?"

Mrs. Brown shook her head. "No. Luther was brave but not reckless. He didn't take foolish risks."

"So his being in Wyndham at all must mean someone took him there?"

"So I would surmise."

"Have you a theory about who killed him?"

"I have not."

"Then, may I get your reaction to rumors I've heard about the possible motive?"

"Of course."

"One was that Mr. Dunlap stole a deer that a white boy named Ward Nutchell had shot."

"I have no knowledge of any such thing. And I wasn't acquainted with anyone named Nutchell."

"But you did know people in Wyndham, right? I understand

you helped your mother clean houses there."

"Yes, I met quite a few townspeople that way. Also, Wyndham folk often came out to buy eggs, chickens, and produce from families in Bryson's Corner. My father was known all around the area for his strawberries and tomatoes."

"What do you think, then? You believe Dunlap was killed over a deer?"

"I'd known Luther Dunlap since childhood, Miss Wills. He wasn't a thief."

Juanita mentioned another possible motive, a quarrel that had begun when a white boy beat Dunlap's dog.

Mrs. Brown frowned reflectively. "That one rings truer. Luther thought a lot of his hound, and I remember it turned up badly injured not long before his death. I never heard him say whom he considered responsible." She turned to her daughter. "Perhaps you would bring us some of that delicious cherry pie you made today, dear. Would you prefer coffee or tea with it, Miss Wills?"

"Either, if it's decaf. If not, water's fine. But, as for the pie, my doctor thinks she put me on a diet yesterday."

Mrs. Brown smiled. "It's your choice, of course, but I recommend the pie. My daughter's an excellent baker."

"I guess a small piece won't hurt. I'll be extra good tomorrow."

Mrs. Cousins stomped across the glossy hardwood floor and down a hallway, her steps fading with distance. Juanita considered the unlikely pair. Mrs. Brown was a petite but shapely woman, dark as walnut, the daughter tall, square, and caramel-colored. Their attire also contrasted, the latter wearing a roomy jumpsuit, the former in a bandbox-neat pleated skirt and blouse.

Their home showed evidence of loving attention from one or both. Surfaces gleamed, furnishings were placed for maximum coziness, crisp curtains adorned windows, lacy doilies covered every available flat area. Framed pictures sat neatly aligned on a table by the couch.

One old black-and-white photo of a teenaged girl appeared to be a likeness of Leona Brown herself. Though grainy, it revealed the same curvaceous mouth, the tip-tilted eyebrows, the deep skin tone. She had been a beauty, and still was.

"Now, Miss Wills—" Mrs. Brown lowered her voice—"I believe you're working up to asking me about another bit of gossip that circulated then, that Luther was killed because of a rivalry in love. One that involved me."

Juanita almost crumpled with relief. She had dreaded this part of the interview. "I did hear Mr. Dunlap and a white teenager were both interested in you."

The lovely old face lengthened. "It's one of the great sorrows of my life that I didn't more strongly deny that story, both before and after Luther's death."

"So it wasn't true?"

Mrs. Brown sighed, a world of regret in the sound. "I'll tell you the truth, Miss Wills, but you mustn't pass it on, nor put a word of it in your book."

"I—if it's relevant to the murder, I'd have to inform the police."

"It's not. And I assure you, it has no place in a history of Wyndham."

"Okay, then."

"Luther Dunlap and I were never a couple. I was, however, seeing someone in Wyndham at the time. A married man."

"Oh."

"I was actually grateful when that rumor about me and a white boy got started, since it hid the truth." Mrs. Brown shook her head sorrowfully. "The young don't look ahead to consequences, you see. They only perceive what works in their favor at the time."

"I doubt you could've prevented what happened," Juanita murmured. "People believe pretty much what they want to believe."

"But I didn't have to *encourage* the falsehood. When Luther was killed—in that terrible way—many people blamed me. I did, myself, though for a different reason than others did. My daughter suffered while growing up because of her mother's reputation."

She paused, then went on. "I've tried to make amends. I finally told my daughter who her father is, though I made her promise not to contact him. He and his family moved away years ago but still have ties to people in Wyndham. He's a nice man, weak but sweet, and I don't want the father of my child bothered." One wrinkled hand smoothed a pleat. Tears gathered in the aging eyes. "But the damage done to Yvonne and to our relationship may be irreparable.

"You'll have noticed her language differs greatly from my own. I was taught to speak correctly as a child and found proper speech important in my teaching career. Yvonne deliberately uses poor grammar, slang expressions, anything to differentiate herself from me." The elderly voice shook with emotion. "Oh, my daughter loves me, Miss Wills. Yvonne's very tender in caring for me. But she still resents my long silence."

Embarrassed, Juanita said softly, "I'm sorry if my coming here causes a problem between the two of you."

"If you can discover and reveal what really happened to Luther, it will be well worth it."

"Do you have any idea, then, who the girl would have been? If a love triangle did lead to Mr. Dunlap's death?"

"I recall seeing a couple of young white women at his place—at different times, not together—but have no idea what their names were. One was tall and had long, light-colored hair. The other was shorter and dark-haired. Both pretty."

Mrs. Cousins returned, bearing a laden tray. She plopped a steaming mug and a saucer of pie on the coffee table in front of Juanita, served her mother, and carried her own food to her chair.

"Thank you, Mrs. Cousins." Juanita tried the pie, shivering with delight at its crisp pastry and tart-sweet filling. "M-m-m, wonderful."

Mrs. Cousins didn't exactly smile, but her frown eased. For a few minutes, they concentrated on eating. Then Juanita set down her empty plate and took up her tablet.

"I heard another possible motive for Mr. Dunlap's death," she said. "Revenge for his victory in an inter-school track meet against Wyndham."

Mrs. Brown smiled broadly. "Oh, yes. Luther won the 100-yard dash, the pole vault, and the broad jump. That made everyone in Bryson's Corner proud, I can tell you."

"I assume Wyndhamites weren't happy about those losses?"

"That's gross understatement. Some were enraged. I believe this theory of Luther's death is the one you should focus on."

"Really. Do you recall anyone in particular being angry?"

Mrs. Brown sipped coffee, looking thoughtful. "One of the women my mother worked for was a Mrs. Tubbs, and her whole family was absolutely incensed. The Tubbses hated having Bryson's Corner even *compete* against Wyndham, much less have the temerity to *win*. It didn't help that the son, Lonnie, was one of those defeated by Luther in the foot race."

"Lonnie Tubbs . . . that name's familiar. Doesn't he own a lot of real estate in and around Wyndham?"

"Yes, he appears to have done well for himself."

"I'll try to talk to him. Anyone else you think of?"

"Lonnie ran around with a couple of boys. Let's see now, one's name was Arnold—Vincent Arnold. Yes, that was it, Vince Arnold. The other was . . . Simon Simms."

"The fussbudget accountant?"

Mrs. Brown chuckled. "I don't know Mr. Simms as an adult, but he probably would be like that now. A nervous lad, I recall."

"And Vince Arnold?"

"He impressed me as a sly type, largely controlled by the Tubbs boy. I don't know if he'd still be around."

"Did you ever hear those three boys mention Luther Dunlap

by name?"

"Once. The Arnold boy was upset over someone's putting sugar in his gas tank. He blamed Luther."

"I heard Dunlap did that to retaliate for the beating of his dog."

"So, that was the connection. Both Vince and Lonnie used the word 'nigger' freely that day, I remember."

"What about Simon Simms?"

Mrs. Brown stared into her cup. "He was more restrained. As if he didn't concur in the others' attitude but wouldn't cross them."

"Going along's just as bad," Mrs. Cousins said with a loud sniff.

Having forgotten her presence, Juanita jumped.

"Don't be so harsh in your judgments of people, dear," Mrs. Brown reproved mildly. "None of us is perfect. And we all would do some things differently if given the chance."

Juanita looked from mother to daughter, wondering if their dialogue referred to more than the behavior of teenaged boys a half-century ago. Mrs. Cousins removed plates and cups and carried them to the kitchen. Juanita asked a few more questions but learned little else. Mrs. Cousins returned just as she closed her notebook and rose.

"I appreciate this more than I can say, Mrs. Brown. You've given me several leads, and hearing your recollections has been invaluable." She turned to her hostess. "Thank you for the coffee and pie, Mrs. Cousins. I've never had better."

The daughter did smile then, a tentative grimace that widened to a grin. "Thanks. I enjoy baking."

"You're both gracious to let me take so much of your time. Can you think of anyone else I could talk to here in Bryson's Corner, Mrs. Brown? Someone who'd know about those days?"

The old woman placed a finger at her temple. "Garvin McCoy. Garvin's a little older than I, and of course would have seen events from a male perspective. Also, he knew Luther quite well."

Mrs. Cousins said a polite but restrained goodbye and excused herself to check on something in the kitchen.

"Thank you for the suggestion," Juanita addressed her mother. "But I'm . . . not sure Mr. McCoy will talk to me." She told of their brief encounter.

Mrs. Brown shook her head and laughed. "Garvin has his ways. But if he were convinced it was important—"

"I hate to trouble you further, but could you—maybe—convince him to talk to me?"

"I'm afraid not. He's among those who still blame me for Luther's death."

Juanita left the house, elated over having learned so much from Leona Brown. On a whim, she drove past the McCoy place, three blocks along the same street as the Cousins'. If Garvin should be outside, she might stop and try to persuade him to talk.

But on reaching that block, Juanita saw that the McCoy residence had a shut-up, drawn-in look, unlike its welcoming face on her earlier visit. The park bench on the lawn next door sat deserted, even the tabby cat nowhere around. The Davis house appeared dark and desolate, as if mourning its deceased owner.

Nine

Thursday evening, Juanita arrived home from the library to find her round oak dining table set with good china, place mats, and candles. Martha said dinner was ready to serve.

"What a lovely surprise," Juanita said. "How'd you know I wasn't in a mood to cook and was tired of takeout?"

"It's about time I did something to repay all your kindness."

"Don't be silly. You've been doing dishes and other chores. Besides, you're great company. I'll wash my hands and be right back."

When Juanita returned, she found a full plate at her place. She sat across from Martha and inhaled a temptingly fruity aroma.

"Smells good. What is this?"

"Chicken cutlet with raspberry vinaigrette, couscous pilaf, and asparagus-and-hearts-of-palm salad."

Juanita sampled each dish, relishing the tangy and nutty flavors, the crisp and soft textures.

"You're a great cook, Martha! I'd better not eat all this, though. The old diet, you know."

"The chicken's 145 calories, the pilaf 175. The salad, including dressing, is about 80."

"Go on! It's all too good to be low cal."

"After my third husband suffered a heart attack, I educated myself about low-fat diets and found some great recipes. I hope you don't mind my rummaging through your cupboards and refrigerator."

"Not if this is the result. Are you in cahoots with my doctor to make me healthy in spite of myself?"

Martha smiled, then sobered. "Juanita, you mentioned you . . . were doing an interview for your history last evening. How'd that go? I fell asleep before you got home, and you were so rushed this morning."

"Great. I got a couple new leads. Did you know a Lonnie Tubbs, Martha? He's big in real estate around here now, though I've never met him. Ran around with Simon Simms and Vince Arnold in high school, I understand."

With great deliberation, Martha sliced off a bite of chicken, her hand trembling slightly. "It was a small high school, so I knew them all. But we didn't . . . move in the same circles."

"What did you think of them?"

Martha patted her mouth with her napkin. "Lonnie was . . . full of himself—something of a bully. Vince was . . . a sneak. He followed Lonnie's lead in everything. Simon—well, you never knew about him. But Lonnie was a—a known troublemaker, and Simon was thin and weak-looking. He may've hung out with Lonnie in order to seem tough himself."

"For not moving in the same circles, you seem to have a clear idea of their characters."

"Like I said, it was a small school. How's Leona Brown? Doing well?"

"Did you know her?"

"Not well. Mother used to send me out to Bryson's Corner sometimes—to buy tomatoes from her dad."

"She seemed fine last night, but I gather she's in frail health."

"Sorry to hear that."

A thought occurred to Juanita. "You went to Bryson's Corner to buy tomatoes? Ever buy eggs from Luther Dunlap?"

"No."

Had that answer come a little too quickly? "I understand some Wyndhamites did. A couple of girls, especially, were seen hanging out there."

"I . . . wouldn't know about that." Martha sat a few moments without eating, her expression troubled. "How's . . . my sister? Ready to move home?"

Juanita grinned. "Not yet. Mavis is worried about the wiring, but the electrician she called to check it is busy on a new subdivision. He hasn't gotten to her job."

"And she won't call someone else."

"Of course not—way too simple. It's sad she's not spending time with you, after you came so far."

The slender face blanched. "I seem to've worn out what little welcome I had. But I can't force her to want me around. Maybe when she's back in her own house . . . Oh, who'm I kidding? I should leave town—that's what would make her happy."

"Don't give up yet. Just when I decide Mavis is a block of granite, she shows me a softer side. She'll come around, you'll see."

"I hope so, but—"

Martha served squares of pumpkin cheesecake. The soft, sweet confection sat delectably on Juanita's tongue.

"I don't want to know the calorie count on this."

"Only 120. Fortunately, you had bought skim milk and low-fat cream cheese right after talking to Dr. Sweeney."

"I didn't mean to actually eat any of that stuff."

"Well, you have now."

They ate and sipped coffee in silence for a time.

"Martha," Juanita finally said, "I want to respect your privacy, but I have to admit I'm curious about this thing between you and Mavis. You said the two of you had been close. So was she upset when you left after high school?"

Martha's eyes moistened. "She . . . begged me not to go. But I . . . just had to. I wrote her when I got settled in Kansas City, explained I still loved her but had . . . really needed to leave." She caught back a sob. "I guess she saw my going as a . . . betrayal. Anyway, I didn't hear back. She was only eight then, couldn't write well yet, but she could've had an adult help her. Mother would've."

"But you did hear from her eventually?"

"Not till Mother died several years later. Then a few years after that, when Father passed. Terse notes, both times.

"I came back for a brief visit about twenty years ago but got a cool reception. After that, I didn't always keep her up on my address changes."

"That's so sad. But as long as you're both still alive, there's hope."

"I don't know . . . ."

They did the dishes and watched a TV sitcom, then set out for an evening stroll. Rip capered at the end of his leash, occasionally stopping to investigate an odor on sidewalk or grass. A bright moon illuminated their route.

"I suppose in time I could come to enjoy exercise," Juanita said. "I do like walking to work and back."

"Rip seemed to miss his outing last night. I thought of taking him by myself but wasn't sure I could control him."

"He can be a handful. We'll make it up to him with an extra-long walk tonight."

As if to prove Juanita's assessment of him, the dog began to bark at a cat lurking under a bush they were about to pass.

"Hush, Rip," Juanita said. "Can't take you anywhere."

Behind them, a motor started and a vehicle idled along to their rear. Juanita started to turn and see if the driver needed directions. But just then, the cat took off running and Rip lunged at it, jerking her almost off her feet. She staggered against Martha, who fell, catching herself on a tree stump beside the sidewalk.

A sharp crack sounded, and an ancient beige pickup surged past them. It zoomed to the next corner, screeched around it, and raced from sight.

Juanita righted herself and hauled on the leash, stopping Rip where he stood. "You okay, Martha? That . . . sounded like a shot."

Martha clung to the stump, visibly shaken. "I'm . . . fine. It must've been . . . that pickup backfiring." With obvious effort, she stood upright and brushed herself off.

"Maybe." Juanita stood a moment, watching the capering dog at her side. The enormity of the other possibility began to sink in. "You know what, Martha?" She steadied her voice with an effort. "I'm tireder than I realized. Let's go back. Sorry, Rip." She tugged him in the direction of home.

With the cat gone, he went without protest. They walked briskly, Juanita making desultory attempts at conversation as her eyes strained to see into shadows. Martha replied in monosyllables. The pickup didn't reappear, nor did any other vehicles pass.

When they reached home and Juanita had locked all the doors and hung up her sweater, she realized her hands were shaking. Martha looked drained of energy. Juanita suggested a nightcap of hot chocolate.

"Sorry, I'm . . . beat," Martha said in a quavery voice. "Think I'll . . . read and . . . have an early night."

"Okay. Me too."

Juanita checked all the doors and windows again.

"Wayne would be proud," she told Rip, as they walked to her bedroom. "Such caution would satisfy even him. I don't want to scare Martha, but I think that was a rifle shot. You were making a fool of yourself about then, so I can't be sure."

He flopped onto the floor, watching complacently as she sat on the bed and lifted the phone receiver from the nightstand.

Wayne was off duty tonight, so Juanita dialed his home number, planning to tell him her worries. But just as the ringing began, she remembered he'd mentioned a get-together of old Army buddies tonight in Sand Springs. Men were flying in from New Jersey and California for the occasion. Wayne would undoubtedly be late getting back.

She waited through four rings until the answering machine came on, then left a brief message asking him to call if he got home before midnight. She considered phoning the police station to report the incident but decided to wait and talk to Wayne. She took a sheet of paper and jotted down all the details she could recall of the experience, then sat staring thoughtfully into Rip's liquid brown eyes.

"If that was a shot—why, Rip? Have I learned something important about the Dunlap killing, maybe from Leona Brown? Or am I about to?"

The dog nuzzled her knee, as if offering what comfort he could.

Ten

The next day, Juanita drove to the neat tan-brick building that housed Wyndham's police station, having called first to learn Wayne would be in. She was no surer today about what she'd heard last evening but needed to talk to him about it. Too, it provided a good excuse for carrying out a plan she had conceived. The day was sunny and dewy after an overnight rain. She could have walked from the library, but her car was necessary to her scheme.

At the station, Juanita greeted the diminutive records clerk, Ruth Sloan, through a microphone at the glass security panel and said she needed to see Wayne. He was in the chief's office, Ruth replied, but Juanita could come in and wait. Ruth buzzed her into the secure area, and she started past the small front office to speak to her dispatcher friend Louise in the room beyond. But as a thought occurred, she turned back.

"Ruth the Sleuth" was the employee who had offered Wayne the *adipocere* theory about the body in the ravine.

Finding the chair beside Ruth temporarily vacant, Juanita sat and waited for her to glance up from her task. Seeing Louise through the large window into the dispatchers' room, Juanita waved. Ruth finished jotting a note on a message pad and looked expectantly at Juanita.

"Read about any interesting poisons lately?" Juanita said casually.

The tiny clerk leaned back and smiled. "How'd you know I've been reading about poisons? Did Lieutenant Cleary mention it?"

"I believe he did. Anyway, I remembered you like reading about crime."

Ruth's wide grin nearly split her small face. "Ever heard of a weed called corn cockle?"

Juanita pretended to consider. "You know, I have. Just recently, I think. Now, where'd I hear about that?"

The records clerk gave a conspiratorial wink. "It's been in the paper and on the radio. That autopsy of the old black fellow? *I* was the one who suggested they check for corn cockle!" Her hands clasped her thin upper arms in a congratulatory self-hug.

"The elderly Bryson's Corner man? Really? That was your idea?"

Ruth nodded enthusiastically. "Most of the guys—all but Lieutenant Cleary—either groan or get that 'here we go again' look when I make a suggestion about a case. And I admit my ideas haven't always panned out. But this one sure did!"

"Excellent! Good for you."

"I didn't really think Lieutenant Cleary'd follow up on it—he seemed a little impatient when I mentioned it," Ruth confided. "But he passed it on to the medical examiner, and you should've seen the looks on people's faces when the autopsy results came back *positive* for corn cockle! They treat me with new respect now, I can tell you."

"The department's fortunate to have you. What in the world made you suspect corn cockle in the Davis case, though? I understand that's a rare cause of death in humans these days."

Ruth chuckled. "Partly, it was dumb luck. I come from a long line of wheat farmers, and at reunions, the old folks like to sit around and tell family stories. One they always tell goes back several generations, to Portia Wilcox, who baked a week's worth of bread for the family every Saturday, using their own wheat she ground herself. But during one harvest everybody was working daylight to dusk like they did—Portia too, right beside her menfolk—and she evidently got in too big a hurry with grinding the flour that week. The whole family—except one kid who'd gone home after church with a friend—got sick and died a few hours after eating Sunday dinner. Bread poisoning occasionally happened in those days, and Portia realized before she passed, what she must've done. She carried on something awful, they said, watching her babies die, knowing she and her husband would too.

"I've heard that story lots of times. So when I read about corn cockle in my book on poisons, I remembered Portia. And Mr. Davis's symptoms sounded kinda similar."

"It was brilliant detective work, Ruth," Juanita said with a smile. "Brilliant."

"Thanks. I felt pretty proud, myself."

A female chaplain who regularly helped at the front desk entered from the hallway and greeted Juanita, who stood and yielded her chair. Juanita waggled her fingers at Ruth and sauntered on to the dispatchers' office.

"Hey, Louise," she said on entering. "How's it going?"

Louise Bright, a middle-aged, heavy-set Cherokee, turned from a computer screen and deadpanned, "I'm sittin' up and takin' nourishment."

Juanita grinned. "Glad to hear it." She enjoyed Louise's sense of humor, which stood her in good stead in the mostly-male world of the Wyndham Police Department. "Justin liking his classes at Okmulgee Tech?"

"Yeah. He's always been good with his hands, and being away from Mom makes him feel grown up. I miss him during the week, though."

Louise turned to answer a call, and Juanita spoke to the other 911 operator. They conversed pleasantly a moment, then the second dispatcher got busy too.

Wayne came along the hall, poked his head in, and grinned a hello at Juanita. "Sorry I didn't get back till late last night, babe—this morning, rather. We talked till after one. Like some coffee? It's not great, but it's hot. At that, it's better'n when we had the vending machine."

"Sure."

He filled a mug and a paper cup from a carafe in the break room, handed her the cup, and motioned to a detectives' room down a hall. A new police chief had recently reorganized the department, redefining procedures and shifting some responsibilities and offices. Since Wayne respected the new chief and felt many of the changes were needed, he had adjusted to losing his small office and sharing this larger one with other detectives. Since the move, Juanita had noticed his officemates were often out on a case or busy in an interview room or elsewhere, and to her relief, she saw no one else about now.

"Ruth said you sounded serious when you called this morning, babe," he said when she was seated across the desk from him. "What's up?"

She recounted the incident of the evening before, while he listened attentively and typed information into a computer. When she paused, he leaned back in his chair and studied her.

"Sure it was a shot, babe? Could've been that old pickup, like Martha said."

"I've heard vehicles backfire, and I've heard gunshots. This sounded like a rifle."

"Why would anyone be shooting at you?"

"I don't know. I couldn't see who was in the pickup—might've just been teenagers getting their jollies—but I have wondered if it was connected to this history of Wyndham I'm working on."

Wayne sipped coffee. "You been looking into anything lately besides that old killing?"

"No. But if Samuel Davis was poisoned deliberately, not accidentally—"

"We're looking into that possibility."

"—if he was, Wayne, maybe he was killed to prevent his talking to me."

He smiled without humor. "You could be making yourself a little too important here."

"I hope that's *not* why he died—I sure don't need the guilt—but if it was, then I may be getting too close to Dunlap's murderer. Or the killer's afraid I will."

"Let's not overdramatize this, Juanita. But call it 'research,' call it 'amateur detecting,' or whatever you're doing, that history's an excuse for you to pry into other people's business. As you should've learned already, that can make folks mad. Why don't you give up this book idea?"

Juanita felt a surge of annoyance. "This is how you protect citizens who come to you with problems? Tell them their troubles are their own fault?"

Wayne grimaced, hazel eyes dark with irritation. "Juanita, I am going to investigate your complaint. All I'm saying is, people shouldn't take foolish chances, then come crying to the law over the consequences. You need to have a care for your own safety, too."

"Shoot, Wayne, name me an activity that's completely risk-free these days. Driving to the grocery, eating food you buy there, drinking tap water—or bottled, for that matter—even sitting on your own couch—"

"That argument didn't wash the first dozen times you used it, and it doesn't now. You know what I'm saying. And you know I'm right."

Juanita considered flouncing out in a huff. Trouble was, she hadn't yet accomplished her other goal. She forced a smile.

"Angry words won't get us anywhere, Wayne. Especially the same ones we've used before."

"Agreed. But speaking of that old case, have you found out anything I need to know? Anything that could've led to someone's shooting at you? Assuming it was a shot, of course."

Juanita thought a moment. "If so, I don't know what it is."

"Describe that pickup again, babe, in detail. Too bad you didn't get a license number."

Quashing a smart-aleck remark that rose to her lips, Juanita repeated the description in somewhat different wording and watched Wayne type a few more characters.

"That all you remember?" he asked, when she'd stopped.

She nodded. "Yes. I sure hope you find that driver." She took a deep breath. "Could you do me one more little favor while I'm here, Wayne? My car has been making an odd sound lately. Can you listen to it and see if you can figure out what's wrong?"

"Better take it to Wagoner's. Bud's a much better mechanic than I am. And that's his job."

"The problem isn't constant, though. I'm afraid if Bud doesn't hear anything wrong, he'll think I'm nuts."

Wayne glanced at his watch. "Guess I could take a minute. Let's go outside, and you start it up."

"Actually, Wayne, you'll need to drive the car a while. It doesn't make the noise when the motor's just idling. Here you go." She handed him a ring of keys, one held separate from the others.

Wayne rolled his eyes. "Okay, let's go."

"I'd better not ride along. I'd be tempted to talk to you, maybe keep you from concentrating on the engine."

He gave her a steady look. "At least tell me what I'm listening for."

"It's just a funny whining. Or a clanking."

"A whine *or* a clank? Juanita—"

"Well, I don't know what to call it. That's another reason I don't want to take it to Bud till you've checked it. You can tell me how to describe the sound to him."

Shaking his head, Wayne strode out. Juanita heard the side door shut. Going to the window, she watched as he got into her car, started it and drove from the parking lot. Now, if none of the other detectives came back for a few minutes . . .

Juanita went to the door of the detectives' room, looked both ways along the hallway, then quickly slipped over to the file cabinet behind Wayne's desk. Heart pumping with excitement, she opened a drawer marked "A–M" and began to flip through folders. Soon, she found one with Luther Dunlap's name on it.

The file felt surprisingly slender. With sweaty hands, Juanita opened it. The few sheets inside had been photocopied, as she knew was often done with old, brittle originals. She ran her eyes rapidly over the pages, noting that few people had been questioned, and those interviews not extensive.

Hearing footsteps approach down the hallway, Juanita grabbed her capacious handbag, thrust the file inside, and shut the purse and cabinet drawer almost in one motion. She was sitting in the chair before Wayne's desk, legs crossed, as a lean young man strode in the door.

"Oh, hi, Juanita," Graham Frye said with a grin, tossing a file folder and a notebook onto the desk beside Wayne's. He removed his blazer, hung it on his chair, and sat down facing her. "You waiting on Wayne?"

"Yes, he's gone to check something on my car. It doesn't sound quite right. How's the new baby? And how's Penny?"

She had spoken a little too animatedly, Juanita realized. But he didn't seem to notice.

"Both great." He rubbed weary-looking eyes and ran a hand over his light-brown buzz cut. "Hope the little devil gets his days and nights straightened out soon."

"Keeping you up, is he?"

Graham nodded. "Some. Bothers Penny more'n me—she's a lighter sleeper. I pretty much die, soon's my head hits the pillow.

'Specially since I've been working late the past couple weeks."

Juanita smiled and nodded. He opened the folder and selected a paper. She picked up her purse and rose.

"Women's room's that way, right?" she asked.

He glanced up and nodded, then resumed studying the file. She left the detectives' room and strolled down the hall to the women's restroom.

Seeing no one around, Juanita opened the door, then shut it with a thump. She crept on down the passage, relieved not to meet any police personnel, and slipped into a supply room at the end. She was in luck, no one here either, and no "Out of order" sign on the copy machine. It was a fairly old model, a back-up for the high-speed copier in the records room, but it should serve her purpose.

Duplicating the slim file took only minutes. Juanita shoved folder and copies into her bag and soft-toed her way back to the restroom. Gliding inside, she flushed a toilet, ran water in the sink, and came out, closing the door with a thud. She strolled back down the hall to the detectives' room, wondering how she could return the Dunlap file to its drawer with Graham still there.

As she resumed her seat by Wayne's desk, an idea occurred. She began coughing, over and over as if she couldn't stop.

"You okay, Juanita?" Graham asked in a concerned voice.

She pretended to strangle, then croaked a single word, "Water!"

He jumped up and ran into the hall. Still hacking, she wrenched open her purse, grabbed the folder, slid open the file-cabinet drawer, and with trembling fingers wedged the Dunlap file into its proper place. She shut the drawer and sat again, gasping harder now. Graham hurried in and pressed a paper cup filled with water into her hand. She drank it, pausing occasionally to cough as if the reflex hadn't fully quieted.

Finally, she wiped her eyes and wheezed, "Thank you, Graham.

That really helped."

She sat silently gloating until she heard Wayne slam the side door. A moment later, he entered the detectives' room and came to stand, hands on hips, in front of Juanita.

"There's not a durned thing wrong with that car that I could hear. Purrs like a contented cat."

"Really?" she said, eyes wide and innocent. "Sure you gave it a good enough try?"

He glared at her.

"Okay, then, thanks for checking it. I'll just have to wait and see if it does it again, then take it to Bud."

She told Wayne and Graham goodbye and waved to Louise and Ruth on her way out. Feeling guilty but triumphant, she parked near the library, took the Dunlap papers from her bag and paged slowly through them.

A queasy feeling inched upward from the pit of her stomach. Very few people had been questioned in 1959, and those few hadn't been pressed hard. Allegations had not been followed up. As for providing names of potential sources, the file was no help. Many interviewees were identified only as "young nigger gal" or "middle-aged white man." Some entries were illegible or unclear.

As for recent activity, there was none. *Nada*.

No wonder Wayne had refused to let her see these records, Juanita thought. He hadn't been on the force in the 1950s, of course. And cops did have that tradition of the "blue wall," refusing to discuss police business outside the department. Still, he had no right to protect the Wyndham Police if that meant failing to get to the truth in a murder case.

It hurt that he hadn't felt he could trust her. She did have a lively curiosity, but he knew she could keep a secret when necessary.

But could she in good conscience keep this one? The public had a right to know how their local government was functioning.

Or not functioning.

What was her proper course now? Bring the matter before the City Council? Talk to the media? Demand a full investigation of the police department? She hated the thought of causing trouble for anyone on the force, but this . . .

Steady, though. There might be a reasonable explanation. Before she did anything drastic, she needed to know more.

The sick feeling rose all the way to her head, making it pound like a piston. Given the racial attitudes of the 1950s, the shoddiness of the initial investigation might not have been all that unusual. Much more troubling was the fact that little or nothing seemed to have been done *since* to right that old wrong.

Not even, as far as she could tell, by Lt. Wayne Cleary himself.

But this case would get solved, she vowed. If she had anything to say about it.

Eleven

Wayne called late that morning to say he could come by for lunch and asked what he could bring her. By that time, Juanita had convinced herself there was a good reason the Dunlap file was scant. Wayne wouldn't simply ignore an old murder, or let others do so. Not if any chance existed of solving it. Someone must have removed papers from the file to work on the case and not returned everything yet.

Unfortunately, she couldn't ask Wayne, given the underhanded way she had learned how skimpy the folder was.

He arrived soon, bringing the takeout salad she had requested and a large bag reeking tantalizingly of hamburgers and French fries. Juanita sat across her office worktable from him, trying to relish the flavors of raw veggies and low-fat cheese. Martha's skill with low-calorie ingredients last night had left Juanita optimistic about her diet. But now, watching him devour his second hamburger and a tall chocolate milkshake, she felt herself weaken.

"How's about giving me a bite of your sandwich, Wayne?"

"Can't. Sorry."

"A sip of your shake?"

"Nope. If you blow your diet, it's not going to be my fault."

"How'd you like to have an irate, hungry librarian jam French fries into every orifice of your body?"

"Pleasant as that sounds, I'll pass."

Juanita thrust a plastic knife into his face. "Hand over that burger, Cleary."

With a grin, he passed her his remaining third of a sandwich. She took a large bite, returned the rest, closed her eyes, and slowly ground meat and bread between her teeth. Grease and sodium had never tasted so good.

"Thanks. I needed that."

"Want more?"

"No. And don't tempt me any further."

"See, that's what I mean. I surrender my food under protest—at knifepoint, mind you—and then get the blame for your going off your diet."

"Seems fair to me."

"It would. Anyone been shooting at you since I saw you earlier?"

"Don't make fun. That did sound like a shot."

"Might've been one."

"Try to contain your horror at the thought."

"I've felt the urge to draw a bead on you myself a few times, babe." Wayne wiped a napkin across his mouth, leaned over and planted a kiss on her forehead. "You know, if someone did fire off a round that night, you might not've been the intended target."

"I admit Rip can be annoying, but . . ."

"Funny. What about Martha?"

"I doubt many people even know she's around. She hardly stirs outside. It's true her own sister isn't thrilled she's here, but a sniper Mavis isn't. Not with a rifle, that is."

"Maybe Martha made an enemy years ago, one who's been thirsting for a chance at revenge."

"That'd be some grudge, to last over forty years."

"A good feud can last for generations. Remember the Hatfields and McCoys?"

"But Martha's such an innocuous type. I can't imagine her ticking anyone off that badly."

"You know what the neighbors of serial killers always say: 'But he was such a nice fellow—never gave anyone any trouble.'" Wayne slurped the last of his drink and tossed the cup into the trash. "I went by your house after you left the station this morning and got Martha's version of the 'shooting.' Pretty much a wasted trip. She confirmed she thought that sound must've been the pickup backfiring but otherwise gave me nothing."

"You bothered my houseguest? Without telling me?"

"I don't have to clear investigative procedures with you, Juanita. You did want me to check out your report, didn't you?"

"Of course. But I assumed you'd do something besides grilling the one person, other than me, who couldn't possibly have fired the shot."

"How much do you know about this new buddy of yours, Martha the Close-Mouthed? You meet her one minute and ask her to move in the next."

"She's related to Mavis. That alone arouses my pity."

"Well, I'd like to know why she suddenly left town after high school. I asked her, but she just referred vaguely to 'small-minded people here.' You ask me, she'd grabbed another girl's boyfriend and the jilted female was making things too hot for her."

"Men! Not all women's decisions have to do with males in their lives." Juanita balled her napkin, threw it into the trash.

Wayne rolled his eyes. "But some do. Ask her about it."

"She's my guest. I can't say, 'By the way, Martha, is an old rival of yours still gunning for you? And *me,* if I happen to be in the line of fire?'"

"Tact isn't your strong suit, but I bet even you could put it more delicately. Seriously, Juanita, you may have a better chance of finding out something than I did—maybe get through that guard she's erected."

"I'll think about it."

"That's a start."

To placate her conscience over copying the Dunlap file, Juanita decided to share with Wayne some of what she had learned about the old case. She mentioned the four motives she'd heard about, then summarized her interview with Leona Brown. He watched her without expression. Finally, she stopped and waited for a reaction.

"That it?" Wayne said.

"Yes. Did you—" she struggled to phrase the question without giving herself away— "know any of that before?"

"Maybe. I can't tell you what the police knew or didn't know, Juanita."

"But it wasn't easy getting some of that information. Surely you can say if it helps or not."

"It's always helpful when citizens come clean with the police. Thanks."

"You're welcome. I think."

"I'm sorry Wayne bothered you today, Martha," Juanita said as the two of them sat in the living room after dinner. "He had to question you, of course, but I hadn't thought to warn you he would."

"He's just doing his job." Martha laid the book she'd been reading in her lap and stared into space a long moment. "Tell me, Juanita, have you . . . known Lieutenant Cleary long?"

"Couple of years."

"And you trust him?"

"With my life. Why?"

"No reason. That's good. Very good." Martha took up the novel.

In view of Wayne's urging to draw her houseguest out, Juanita decided she couldn't let the conversation stop there. "Martha, do you still think that wasn't a shot last night? It really sounded like one to me."

"I . . . haven't heard that much gunfire," said the soft voice from behind the book. A minute later, Martha laid the novel down and looked thoughtfully at Juanita. "They do say that the simplest explanation is usually the correct one. Something like that, anyway. The pickup could've backfired. Old vehicles do."

"Suppose it was a shot, though, just suppose. I know this sounds awful, but is there anyone who might think they had reason to shoot at you? Someone who knew you from years ago?"

Martha sat with eyes closed for several moments, swallowing a couple of times, color rising to her cheeks. "No," she finally said and picked up her book.

The conversation seemed to be over, but it left Juanita with questions. What was troubling this gentle woman? And why had she asked that about Wayne? Did she have some reason to suspect he *wasn't* trustworthy?

Juanita had spoken truthfully just now—she *would* trust Wayne with her life. But she couldn't erase from her mind the nagging question that inadequate file had raised.

Twelve

As Juanita stood in the WCC classroom the following Tuesday evening, talking with Doug Darrow while waiting for Books to begin, she looked up and noticed someone standing hesitantly in the doorway. A heavy-set black woman.

Althea McCoy. Juanita hurried over to her.

"I'm glad you could come, Althea. But I thought you said you wouldn't have time."

"I don't, really." Her eyes darted around, brightening as they reached dreadlocked Matrice Marlow, a vivacious WCC student who attended Books meetings for college credit.

Juanita realized then how "white" the gathering might seem to Althea. The Books membership had earlier included a black male WCC sociology teacher and the Japanese widow of a World War II veteran, both of whom had now moved away. Juanita usually didn't notice the racial makeup of groups but suddenly realized that might be because her own race was usually in the majority. Matrice never seemed bothered at being the lone African-American among many Caucasians. But Matrice was outgoing and self-assured to the point of dominating any gathering. Althea might well feel differently. Uncomfortably, Juanita recalled her own nervousness when in Bryson's Corner to see Davis, and even when she'd been with Leona Brown and her daughter. But Bryson's Corner had been unfamiliar territory, her welcome there uncertain. Had her minority status also been a factor?

She didn't think so, but the thought gave her pause.

"I decided this might be a good break from my usual grind," Althea went on, her smile tight. "Besides, I wanted to ask—that diary you mentioned—is your offer to let me see it still open? Maybe it could help with my paper, after all."

"Sure. We can run over to the library after this meeting."

Althea's tense expression relaxed. "That would be great. I called the library yesterday to check your hours, and the young man said you're open late Thursdays and on Saturdays. But I have a class Thursdays and work Saturdays. Our schedules just don't mesh."

"No problem. Glad you could come tonight. Let me introduce you to our moderator."

They crossed the classroom to the teacher's desk, where Katherine Greer sat in regal dignity.

"Glad to meet you, Miss McCoy," she said warmly when Juanita had made introductions. "Have you read *To Kill a Mockingbird* before?"

"A couple of times."

"Good. We're glad to have you join us. Please help yourself to refreshments." Katherine indicated a table near the window that held two coffee urns, cups, saucers, napkins, and a large platter of dark squares.

Juanita served Althea, poured a cup of decaf for herself, and added a single rock-hard brownie to her own saucer.

"Forbidden fruit," she said. Lowering her voice, she added, "Luckily I can resist gorging on Bonnie Allen's cooking. Now if it was Eva Brompton's turn to bring food . . . . Bonnie's a nice lady but tends to overcook everything."

Althea nibbled at a brownie and finally crunched off a sizeable bite. "This definitely could've used less oven time."

"Even so, my sweet tooth appreciates it."

"Time to begin, people," Katherine said in her cultured but firm voice. The dozen or so individuals ceased chattering and found chairs at library tables placed in a semicircle facing Katherine's desk. Juanita and Althea sat at one end of the arc beside Eva and Cyril Brompton, both of whom welcomed Althea heartily. She responded with a reserved smile.

"*To Kill a Mockingbird* was originally published in 1960," Katherine began, "and was considered somewhat daring then in terms of its portrayal of the races. Reading it now, does the novel hold up, or seem dated?"

"Oh, I think it's wonderful," said Eva. "This is the fourth time I've read it, and I like it better each time."

Katherine smiled. "Can you tell it was written in the 1950s, not just last year?"

"Absolutely," came Matrice's scornful reply. "The attitude towards black people is paternalistic throughout, even on the part of the 'good' characters."

"Can you give an example, Miss Marlow?"

Matrice thumbed quickly through her copy of the novel. "Okay. Atticus Finch says, 'There's nothing more sickening to me than a low-grade white man who'll take advantage of a Negro's ignorance . . . .'

"It's true Finch is repudiating the white guy's behavior, but he just assumes blacks will *naturally* be more ignorant than whites."

"That would've been a fair assumption in the thirties, when the story takes place," offered Cyril. "Plenty of whites were poorly educated then, but blacks were even more likely to be. Especially since schools were separate and anything *but* equal."

"That's not the only example," Matrice went on, her dreads swinging with each emphatic nod. "Atticus doesn't correct his daughter when she uses the insulting epithet 'nigger.'"

"Cyril's right, though," said Doug Darrow. "The period a story's set in is important."

He sat facing Juanita at the other end of the semicircle, as usual dressed in army T-shirt and fatigue pants. When Juanita had asked him once why he preferred military garb for leisure wear given his pacifist leanings, he'd said, "These clothes are comfortable, and gung-ho warmongers shouldn't be the only ones allowed to wear them."

He now sat up straighter. "The 'n' word was in common use in the 1930s, and it wasn't always meant derogatorily."

"So *you* say," said Matrice. "You weren't the one getting called 'nigger.' Besides, the fact everyone does something doesn't make it right."

"All true," Doug conceded. "No question it's a loaded word. I'm just saying that, when Scout uses it, she doesn't intend to demean black people."

"This young woman's right," Althea put in. "Whites will never understand why that word offends us so much."

Matrice grinned at Althea and gave her a "thumbs-up" sign. A moment of silence followed. Then Meador, with a nervous smile, spoke.

"But if you insist we'll never understand, what hope is there that the races can ever be friends?"

"I'm not sure we can," said Althea. "I think there'll always be suspicion and distrust on our part, based on the past few *hundred* years."

"But I'm not the one who enslaved your ancestors."

"Your great-great granddaddy did."

"I doubt it," Meador muttered. "No one in my family's ever been rich enough to own land, much less slaves."

"To get back to the novel," Katherine said quietly but resolutely, "it's true that the offensive word 'nigger' appears in the novel several times. As Miss Marlow correctly points out, even 'good' characters use it. And earlier books—Mark Twain's *Huckleberry Finn* for one—have been the target of book-banning efforts because of it. How much allowance should we make for a story's time period? Or should we always insist on 'political correctness,' as seen from the viewpoint of a later, presumably more enlightened, age?"

"Writers have to try to make their characters sound authentic," said Juanita. "Huck Finn uses the word because that's what people said then. It's not meant as a put-down of Jim, whom Huck genuinely admires."

"Again," said Matrice, "that's easy for you to say."

"I really think you have to consider the overall tone of a book," Juanita went on, irritated in spite of feeling sympathy for the younger woman's position. "It isn't black people who're shown in a bad light in either novel. In both, the racist actions and words of whites are criticized."

"There've sure been lots of changes in race relations since 1960," noted Cyril, ever the peacemaker. "This book came out before the Voting Rights Act and other big civil-rights laws, remember."

"In fact," said Juanita, "it may have been a factor in their getting passed. It certainly called attention to the fact the law wasn't color-blind."

Katherine nodded. "Going back further in history, there's a legend that Abraham Lincoln said on meeting Harriet Beecher Stowe, 'So this is the little lady who made this big war.' Can we go so far as to call *To Kill a Mockingbird* another *Uncle Tom's Cabin?*"

"That might overstate its impact," said Juanita. "By the late fifties, lots of forces were pushing for greater racial equality. This book was one of many voices. But I do think it helped—especially since it won the Pulitzer."

Althea cleared her throat and folded her arms, overhead light glinting off her shiny bracelet.

"Have you a comment to make, Miss McCoy?" Katherine asked politely.

Althea started to speak, then shook her head.

"Literature and the political climate of a country always

influence each other," Katherine went on. "Harper Lee's novel looks back to the 1930s, twenty-some years before it was published. We're now looking back on *it* from nearly a half-century after its publication. How had society's attitudes changed from the Depression years to 1960? And how are they different now?"

Cyril said World War II had had more impact on race relations than any legislation since. Doug disagreed, saying that laws passed during the 1960s had shifted the racial landscape almost as much as had the Civil War. Others in the group took sides, and a spirited debate followed. Finally, Katherine raised a hand for quiet.

"Thanks, everyone. We've run past our usual time, but it's been a stimulating discussion. Remember to get your copies of the Amy Tan novel we've chosen for next time."

Several people left. Others lingered in small groups, continuing the discussion.

"It was great to see another sister here," Matrice said to Althea. "And you and I seem to think a lot alike. Want to meet for coffee some time?"

"Love to, but I'm snowed. We can exchange phone numbers, though."

"Great. I'm way busy, too—classes, part-time job, cheerleading practice, games—but let's find the time."

They traded numbers, and Matrice left.

"I'm glad you came, Miss McCoy," said Katherine. "I hope you'll join us again."

"Thanks. It's been interesting."

Juanita and Althea walked out together, then drove separately to the library. Juanita led the way in her car, Althea following in a bronze Taurus. They parallel-parked under a street light on West First, near one end of the library building. Oaks and evergreens, the former dropping leaves, cast subtle shadows across yards in the mostly-residential neighborhood. Draped, lighted picture windows in modest frame houses suggested giant eyes in a row of Cyclopes.

Juanita unlocked the west entry, having remembered that the front door was hard to open. She kept forgetting to have Meador treat the lock with graphite.

They stepped through the door into the west-wing stacks, a huge room filled with rows of tall bookshelves. Subdued after-hours lighting made softly glowing paths of the center and outer aisles, with darker blobs of shelf units and connecting corridors between. Juanita shivered. Much as she loved her library, she sometimes felt "spooked" in the empty stacks at night. She flipped a two-way switch on a panel just inside the door, illuminating brighter overhead fixtures, and led Althea through the wing and into the main reading room, turning on more lights as they went. When empty of people, the reading room always struck Juanita as a little sad, like a vault of unused treasures.

In her office behind the checkout oval, Juanita took a key ring from her desk drawer. They then went to the east wing, up a set of steps, and past more rows of full shelves to a storeroom at the end of the building. Unlocking the door, Juanita switched on an overhead bulb and ushered Althea inside. Shelves of bound volumes, dusty and unused, lined the cubicle, with multiple cartons piled in front of shelves. A table and two chairs occupied the narrow center space.

"People sometimes leave us their cherished libraries," Juanita remarked. "Unfortunately they don't always check with us first to see if we want them or have space to house them. Let's see . . ." She examined notations lettered in Magic Marker on sides of stacked boxes and stopped at one labeled "Stevens Collection, Corbett Diary." Opening it, she plucked out several red-backed ledgers.

"Here's the journal. Journals, I should say. Maizie's ancestor, Jane Corbett, was a prolific writer and kept at it over many years." Juanita checked dates written on the front covers in faded ink. "Let's see, was it 1842 when Dickens first came to the U.S.?"

"Right."

Juanita brushed dust off a volume and handed it to Althea. "Here's 1842. Jane visited her cousin in Cincinnati at a time Charles Dickens was there. Both women were fans, and it happened that the cousin knew the wife of a schoolmaster Dickens met while visiting a Cincinnati school. Dickens took a liking to the man, who was a great reader of his work and agreed with him that he should be paid for his work in America as he was in England. That was Dickens's hobbyhorse on that trip, you may recall, the need of a strong copyright law here.

"Anyway, Dickens accepted an invitation to dine at the teacher's home. And when Jane's cousin learned her idol would be there, she wangled an invitation for herself and Jane. Read this. It's a fascinating account."

Althea hefted the slim volume. "But you say this can't be checked out?"

"That's the stipulation, I'm afraid. However, I could photocopy portions for you. Why don't you look it over and let me know which pages you need. I'll go turn on the copy machine."

She went downstairs, switched on the copier, and killed some time answering a letter received that day. When she returned to the storage room, Althea was smiling, her face radiant.

"This is wonderfully detailed! It describes the excitement in Cincinnati over having a famous author visit, the talk at table about a Temperance Convention parade Dickens saw there, and the private reading he consented to give after dinner. Even tells how his voice broke when he read aloud a passage from *Oliver Twist* about the death of Nancy."

"So it'll help with your paper?"

"You bet! Quoting a source no other researcher has used should really impress my prof. Can you copy from here to here? Then this later passage, where she refers back to that night?"

"Sure. Let's go do that."

They went downstairs, where Juanita made the copies and collected the copy charges.

"Thank you, Miss Wills," Althea said formally, her earlier reserve returning. "I appreciate this very much."

"Juanita, please. Glad to help. Is your dad doing okay?"

"He's fine." Althea folded and unfolded the copies. "I really don't think he knows anything that could help you."

"Maybe not."

"Still—you have done me a huge favor. If he did talk to you—not saying he will—would—could you keep his name out of it? Not mention it in your book?"

Juanita frowned. "I'd have to find another source to quote for whatever information he might give me." Seeing the worry in Althea's face, she added, "I'll try."

"I'm relying on you, Miss Wills. I don't want Daddy bothered, and he would be if people knew he'd given information about that old crime. But he may not even meet with you. Daddy's got a mind of his own."

"You'll withdraw your opposition, though? Wonderful! Thanks a lot." Juanita paused. "Maybe if you asked him to see me…?"

Althea stiffened. "I won't plead your case for you—I still think it's a bad idea—but I won't oppose you."

"I'll settle for that."

After Althea left, Juanita replaced the journal in its carton, turned off lights, and re-locked the storage-room and west-wing doors. She and Althea seemed to have reached an uneasy truce, she thought. However, "uneasy" seemed an important part of the phrase.

Thirteen

"I have good news," Juanita said when Robert Norwood answered her phone call the next day. "Althea McCoy says if I can get her dad to talk to me, she won't object."

"Really? What kind of spell did you put on her?"

"I lucked out. We happen to have a book she needed, one no other library has."

"I'm impressed. Guess I haven't been spending enough time in that warehouse of wisdom you run."

"The first step in reforming is to admit you have a problem. You had any luck convincing Garvin?"

"He seems to be weakening. I think he likes the idea of doing something behind his daughter's back."

"So, can we keep it from him that she's consented? Just kidding."

"I'll head out there tonight, see how things stand."

"At least you won't have to avoid Althea now."

"Well . . . I don't know that I'd go that far."

"What is it with you two, anyway? Why don't you get along?"

Robert chuckled. "You are a snoop, aren't you? Not that it's your business, but I once asked Thea out. She turned me down like a wool blanket on a hot night."

"Oh."

"And even a jock can figure out what that means. She doesn't like me."

"Maybe there's another reason she said no."

"Forget it. I'll see what I can do with Garvin."

"Good luck."

"Hold onto your chair, Juanita," Robert said when he called that evening. "Garvin's agreed to meet with you."

"Great! When and where?"

"Saturday, his place." Robert cleared his throat. "He made conditions."

"Uh-oh."

"He wants me there. And he doesn't want Thea present."

"Is that okay with her?"

"She wasn't thrilled—maybe because you went through me—but seems to figure she owes you. So I'll pick you up at two o'clock Saturday."

"Good. I'm very grateful, Robert."

"No offense, but I didn't do it for you, Juanita. This is for the Luther Dunlaps of the world—and all the people who care about them."

"I know. Thanks, anyway." Juanita hung up the phone, then saw her houseguest was watching thoughtfully from an easy chair, romance novel in hand. "Great news, Martha! Garvin McCoy will talk to me about the Dunlap murder."

"Really? I didn't think—"

"I didn't expect he ever would, either. This could be the break I've needed."

"Terrific," Martha said faintly and retreated behind her book.

Juanita decided not to point out that the shirtless Adonis and the throbbing-bosomed heroine on the novel's cover were standing on their heads, as if their love story didn't fully engage Martha's attention at the moment.

Fourteen

After work Thursday, Juanita accompanied Meador and State Representative Claude Gilroy to Buffalo Flats, a small town forty-five miles west of Wyndham where the candidate was to speak.

"Come with us, Juanita," Meador had begged the day before. He had become friendly with Gilroy's secretary and had formed the habit of stopping at the Representative's insurance office/campaign headquarters over his lunch hour. "You'll help swell the crowd."

"What a way to invite someone who's struggling to diet."

He grinned. "You're looking thinner every day, boss."

"Too late. Speaking of that, how do you keep your slender figure? Working out at the gym a lot?"

"Not so much lately. I've been riding my bike with a buddy who's training for a big race. That's an exercise you'd probably enjoy, Juanita. Not racing, I mean, just riding."

"Maybe."

"And I mostly eat supper with my landlady, who's into Weight Watchers. She occasionally makes something I don't like, but paying her a little extra for meals is lots cheaper'n going out all the time."

"It does help to have a diet or exercise buddy. Martha's cooking may just save my life. Drat! That's something I'll owe Mavis for, indirectly. Don't tell her I said so, though, okay?"

"Not if you come with us tomorrow. Please, Juanita. The audiences haven't been all that great in some of these little places."

"Wonder why. Suppose other people detest political speeches, too?"

"They're part of the process of choosing our leaders."

"Mm."

"Gilroy's more interesting than most politicians."

"Mm."

"Do this for me, Juanita, and I not only won't tell Mavis what you said about owing her for Martha's cooking, but I won't be late to work for a whole month."

"I must've misheard. I thought you just offered to accept a bribe to do what you should be doing anyway."

"Ha, and ha. Will you come?"

Juanita had heaved a long sigh. "I guess so. Don't ask me why."

Now she was regretting her decision. After a light lunch and no time for dinner, her stomach was growling its emptiness. And besides dreading the coming campaign speech, Juanita had had to hear Gilroy talk almost constantly since she had climbed into the passenger side of his white Cadillac.

"Shouldn't you rest your voice for the speech?" she said during one of his infrequent pauses. "I've heard that people who talk or sing too much can get nodules on their vocal cords or something. You really don't have to make conversation on my account."

Rubbing his globe-shaped nose, Gilroy gave her an amused look. "I think that's the nicest way anyone's ever told me to shut up."

She grinned. "At least you have a sense of humor."

"Politicians have to develop thick hides. We know we're not everyone's favorite people."

"With some reason."

"I like your employer, Meador," Gilroy said, lifting his striking dark eyes to the rearview mirror. "She's direct, says what she thinks."

"Unlike most politicians." Juanita glanced back at her young assistant, saw him tense up, fidget in his seat, and frown. She winked at him, but he didn't respond.

"Surely you believe in the American political process, Miss Wills?" Gilroy said.

"I'm trusting it less and less," she muttered, "the more I watch officeholders bow and scrape to wealthy contributors."

He cupped an ear, reminding her he had a slight hearing problem. She repeated herself in a louder tone.

"Our system could use some tweaking, I admit," Gilroy said, "but it's the best anyone's come up with." He negotiated a curve, his large hands relaxed and sure on the wheel. "That's why it's important for individual citizens to get involved, make their views known."

"Uh-huh. Tell me something: If you heard my opinion about an issue, then an opposing one from a lobbyist for a rich corporation, who would you pay more attention to?"

He chuckled. "I'm guessing if I said 'to you' or 'to both equally,' you'd accuse me of lying,."

"Certainly would."

"Unfortunately, that's the system, until voters make a strong enough demand for change. I have to keep raising money, to get reelected, to continue to do the people's business."

"So it's my fault, eh? You politicians are all alike."

"No. We're not." He turned and looked her fully in the face, his prominent eyes full of sincerity. "I assure you, Miss Wills, I'm a different sort of politician."

She found herself wanting to believe him. "I've heard that

claim before."

Gilroy laughed. "You're a tough sell, Miss Wills."

"Juanita," Meador whined, leaning forward to touch her shoulder. "Tell the Representative about that literacy workshop you went to. He's very involved with literacy efforts around the state, Juanita. She's planning to be a tutor, sir, to help adults learn to read better."

"I don't think—" Juanita broke off as she registered the note of desperation in her young assistant's voice. Perhaps she should encourage what could be a genuine interest in politics, apart from his attraction to Gilroy's secretary. "I do recall you sponsored a bill about literacy last session, Mr. Gilroy, and I've checked into becoming a tutor. The people in Wyndham's literacy program impress me as being dedicated, and I like the fact adult learners don't have to buy their own materials, as I hear they do in some programs."

"Yes, Wyndham's literacy effort is exemplary, supported by employers and by the community."

"I don't know how good a teacher I'll be, but I'd like to help someone learn to love books as I do."

"A worthy goal, Miss Wills. Librarians and reading programs are natural allies, aren't they? Tell me, how's your other project coming along? The book about Wyndham's history?"

"I've made progress—found a few people willing to talk about Luther Dunlap's murder. You'd have been around at the time, Mr. Gilroy. Maybe you recall something that could help."

He didn't speak at first, one hand smoothing his wavy white hair. "That was so long ago. I wish I could help you, Miss Wills, but—"

A grumble rose from her vacant innards. To cover the sound, she asked, "Did you know a Ward Nutchell then? Or Lonnie Tubbs, or Simon Simms, or Vince Arnold?"

Gilroy smiled. "Nutchell was in my class. A juvenile delinquent type, always skipping school or causing a ruckus. He left before our class graduated—went into the army, I heard. The other three I know. Lonnie and Vince sometimes come to my rallies, and Simon does accounting work for my insurance firm."

"Those four have been mentioned as boys who might've been involved in Dunlap's death."

"Really?" Gilroy straightened the cuff of his red Western-style shirt. "Nutchell, perhaps. Seems likely, now I think of it. But the others? No, I can't imagine them killing anyone."

"Did you know them well in high school?"

"In a small school, you know everyone fairly well. Groups of boys, sometimes boys and girls, did things together—'hung out,' as kids say now. But I was a grade behind all those guys except Nutchell, not close friends with any."

"How about girls? Did you have a steady then, play the field, or what?"

He sobered. "I got my heart broken once. But that's high school for you. It happens."

"Tell me about the track meet, when Dunlap won three events and beat all the white boys."

He chuckled. "You've been doing your homework, Miss Wills. Let's see, that was a . . . big day. As you know, in a small town, school events are extremely important. Feelings ran high."

"I hear Wyndham's superintendent took heat for inviting Bryson's Corner to participate."

"That wouldn't surprise me."

"Did you hear a lot of racist comments at the time?"

"Quite a few, I'm sorry to say. It was a different age, not a politically correct atmosphere."

"Ever hear any of those four boys make such remarks?"

"Probably. Though they don't stand out in my mind as being worse than anyone else."

"Ever say such things yourself?"

"Juanita," Meador warned from the back seat, "don't accuse the Representative."

They passed a convenience store, Buffalo Flats One-Stop, then three modest homes set in big yards.

"It wasn't an accusation, just a simple question."

"And one that deserves an answer," Gilroy said. "Miss Wills, I may've said things then that I wouldn't be proud of now—it truly was a different time—but I don't condone racism in any form today." He smiled conspiratorially. "You haven't unearthed an old tape-recording of me using the 'n' word that you're planning to play tonight before my speech, have you?"

"If I told you, that would spoil the surprise." Noticing he was stopping in front of an old rock armory, where a homemade banner proclaimed "Buffalo Flats Fun Night," she said, "We seem to be here." Light poured from the open door, people milled about inside, and Juanita could see long tables holding platters and bowls. "Oh, are we being fed tonight?"

"I like to schedule my talks at community events when possible, to help attendance." Gilroy got out, circled the car and gallantly opened her door. "Tonight the Buffalo Flats folk are holding their monthly potluck and games evening. I'll be speaking after dinner."

Meador handed him a camera and a blue plastic cake holder from the back floorboard, then crawled out himself.

"Thanks, son. I've brought a modest offering myself, Miss Wills. Baking's a hobby of mine. And from experience, I can tell you the local cooks here are outstanding."

"Great. Let's go."

But Juanita had to contain her eagerness a while longer. The trim blonde woman who greeted them thanked Gilroy effusively for the cake he handed her and explained, "I hope you-all aren't starving. The young folks have a volleyball game going, and we won't serve till that's over. But I can get you some iced tea or coffee."

The cavernous room felt over-warm to Juanita, so she requested tea. She looked about, trying not to focus on the tables in the center holding dishes covered in plastic wrap or foil. Aproned women bustled around, adding or arranging items. At one end of the long room, rows of metal chairs faced a podium. Small tables surrounded by more folding chairs sat along one side, a couple of them occupied by elderly men playing dominoes or checkers.

"Would you like to take a seat, Miss Wills?" Gilroy asked when their hostess had brought them drinks. "Meador and I are going out to watch the game."

Juanita touched the cool glass to her cheek. "I'd better go, too. Or I'll embarrass us all by raiding that food this minute."

Behind the armory, between spreading pecan trees, a net had been strung to form a makeshift volleyball court. Players ranged from adolescence to fifty-plus, the teams being encouraged by spectators surrounding the court. Not far away, children played tag and hopscotch. Gilroy snapped photos of the wholesome, Norman-Rockwell-like scene.

Juanita soon spotted the team stars, two teenaged males facing each other across the net. Shirts off, upper bodies glistening in dying sunlight, they eyed each other like dogs claiming the same bone. Overheard comments told her the stocky white youth with tight carroty curls and a full-lipped pout was Todd Granger, the lanky black one with the ironic grin and studs in his ears and eyebrows, Martin Moseley.

A studious-looking girl on Martin's team slammed an expert serve over the net. It bounced off the wrists of a gangly boy on Todd's side. A tall female set it up for Todd. The sphere hung in the air, then he spiked it hard just out of Martin's reach. A roar came from the sidelines. Todd did an impromptu jig. Martin watched with clouded face.

The ball was put in play. One side scored a point, then the other, until the contest tied at 14–14. A slender Latino boy on Todd's team served. The ball went off three sets of hands on the other side. Two alert guys returned it. Control changed back and forth, both star players in the thick of a hard-fought battle.

Finally, Martin's team pulled ahead by one.

His side served. A stout defender lumbered towards the net, stumbled, reached an arm out, and barely tipped the ball. His bookish teammate got her hands underneath and lofted it high. With a spectacular jump, Todd returned the ball.

This time Martin was ready. Leaping high and writhing in a half-turn, he slammed the ball to the earth in the other court, barely missing Todd's toe. Cheers erupted from supporters. Martin's fellow players grabbed him, lifted him to their shoulders, chanting "Mar-tin, Mar-tin!"

Todd's teammates eyed each other dejectedly, then one after another congratulated him on a good game. Twisting away, he stalked off the court.

Players and spectators called children from games and drifted towards the building. Gilroy had taken action shots during the volleyball play and now photographed individuals and groups, including Juanita and Meador. As they worked their way towards the armory, the legislator greeted and shook hands with people.

Soon Juanita sat at a table happily munching portions of five entrees and three side dishes, with a wedge of buttered cornbread. To her deprived palate, it all tasted heavenly. The other women at her table—one white, one black—were among the cooks, and she complimented the delicious spread.

Most diners, she noticed, had divided off by race. Only one table besides her own was integrated, with four middle-aged males—two African-American, one Latino and one Caucasian—chatting amiably. Young people huddled with others of their own color, mirroring a trend of returning segregation seen on college campuses in recent years. Race relations had improved greatly in some ways since the 1950s, Juanita thought—in other ways, not so much.

The volleyball stars occasionally glanced at each other across the few feet separating their groups. Martin grinned cockily, his slim dusky face radiating good cheer. Todd pursed his thick lips, his brown eyes chilly. They could be Luther Dunlap and one of the white boys he beat at track decades ago, Juanita thought.

For dessert, she couldn't choose between peach, coconut, and pecan pie, so ate a small slab of each with coffee. The cakes looked great, including Gilroy's—German chocolate, one of her favorites—but she couldn't manage another bite. Miserably full of both food and remorse, she went outside for some air. Stars sprinkled a black sky. Chill air cooled her perspiring flesh.

"Pretty night, isn't it?" Meador had followed her.

"Very clear."

"Great victuals."

"Makes me long for the old Roman days, when you overindulged, visited a vomitorium to hurl your cookies, then ate more." She sighed. "Now I guess we have to pay the toll."

"The speech, you mean. Gilroy's a good guy, Juanita. He cares about people in his district. He's always asking how I am, and you and Mavis, and what's happening at the library . . . ."

"He seems to've made quite an impression on you."

"I think politics may be my real calling. I want to make a difference, the way he's doing."

"Then I hope you reach your goal. In the meantime, let's go get this over with."

Fifteen

A nervous man in an ill-fitting seersucker jacket gave Gilroy a reverent introduction. Then the speaker stepped to the microphone, beaming at the people seated in folding chairs.

"My good friends," he said.

"First lie of the speech," Juanita muttered. She and Meador sat at one side of the room. "I doubt he even knows most of the people here."

"Sh-h-h," Meador warned out of the corner of his mouth.

"It's an extraordinary privilege to be back here in . . ." Gilroy hesitated. " . . . Buffalo Flats."

"Forgot where he is," Juanita murmured gleefully.

"Shut up, Juanita," Meador whispered fiercely, then added a milder, "please."

Gilroy spoke at length about the people of Buffalo Flat, the phrases "good old American values" and "the kind of folks that make this country great" recurring often. Meador's round face wore a proud smile. The speech also seemed to be going over well with others. Juanita bit back a caustic remark about gullible voters.

The speech was practiced, professional, sometimes folksy,

telling about the agenda Gilroy had pushed in the last legislature, which ranged from tax relief for farmers and small businesses to updated regulations on wildlife management. Listeners often nodded agreement.

His voice changed, became throaty, as he mentioned his effort to increase state funding for literacy councils. His bill had failed by a mere three votes, he noted with a puckered brow.

"Most of us don't realize how many men in this very county read too poorly to get *or keep* good jobs to support their families. Teenagers are afraid to apply for drivers' licenses because they can't study the manual. Women can't read stories to their young children."

His penetrating eyes softened, glittered moistly. "They're people like you and me, ladies and gentlemen, but destined to remain all their days on the fringes of society." His voice broke.

Juanita noticed tears in many hearers' eyes. She swallowed a lump in her own throat.

"Someone has to do battle for those without big incomes or fancy degrees, the kind of folks who made and continue to make this country great." His voice grew combative. "I've done that in your state legislature. But we also need *national* leaders to carry the fight."

Juanita felt torn between scorn for his trite phraseology and a hope that Gilroy meant what he said. She was beginning to understand what attracted Meador to him.

"People often go to Washington and lose touch with their constituents," he went on. "The laws they enact take away rights from the working men and women who sent them there.

"And that's wrong!" He brought a fist down hard on the lectern.

"So I'm here tonight, ladies and gentlemen, not only to socialize with you fine folks, but to ask your views on something. Our fine Senator Cunningham may not run again because of poor health, and some have been kind enough to suggest I run for his seat. I need you-all to tell me if I should or not." Gilroy smiled self-deprecatingly. "If you prefer I stay in the Oklahoma House, I will. But if you think I can help more in Washington, I need to know it."

His shoulders sagged. "I hate talking about money, folks—purely detest it—but it costs a lot to run a campaign today. And I'd need to be able to be competitive, to make a real race of it."

"Now we get to it," Juanita couldn't resist commenting softly.

"So if you want me to represent you in our nation's capital, I'd appreciate contributions. I have a young friend with me this evening—stand up, Meador—as fine a young fellow as I've met in all my years in government. He'll be at the table by the door as you leave and will be happy to receive whatever you can donate, cash or check, and give you a proper receipt."

Horrors, Juanita thought, Meador's the *money* man. Visions of errors in library petty-cash records made by the fine young fellow danced in her head. But he glowed with self-satisfaction, rising and waving to the crowd, clearly relishing his role of apprentice statesman.

"Also with me tonight is Juanita Wills," Gilroy added, "head librarian at Wyndham Library, a dedicated public servant who also serves her community in other ways. Why, she's becoming a literacy tutor herself! I'm proud and flattered she came this evening. Stand up, Miss Wills."

Annoyed at being made to appear his political supporter, Juanita stood and half-heartedly waggled her fingers. Gilroy soon sat down, to loud applause and obsequious thanks from the man in seersucker. Clapping was long and enthusiastic. Audience members rose, several crowding around the Representative. He cupped an ear as an elderly female spoke to him and pumped his hand. Meador and Juanita made their way to the door, where he sat at a table where a sign on a wicker basket read pointedly, "Contributions."

She went on out.

Gulping cool air, Juanita considered what had happened. She felt used. On the other hand, she should probably have foreseen how her presence could be interpreted.

A raised voice drew her eyes to a corner of the armory. Three young males—all white, although the yard light gave a faintly non-Caucasian cast to Todd Granger's ample lips and taut curls—stood with lit cigarettes. As Juanita watched, Todd made an obscene gesture at two young black men leaning against a parked car. One of them, Martin, grinned cheekily back, then resumed his conversation.

Todd's buddies spoke softly to him, seemingly urging him to some action. He left them and sauntered towards the blacks, his friends following at a distance. At Todd's approach, Martin turned and raked him with a look that managed to be both deadpan and challenging.

"Uh-oh." Juanita shrank into the shadows. "Where's a cop when you need one?"

Martin stood erect and ambled two steps towards Todd. They circled each other, exchanging words too low for Juanita to hear. Tension sparked in their body language. Todd's hands rested indignantly on his hips. Martin's arms lay folded across his chest but appeared flexed and ready. The shoulders of both were high and braced, like cats arching their backs. Juanita almost believed they were Luther Dunlap and one of his white adversaries.

She was about to step inside to summon help when Todd doubled a fist and threw a punch at Martin. His opponent side-stepped, and the blow missed. Todd sprang at Martin, pummeling him with both hands. Martin landed a right in Todd's solar plexus. Todd faltered, nearly fell. The onlookers, two white, one black, moved menacingly closer. Todd regained his footing and ran at Martin again, this time striking him hard in the chest.

"Stop it!" Juanita said in her best severe-librarian voice. "No brawling! I mean it!"

The five froze in place, then turned as one, searching for the speaker. Juanita stayed hidden. The principals glanced towards their pals as if awaiting a cue. Todd's fierce expression slowly changed to one of calculation. He turned away, flinging words back at his rival.

"This ain't over."

"Any time, any place," Martin cried, clutching his chest.

The whites returned to the corner of the armory. Martin and his chum lounged on the hood of the auto.

Juanita sagged against the wall of the building, shaken by what she had witnessed. She folded her arms and tucked suddenly-icy fingers under them. She realized she was trembling all over, with frustration, annoyance, and yes, fear.

"Nigger!" someone yelled.

She looked up, saw the two groups glaring at each other, but couldn't tell who had shouted the epithet. Or at whom.

Taking a deep breath, she went inside again. Meador was busily writing receipts, the basket half-filled with checks and greenbacks. The candidate stood near the podium, holding forth to half a dozen people. Spying the blonde woman who had greeted them initially, Juanita asked if the county sheriff or a deputy was present.

"The sheriff?" The woman's voice dropped to a whisper. "Why do you need *him*?"

"There was a little disturbance outside. No one got hurt, but the sheriff should be told."

"Oh, dear. A fight?"

"It's over now. I just need to let him know."

"I did see him earlier—oh, there he is. Come with me." She led Juanita across the room to where two men stood near a table holding big coffee urns. "Milt," she said to the taller one. "Could this lady speak to you a minute?"

"'Scuse me, Tubbs," the man called Milt told his beefy companion, setting down his cup. The blonde introduced him as Sheriff Milt Eggerton, then left. The sheriff shook hands formally and dragged two chairs to an unoccupied corner, where they sat down. Juanita decided his solid handshake and sad eyes inspired confidence. She told him about the altercation and the earlier competition on the volleyball court. He nodded.

"Those boys've been spoiling for a fight," he said grimly. "Caused trouble at a couple basketball games last year. 'Preciate you filling me in, Miss Wills. I'll go settle 'em down."

They rose. As something he'd said earlier sank in, she sat again. He politely followed suit.

"Sheriff," she said, "you were talking to someone named Tubbs before. That wouldn't be *Lonnie* Tubbs, would it?"

"Sure would. Want me to introduce you?"

"No, I won't bother him when he's socializing and politicking. I just need to talk to him some time about a research project I'm doing."

"Come on over. If Lonnie can help you out, I'm sure he'd be glad to."

Checking that Gilroy and Meador were still occupied, Juanita followed Eggerton to where Tubbs now stood by a short, thin man with scraggly white hair, in scruffy jeans and a faded denim shirt. At their approach, the smaller man moved off. Eggerton introduced Juanita to Tubbs, a huge red-faced man with gray hair, big ears, and deep blue eyes. The sheriff excused himself and headed for the door. Juanita told Tubbs about the history she was working on.

"That sounds like a real good thing to do, ma'am." His jovial grin didn't quite reach his sapphire eyes.

"Right now I'm looking into an old murder case," she said, watching his expression. "Luther Dunlap's death."

He blinked rapidly several times. The smile now looked set in place. "Luther Dunlap, you say. Black fellow, got killed in Wyndham?"

"Yes. Could you tell me what you remember about it?"

"Let's see, that'd've been when I was in high school. That was a real long time ago, ma'am."

"I know. But it would be a great help if you'd tell me what you can recall about those days."

"Ma'am, I'll sure do my best. Let's go set over there outa the way."

They returned to the seats she and Eggerton had occupied, and she took out her small notebook and a pen.

"Fire away," he said, his expression good-humored and ingenuous.

"Did you ever meet Luther Dunlap?"

Tubbs stroked his chin. "Once. His old man worked on my folks' farm, time to time."

"So you knew his dad?"

"Not really." Tubbs grinned. "I usually managed to have ball practice or something that kept me from helping around the place. Old Dunlap was a man of few words, anyhow. Never said nothing that wasn't about the work we was doing."

"How did you happen to meet Luther?"

"Went with my dad when he drove out to Bryson's Corner looking for hands to hire. Old Dunlap had been recommended to him, but Daddy wanted to see how he kept his own place. Said you could tell a lot about a fella by that. He musta been satisfied. He hired the old man."

"And you met Luther that day?"

"Yeah, he was helping his dad work their garden. Tall, lean guy. Not friendly."

"I understand you competed against him in a track meet held not long before his death."

Tubbs's eyes flickered. "Yes, ma'am." He hesitated. "And if you know that, I s'pose you know I lost to him, like several other Wyndham guys. But I didn't have nothing to do with him getting killed."

"What do you recall about the night he died, and about your own whereabouts that evening?"

Tubbs shook his head impatiently. "Ma'am, could you recollect details of what you did one night forty-some years ago?"

"Not unless I had reason to. But when a big event happens—like the Kennedy assassination, or a sensational murder in your own small town—you compare notes with others about where you were and what you were doing at the time. Right?"

"We probably did. But I sure can't recollect after all this time."

She studied his artless eyes and solemn mouth. Why did she feel a smirk lay behind that innocent expression?

"What else can you tell me about Luther Dunlap, then? Besides his abilities in track."

Tubbs looked thoughtful, then slowly grinned. "Seems like some 'a the gals thought he was good-looking."

"Wyndham girls?"

He shrugged. "Day of the meet, he was warming up for the foot race, and several gals was standing around whispering 'mongst themselves. One said he looked like he might could run pretty fast, another said he couldn't beat the Wyndham boys. But all of 'em had their eyes glued to him."

"Who, for instance?"

He chuckled. "You're going back a ways, Miss Wills. Let's see, now. Hattie Stevens, of course, Miss Hot Pants herself. And Phyllie Campbell."

"Phyllida Campbell? Simon Simms's secretary?"

"Yeah. Phyllie liked all the fellas. She had a reputation, that one, nearly as much as Hattie."

"Mousy little Phyllida Campbell?"

Tubbs grinned. "Might be more goes on in that office than accounting, you know? Besides, she wasn't then—mousy, I mean. A real party girl. Took her out myself a coupla times."

"Did you ever hear gossip that linked her name with Dunlap's?"

"Nope." Tubbs pulled at an ear. "And I don't recollect who else was in that group of gals either. Wait, I do, too. Grace Hendershot. Even Missy Stuck-Up Hendershot looked as if she could eat the guy up."

Juanita nearly dropped her pen. Gracie Hendershot. And Grace's bread had poisoned Samuel Davis, just before he might have revealed the truth about Luther Dunlap's death.

Perhaps she wasn't so innocent after all.

Sixteen

Juanita asked more questions of Tubbs, trying to pin him down on his movements the night of Dunlap's death, but his vague replies neither intensified nor allayed her suspicions of him. She had the distinct impression he was having fun at her expense, and wondered how much faith she should put in anything he told her.

During the return to Wyndham, while Meador and Gilroy crowed about the amount collected that evening, she considered her next move. She didn't know how to reach Vince Arnold, another in the trio Leona Brown had mentioned as possible suspects—the Wyndham phone book didn't contain a listing for him—but she *could* question Simon Simms. Again.

And she could check out Phyllida Campbell.

Martha was already in bed when she got home, but at breakfast the next morning, Juanita broached the subject of her investigation.

"I met Lonnie Tubbs last night," Juanita said, casually smearing low-fat cream cheese on half a whole-wheat bagel. "Not sure what to make of him."

Martha eyed her over the coffee cup she was draining.

"I can see him being a bully when he was a kid, like you said."

"Mm."

"But people can sometimes change over time."

"Mm. More coffee? I'm having some." Martha held the pot near Juanita's cup.

"Guess not. I'll be drinking more at work. Tubbs did mention a few women he thought could've been interested in Luther Dunlap."

Martha almost dropped the carafe, clinking it against Juanita's saucer.

"Phyllida Campbell was one."

Martha let out a breath, lifted the pot with a steadier hand, and poured herself a refill. "Phyllie? Really?"

"Tubbs said she was considered wild then—hard as it is to imagine now."

Martha smiled sadly. "I suppose she was a bit fast."

"And a Hattie Stevens."

Martha looked thoughtful. "Yes, I remember Hattie. Her mother worked in the cafeteria—not a nice woman. Hattie was okay, pleasant to talk to, but *quite* fast—for those days."

"And Grace Hendershot? Her too?"

"Mm . . . no, I wouldn't say so. Grace had an aloofness about her—not indifference, but an air of detachment that I admired. That quality made her—"

"Yes?"

Martha shrugged. "I don't know . . . ."

"How well did you know Grace then? And Phyllida? And Hattie?"

"I didn't know Hattie well, just visited in the lunch line and such. I suppose I was friends, of sorts, with the others. We didn't spend lots of time together, but we got along."

"And they were all friendly to each other?"

"Far as I recall."

"Martha, you don't have to answer this, but I'm curious. Why did you come back to Wyndham?"

"You asked me that before."

"But why return *now*, after so many years?"

Martha's eyes fell. "My third husband died a few months ago. I thought . . . it was time."

"To come home."

"Yes. There's a season for everything, isn't there? It just seemed right to come back now." Martha rose and began to place utensils and plates in the dishwasher, signaling the end of the conversation.

On reaching work that day, Juanita called for an appointment with Simon Simms, and got one for mid-afternoon. She arrived early and waited in the outer office, watching Phyllida Campbell work away on a computer. Today the secretary wore the same gold earrings and a tan shirtwaist, almost the twin of the navy one she'd worn on Juanita's earlier visit, that set off her twig-slim frame and tawny hair liberally sprinkled with silver.

"Excuse me, Miss Campbell," Juanita said, when the flying fingers paused on the keyboard, "have you lived in Wyndham all your life?"

Phyllida swiveled to face Juanita and crossed her hands on the desk. "Pretty much."

She had probably been a cute teenager, Juanita thought. But now, sad eyes and deeply etched facial lines said the years since had not been kind. Juanita explained her history project.

"That's a great idea!" Phyllida's enthusiastic smile lit her face, making it attractive still. "I'm sure lots of people would buy a copy of a Wyndham history. I would, myself."

"That's good. You might be able to help with some of the research."

"I'll try."

"Do you recall when Luther Dunlap was killed?"

The secretary's face blanched, and her hand went to her throat. "Oh! It's a shock to hear that mentioned, out of the blue, after so many years."

"Sorry. Guess I'm too blunt sometimes. Could you tell me what you remember about that death and the circumstances surrounding it?"

Phyllida spread her hands, a gesture of helplessness. "The awfulness of it. The inhumanity." She looked at Juanita, her eyes reflecting horror at the memory.

"Yes," Juanita said softly. She recalled the report of the murder carried in the local paper at the time. Although the reporter had chosen his words carefully, avoiding graphic details that a current tabloid paper would play up, Dunlap had clearly died a brutal death.

"You know what they did to him, don't you?"

"They beat him first."

"And then—" Phyllida's hand curled into a fist— "then they tied his arms—to two fenceposts bordering the track." She swallowed convulsively. "And his legs to—" Her voice failed.

"They tied him to a car," Juanita finished the sentence that Phyllida could not. "He was literally torn apart."

Phyllida buried her face in her hands. She shuddered. Juanita rose and took a step towards the desk, then sat again, instinct telling her this proud woman would resent efforts to console her.

After an interval, Phyllida looked up. "That murder was the—defining moment for my generation. It's when we—had to admit that real *evil* existed—right in our midst." She opened both hands on the desk, palms up, and looked tearfully at Juanita. "Before, you know, we could pretend racism was—someone else's problem."

"Have you any idea who did it?" Juanita asked softly.

Phyllida shook her head. She seemed weary. "School was rife

with rumors. I never heard who the ringleader—" She broke off as Simon Simms entered from the hallway. "Excuse me, I need to finish this." Dashing moisture from her eyes, she abruptly turned again to the computer.

Juanita hadn't heard the accountant approach. She wondered if he'd been standing in the hall listening to their conversation.

"Ready for you now, Miss Wills." He paused by the desk and asked gently, "How's that letter coming, Phyllida?"

The secretary smiled wanly at him. "It'll go out today."

Though the exchange concerned an office matter, Juanita thought it had tenderness in it. Was Tubbs right, that the two had a non-business relationship?

"Good, good," Simms said. "Come on back, Miss Wills. You say you want to discuss a problem at the library?"

She nodded and followed his tall form down the hallway to his office. It looked as before, only now three stacks of folders sat neatly aligned on its right side. He waved her to a chair and faced her from his own across the desk.

"What can I help you with today, Miss Wills?"

"Several of the little chairs in the children's section are in bad shape. And I've no money in my budget for replacements."

He shook his head. "City finances are strained, Miss Wills. Sales tax revenue's down, and the city has to defend that big lawsuit brought by a former employee. I barely managed to keep your appropriation for the new fiscal year at the same level as this one. Why don't you ask the Friends to help?"

Juanita nodded thoughtfully, as if that solution hadn't occurred to her. In fact, this was a typical Friends of the Library project. Coming to Simon about it must make him wonder about her competence, but it had provided an excuse to see him.

"The chairs are wobbly and may be dangerous," she went on. "And we don't have a lot of seating space for the kids to begin with."

"I'm sure the Friends'll help, Miss Wills," said Simms

dismissively, pulling a folder to him and clicking a ball-point pen. "Thanks for coming."

"I appreciate your suggestion about the chairs, Simon. While I'm here, could I ask you a few questions about that old murder I'm researching?"

His eyes narrowed. "I've already said I can't help you with that."

"I know. But before, I just asked generally what you remembered about that murder. Now I have specific questions, regarding information I've gotten from other sources."

"And these other sources would be . . . ?"

"I'm not ready to reveal those names. But I believe my information's solid."

He nodded slowly, one long finger tapping the folder. "All right. Ask your questions."

She said she had been told he'd been friends with boys rumored to have caused Dunlap's death. "Lonnie Tubbs? Vince Arnold? Didn't you run around with them?"

He cleared his throat. "I did know them. We did things together sometimes. I was lonely in high school, too shy to date, and they . . . filled a need. But as for what happened to Dunlap, I certainly wasn't involved. I'm very sorry about that killing."

His wistful tone stirred Juanita's sympathy. Then, she reminded herself he might be lying.

"You must've known Tubbs and Arnold pretty well. Do you think they'd have participated in it?"

"I . . . would rather not . . . speculate."

"For heaven's sake, Simon! I'm not asking if you think they stole a pack of gum. This is murder we're talking about. Please don't protect your buddies if you know *anything* that might help solve that old case."

He stiffened. "They're not my 'buddies,' as you put it. We haven't been friends for a long time. Remember, Miss Wills, you're in *my* office and you came to *me*. I can insist you leave."

"Sorry, I get a little carried away sometimes. It's just frustrating to keep running into walls."

He picked up a stapler, turned it over, and replaced it precisely where it had been. His lips worked as if he was arguing with himself about something.

"I will tell you this much, Miss Wills," he said finally. "The night Dunlap was killed, I was supposed to meet Lonnie and Vince at the pool hall. Neither showed up. I waited an hour or so, then went home."

A thrill of excitement ran through Juanita. "Did they explain later why they didn't meet you?"

"Lonnie said he'd had to doctor sick cattle at his dad's farm and Vince helped him."

"Did you believe the story?"

"I wanted to."

"But you didn't."

"Lonnie was a genius at conning his dad—he could always get out of work. As for Vince, he hated anything to do with animals. But I don't know for a fact Lonnie was lying."

"Did you tell all this to the police right after Dunlap was killed?"

"I . . . don't think I should go into any conversations I might've had, or not had, with the police."

"But this is extremely important. And it's not—" Juanita caught herself just in time. She had almost said the information wasn't in the police file on Dunlap's death. "It's not information most people would've known," she substituted. "Unless, of course, you told your family or friends about it."

"Oh, I wouldn't have done that." Simms stroked his upper lip, with a finger that trembled. "It truly was a different time, Miss Wills. It's hard to make someone who didn't live through it, understand. I was a scared kid. Besides, I had absolutely no proof those boys were guilty. I guess I was glad the case *didn't* come to trial at that time."

"But you would testify if it did now?"

He drew a long sigh. "I'd have to, wouldn't I?"

"Have the police—ever—talked to you about this case?" Juanita hoped her voice didn't betray how much she cared about the answer.

"I don't believe I should discuss that with you, Miss Wills."

"Do you know if Arnold is still in Wyndham?"

"I see him occasionally around town, looking ragged and dirty, as if he leads a hand-to-mouth existence."

"You know where he lives?"

"I don't know if he even has a home."

"Hm. If he's homeless, that would explain the lack of a phone. What about Ward Nutchell? Heard anything of him lately? I'd like to talk to him too."

"No. I didn't really know Ward, though we were on the track team together. I haven't tried to keep in touch with most people from school."

Juanita switched to another angle. "I'm sure you heard the gossip that Dunlap and a Wyndham fellow were interested in the same girl. What can you tell me about that?"

"Nothing. As you say, it was just talk. I don't know if it was true or not."

"If such a triangle existed, who do you think the young woman and the Wyndham man could have been?"

The accountant coughed twice. "I . . . couldn't say, Miss Wills. I can't help you any more, and I have things I need to do."

"Okay, Simon, thanks. You've been a real help."

He rose when she did, his expression pensive, and wished her success in replacing the children's furniture.

She walked the few blocks from Simms's downtown office to the library, a welcome nip in the air teasing of cold weather to come, dry leaves crunching under her sensible one-inch heels. Juanita pondered the interview, trying to decide how to proceed next. She ought to call Wayne. He hadn't shown enthusiasm about her last sharing of evidence, but maybe if she told him what Simms had said about Tubbs and Arnold, Wayne would say more, give her an opening to discuss the sparseness of the Dunlap file.

She also needed to locate Vince Arnold. She didn't know what he looked like—she might have seen him without realizing it—but thought she knew how to find out.

When she reached the library, she telephoned Wayne at the station, fortunately found him in, and summarized her conversation with Simms.

"Thanks for telling me, Juanita," Wayne said. "It's helpful."

"So you didn't already know that those two guys failed to meet Simon that night?"

"Juanita, you realize I can't—"

"'Talk about an ongoing investigation?' I know the wording by heart, Wayne. See you." As she started to hang up in frustration, she heard his voice crackle at the other end, and she returned the phone to her ear.

"Wait, Juanita, don't go away mad," he said. "As you know, it's a citizen's duty to pass on pertinent information to the authorities investigating a case. However, I *truly* appreciate your telling me what Simms said. Thank you."

"That's an improvement. Even better would be to say, 'Thanks, we hadn't learned that information before.' Couldn't you do that?"

"No."

"Then have a nice day." This time, she did hang up.

She went to the corner of the open stacks in the west wing, where was housed a collection of Wyndham High School yearbooks and local telephone books. The most recent years of both were in the reference room, but older ones were shelved here. Running her fingers over spines of school annuals, she located several late-fifties editions and carried them to a nearby carrel. There, she pushed aside a seldom-used extension telephone she'd installed after catching Meador hiding in the stacks, reading on the job once too often. Opening the 1959 annual, she turned to individual senior-class photos, under each of which appeared the student's full name and a nickname: "Moose," "Stretch," "Cutie-Pie," and so on. Presumably, if any youngster hadn't come already equipped with such a moniker, the yearbook staff had supplied one.

Juanita found Simon Simms, thin-cheeked, with dark hair and a solemn look on his acne-ridden face. "Fussbudget" fit him perfectly, she thought. In the row of black-and-white pictures below his, nubile-looking Hattie Stevens ("Kitten") sported a dusky pixie-cut, heavy make-up, and a flirtatious smile. She looked slightly familiar, Juanita thought. Then came Lonnie Tubbs ("Handles"), wearing a cocky grin and a raven burr cut that emphasized his large ears.

Flipping to an earlier page, she found Martha Haney ("Dream Girl"), a genuine beauty with a cap of dark curls and a mysterious smile. Grace Hendershot ("Duchess") wore a pale pageboy and a haughty expression. On a different page, frizzy-blonde Phyllida Campbell ("Phun Phyllie") flashed a bold grin, her scrawny neck protruding from a sedate Peter-Pan collar.

Finally, Juanita found Vince Arnold ("Squirrel"), with sharp features, close-set eyes, and a full head of medium-dark hair slicked back. In those days he'd have been called a "hood," she thought, recalling books and movies from the period. She tried to visualize an older Arnold as he'd look now, and thought she had seen him somewhere. She couldn't think where or in what circumstances, however.

She turned to the junior-class photos. Claude Gilroy ("Gladhand"), with prominent eyes and a sandy pompadour, radiated confidence. Ward Nutchell ("Droopy") seemed somewhat familiar, but perhaps that was because his long, spare face, receding chin, and dishwater-pale hair marked him as ordinary. Had she seen him before? Juanita couldn't be sure.

She glanced through the other annuals, finding earlier portraits of all the youths, then went back to the 1959 book. Paging through group shots of clubs and organizations, she noticed that Tubbs, Simms, and Arnold were in several pictures, always together. Gilroy and Hattie appeared in a half dozen clubs but never together, and neither beside the same individual twice. Had they had lots of friends? Or none?

Other than his class photo, Nutchell appeared only in a shot of the track team, standing between two boys she didn't recognize. Martha and Phyllida were in two group pictures, in one sitting side by side at a large table with the yearbook staff, in the other with the Home-Ec Club, Grace Hendershot sitting between them. Grace appeared in no other group photos.

Nine youngsters on the verge of adulthood. Juanita suspected those fresh faces held the answers she sought. But could they be made to speak?

Seventeen

That afternoon, Meador came back from his regular lunchtime visit to Gilroy's campaign headquarters, bearing a fistful of passes for a carnival ride at the county fair that was to open in Wyndham next week.

"Brandy—the Rep's secretary—said the carnival's 'front man' came around and left a bunch of passes to promote the midway," he explained to Juanita and Mavis as they all sat at the circulation desk that afternoon.

"You two seem to be getting chummy," Juanita commented.

"Brandy's cool. I asked if she'd like to go to the fair with me, but she expects to be busy the whole time it's open."

"Really. It lasts a couple of weeks, doesn't it?"

"Yeah, but her mom always has stuff for her to do evenings."

"She lives at home, then?"

"Yeah. And she seems to wash her hair a lot."

"Oh." It sounded as if Meador was about to get his heart broken, Juanita thought. But no warning she could give him would prevent that.

"I want to give tickets to a couple of my guy friends," Meador went on, "but there're plenty for you and Wayne, Juanita, and you and your husband, Mavis. Martha too. But they're only good for opening night, next Thursday."

"A carnival ride?" Mavis jeered. "Don't be ridiculous."

But it sounded like fun to Juanita. When she mentioned it to Wayne, he said he'd also be up for a fair.

Saturday afternoon, Garvin McCoy eyed Juanita suspiciously as she set her purse on his porch floor. She opened a notebook on a table Robert Norwood had placed by her chair. McCoy perched stiffly on the swing, arms folded across his T-shirted chest. Robert lolled beside him, an arm across the wooden swingback, one foot moving the suspended seat back and forth.

"Thank you for seeing me, Mr. McCoy," Juanita began. "I want my book to tell the truth about what happened to Luther Dunlap, so it's important I talk to people who knew him."

He watched her without blinking, face expressionless.

"I understand you knew Mr. Dunlap pretty well," she went on. "And that you and Samuel Davis were good friends then, too."

His solemn stare began to unnerve Juanita. She took a deep breath. Had she wasted her time and Robert's by pressing for this interview?

"Garvin," Robert said, a note of warning in his voice.

"She ain't asked me nothing yet."

"You're right, I haven't," she said, relieved to finally hear him speak. "What do you recall about the night Mr. Dunlap died?"

Again, that stony gaze. This was impossible, she thought.

Maybe her questions needed to be more specific. "For instance, did you hear him say he was planning to go into Wyndham that night?"

"No. And he wouldn't. He wadn't crazy."

She hastened on. "Then do you know of anyone who might've taken him there against his will?"

"Don't know no names."

"But you do know of someone?"

McCoy looked away, watching the yellow tabby mince across the lawn. The stillness stretched to a minute, then two.

"Tell it, Garvin," Robert said softly. "Luther can't speak for himself. You've got to do it for him."

"She'll sweep it under the carpet. They all do."

"Things've changed since the fifties. And I believe Miss Wills'll tell it straight."

McCoy's eyes returned to her face, and he seemed to consider. He shrugged. "Samuel seen them take him."

Juanita's heart skipped. "He saw someone kidnap Mr. Dunlap?"

McCoy nodded. "Three fellas. Luther lived crost the way there then." He pointed to a house across the street and down half a block. "Samuel and him was over there listenin' to the raddio that evenin'. Luther's ma and pa and sisters went to visit relatives—the boys stayed there. Luther was s'posed to be helpin' Samuel with his schoolwork."

He paused, scratched at an ear. Juanita held her breath, hoping he'd go on. At last, he did.

"Mama had me choppin' wood, or I'd a-been there too. Samuel's folks didn't have no raddio, so he talked Luther into listenin' to a music program. The disc jockey was doin' a tribute to the Del-Vikings, and Samuel was a big fan. 'Specially liked 'Kripp' Johnson."

McCoy looked away into the distance several minutes. Juanita tried not to fidget with impatience.

"Somebody banged on the door," McCoy said. "And Luther went to answer. Samuel heard him say, 'What you doin' here?' Then he yelled back to Samuel he was goin' outside to get rid of somebody.

"Samuel was glued to the raddio, 'cause his favorite song—'Come Go With me'—was playin'. After it ended, Samuel went and looked out the door to see what was goin' on."

McCoy watched a fly light on his jeans-clad thigh, then waved it away.

"Samuel seen two white fellas throw Luther in the back of a old jalopy. Third guy gunned it, and they took off."

Juanita's pen flew. "What did they look like, these white guys?"

"One of 'em what grabbed Luther was big and had real dark hair. Other's was carroty-red, showed up good in the bright moonlight and right under the pole lamp, Samuel said. He couldn't see the driver."

At last, Juanita exulted, real information about Dunlap's killers. "About what time in the evening was this?"

"Program come on at eight-thirty. Guess it would've been near nine."

"What kind of car?"

"Old, dark-colored Ford. Samuel didn't know the year, didn't keep up with cars like most guys. I coulda told if I'd been there, but not Samuel."

"Did he tell all this to the Wyndham Police?"

"Tried to. Went in town next day, talked to some fella at the station. Man wrote it down, but Samuel said he didn't seem too interested. Asked if Samuel knowed the white fellas' names. Looked glad when he said no."

"Do you know if anyone followed up on the information he gave?"

"They was mighty quiet about it if they did."

"You know the name of the cop Mr. Davis told about it?"

"Nope. Samuel was so scared talking to the po-lice, he didn't get the name. Cop's probably dead now, anyway, so long ago."

"What about—more recently?" Juanita struggled to keep her voice steady. "Have you or Davis ever talked to the police about that night?"

McCoy looked at her, one eyebrow raised, and shrugged. "Don't matter. They hide what they want to hide."

Juanita waited for him to say more. He didn't, so she tried again. "Has anyone from the Wyndham Police *ever* asked you or Davis what you knew?"

He glared at her. "I said what I said."

Afraid more pushing would make him clam up entirely, she tried a different tack. "Had Mr. Dunlap been having trouble with certain white boys before that night?"

"Some, time to time, over different things."

"I've heard various rumors about why he was killed. One was that he had stolen a deer off a car hood after a boy named Ward Nutchell shot it."

"That ain't true. Luther Dunlap was a crackerjack hunter his own self. He wouldn't of stole no deer off'n nobody else."

"Okay. I also heard he'd sugared someone's gas tank over the beating of his dog."

"That's so, I think. This kid, name of Arnold-somethin', used to come out here to buy truck outa people's gardens and re-sell it in Wyndham. One time—month or so before Luther got killed—Arnold was down the street loadin' up melons. Luther's hound come around, wasn't botherin' nothin', but that Arnold boy was real scared of dogs, I guess. He hauled off and grabbed a tire iron, started beatin' on the poor beast.

"Luther didn't see it happen, but he heard about it. Some time later, Luther told Samuel and me somebody had dumped sugar in that white kid's tank. Way he said it, we knowed it was him. Said Arnold'd never know who did it. Mebbe he was wrong."

"Could the boy have been *Vince* Arnold?"

"Might've been the name."

"Okay. Another rumor was, there was trouble between Mr. Dunlap and a white boy over a girl."

McCoy's eyes strayed again to the tabby, which now sat on the sidewalk licking a paw. "I heard that."

"Was it true?"

"Luther was good-lookin'. The ladies liked him. Wadn't just

his looks, neither. He treated 'em nice, give 'em flowers he'd growed in his yard. He knowed how to talk to 'em, make 'em feel important."

"Do you know who the girl was? And the other boy?"

"Leona Brown'd never say if it was her, but she didn't deny it. Don't know the man."

Juanita flipped a page. "Did you know of *any* black-white couples around here at that time?"

McCoy's face clouded, as if he recalled something painful or unpleasant. She couldn't resist probing further.

"Forgive me for asking, Mr. McCoy, but were either you or Mr. Davis involved with a white female?"

He turned scornfully towards her, lips firmly set. She decided to shift the conversation before he could tell her to leave.

"Another possibility I heard was that the murder might've been done out of revenge, because Mr. Dunlap won several events in a track meet."

Tension eased from his face. He chuckled. "Them whiteys in Wyndham didn't take to that a-tall. Made Bryson's Corner mighty proud, though."

"I've wondered if that's the reason Mr. Dunlap's body was left on the *track* at Wyndham High School."

McCoy slowly nodded, his eyes on the cat again. "Could be." He fell silent a moment, then went on as if thinking aloud. "Samuel and me was best friends. Brothers, some thought, even if he was lots lighter, even lighter than Luther. But Samuel looked up to Luther, imitated him in lotsa things.

"They got closeter them last months. Seemed like they was keepin' secrets for one another."

Juanita watched in sympathy, thinking that he now seemed to be trying to explain something to himself.

"Used to make me mad when they'd be together 'thout me." He rubbed a withered hand over his fuzzy crown. "I felt real bad after Luther got killed that way, though."

She waited several minutes, but this time he didn't go on.

"Mr. McCoy," she said gently, "I'm awfully sorry about your friend Mr. Davis. Do you think his death was . . . accidental? Or could someone have planned it?"

He rubbed a hand over his face, forehead to chin, and shook his head. "Wish I'd been here. Mebbe I coulda—" His voice broke.

"Could have what?" Juanita murmured, hardly daring to breathe. "Could have called a doctor sooner?"

He shook his head again, then sat gazing into the distance.

Juanita tried again. "Do you—or did Samuel—know a white boy named Lonnie Tubbs? Or one named Simon Simms?"

He gave a long sigh, then looked at her and frowned. "I never. Far as I know, Samuel didn't. I heard of Tubbs, though. He lost to Luther in the foot race. Ain't he the one that's big in property now?"

"Yes, he owns lots of real estate in the county. Simms is an accountant in Wyndham."

"Don't know him." McCoy's eyes, fierce now, fastened on Juanita's. "You think they was the ones killed Luther?"

"I don't know, yet. But one of my sources mentioned hearing Lonnie Tubbs and Vince Arnold once, using racial epithets and grumbling about the track-meet results. Simms used to run around with them some."

McCoy nodded slowly. "Could be. But plenty of people said such stuff. What you need is to find that witness."

"You've lost me, Mr. McCoy. What witness?"

"The one what saw Luther get killed."

"Someone actually saw it happen?" Juanita's pulse raced. "Who?"

"Don't know. Samuel heard about it several weeks later but never would tell me who it was."

"Did he say who he heard about it *from?* Or give you any clues to the witness's identity?"

"Just said it was somebody had the color skin the po-lice would believe."

"The witness was white?"

McCoy smiled, as if the question was too stupid to merit a response.

Eighteen

Over the next few days, Juanita thought about what Garvin McCoy had said about a white witness. She knew she should tell Wayne, but his tepid responses to her earlier confidences left her reluctant. If she could find out who the witness was . . .

She decided to hold off telling him, hoping she'd soon have a real bombshell to reveal. One thing deeply troubled her, the fact that Davis had given information to the Wyndham Police soon after Dunlap's death, yet nothing of that interview appeared in the official file she had copied.

One day while both assistants were manning the circulation desk, Juanita sat in her office thinking about the music that had so enthralled Samuel Davis. Idly she typed the name "Del-Vikings" into an online search engine and clicked on a few of the 160,000 sites that came up.

She learned that the doo-wop singers' complex history had included personnel changes, contract disputes, and internal strife. Over the years, some version of the name—Del Vikings, Del-Vikings, Dell-Vikings—had been used by various groups, and sometimes more than one of these had recorded for different record labels at the same time. First tenor Corinthian "Kripp" Johnson had been a member of the original quintet, formed in 1955 when five black enlisted men at Pittsburgh Air Force Base began singing together in the camp hall. He'd also been a part of some later incarnations as groups formed, disbanded, and re-formed.

"Come Go With Me" had been an early and enduring hit for the singers. Juanita wondered if young Samuel Davis had been attracted merely to the piece's catchy rhythm and the group's harmonic blend, or if the lyrics had also held special significance. Had Davis loved a girl and longed to go away with her? The mother of his son Bill, perhaps? Or had he loved another in 1959?

Maybe there'd been no specific person at that time. Like many adolescents, Davis might have simply been in love with the idea of love. Juanita wished again that she could've met and talked with him before his death.

Thursday arrived, and Martha declined to accompany Juanita and Wayne to the fair, saying she had letters to write.

"Do come," Juanita begged that day at breakfast. "You never go out, and this'll be a nice change for you."

"I don't like crowds, or midway rides. I'm a homebody."

"A world traveler like you?"

"Maybe that's why I like to stay home—I've been away so much."

That evening Wayne picked Juanita up at the library in his late-model Wyndham Police car. The new chief believed that having cops drive cruisers while off duty made the police's presence in the community more visible, and hence helped deter crime. They drove to the fairgrounds at the edge of Wyndham, paid for parking at the gate, and followed a man's wave to a spot in a long line of cars. Juanita nodded to the attendant as she got out. He didn't return the greeting, his close-set eyes darting from Wayne to his official car.

"Evening," Wayne said, meeting the man's gaze without smiling.

Juanita had the impression they recognized each other. Glancing at the man again, she did a double-take.

Slight of build and unshaven, with tangled white hair and a pointy nose and chin, he wore torn jeans and a much-washed denim shirt. She had seen him somewhere recently. Buffalo Flats, perhaps?

"Wait a sec, babe," Wayne said. "I promised a guy at work I'd help him move furniture next weekend, but I'd forgotten that's when the bowling tournament is. Let me call him right quick before I forget."

He got back into the car, and Juanita saw him punch buttons on his cell phone. She studied the attendant again.

Yes, Buffalo Flats. He had been with Lonnie Tubbs. And she had also seen a younger version. Allowing for age-related changes, he could be—

"Excuse me," she said. "Are you by any chance Vince Arnold?"

His squinty eyes widened slightly. "Who wants to know?"

"I'm Juanita Wills, the local librarian. I was looking through an old yearbook recently, and I believe I saw your picture. Class of '59?"

His eyes narrowed to slivers. "Yeah. So?"

"I'm researching a history of the town, and I need to ask what you recall about something that happened during your senior year."

"What would that be?" He scratched his shoulder and half-turned towards an approaching vehicle.

Juanita hesitated, not wanting to scare him off. She wished her approach had been less direct. On the other hand, coyness might not work with him. Anyway, she didn't see how to avoid answering, now.

"The death of Luther Dunlap."

He waved an orange pickup to a spot beside the police car. Juanita moved from its path.

"I'm busy, lady," Arnold growled.

"Then could I talk to you later this evening, after you're finished here?"

"Won't do you no good. I don't know nothin' about that."

"But you were around at the time. It would really help if you could at least tell me what you heard about it then."

Wayne climbed out of the car again. Juanita wished his call had lasted a little longer. Still, whether he liked it or not, she couldn't let this chance go by.

"Well, okay," Arnold said. "Come back around—say, 8:45. Shouldn't be no cars comin' in then."

"Great. Thanks."

Elated over getting his commitment to an interview, Juanita tucked a hand under Wayne's arm and grinned up at him as they walked across the parking lot.

"What was that about?" he asked, clasping his free hand around hers.

"I realize you won't approve, Wayne," she said, "but I hope you won't go all stern about it. That man was in high school here at the time Luther Dunlap was killed. He's agreed to talk to me about it."

"And he is?"

"Vince Arnold. As you—" Juanita stopped. She had almost said, "As you'd know if you'd been looking into that old case." But that wouldn't have helped the festive mood of the evening.

"As I what?"

"Nothing. You're not going to try to keep me from talking to him, I hope."

"Any private citizen can talk to any other private citizen."

"True."

"But I will warn you—again—about the dangers of poking

your nose in where someone might not appreciate it. And if you should learn anything that might be relevant to a *still-open* murder case, you *will* tell me. Right?"

"O-o-okay. But for now, let's go have a good time."

They reached Wyndham Community Building, a large cement-block structure that housed events of area-wide appeal such as Kiwanis Pancake Day fundraisers, domino tournaments, Quilters Society exhibitions, and pre-election political "speakings," where candidates for local and state offices made their pitches to voters. Currently, the huge room held rows of tables displaying entries in agricultural and domestic-science contests: plump grains and melons, home-canned relishes, baked goods, needlework, and craft items. The fair had drawn a big crowd for its opening night, a mixture of farmers and "city folk" in jeans, overalls, print dresses, and other casual attire. Laughter, chatter, the crying of babies, and the shuffling of feet combined into a low din. Aromas of farm produce, home cooking, cologne, and perspiration assailed Juanita's nostrils.

They split up, Wayne heading for the displays of wheat and alfalfa, while Juanita browsed among embroidered pillowcases, crocheted doilies, and knitted sweaters. After a while, they met at a table that held an assortment of fruit pies with wedges cut out. They stood salivating over the flaky pastries and juicy fillings, and Juanita heard Wayne's stomach growl.

"Easy, big fella," she murmured.

"We should get something to eat," he said. "Think I'll start with that deep-dish apple job."

"Make mine blueberry. Or—we could remove ourselves from temptation, painful though that will be."

Juanita turned and almost ran into Grace Hendershot. They all said hello.

"I haven't seen your name on any of the entries, Grace," Juanita said. "Surely you entered your bread-and-butter pickles."

Grace glumly shook her head.

"What about your canned peaches and pickled okra?"

"Nope. I was told not to."

"Told? By whom?"

"Those ladies that run the show. 'In view of the circumstances, Miss Hendershot . . . ,' one of them said. She didn't finish, but I knew what she meant. People think I killed Sa—that man that died. I wouldn't. Didn't."

"That's awful, Gracie. But you haven't been arrested, so you must be in the clear. Right, Wayne?"

He pursed his lips. "You know I can't discuss a case that's under investigation, Juanita."

She gave him a long look. "Excuse me a minute, Wayne. I need to talk to Grace. Alone."

He shrugged and moved a few tables away, feigning interest in a hand-painted birdhouse. Juanita drew Grace to a quiet spot apart from the crowd.

"How're things going, really? Are the police bothering you?"

"They keep questioning me. Mr. Cleary's always polite, but it's like he thinks—" A tear trickled down Grace's waxed-fruit cheek. "And I wouldn't—I couldn't! I don't know, Juanita, I just don't."

"There, there, it'll be all right." Juanita hugged the older woman, wishing she felt as confident as she sounded. She lowered her voice till it was barely audible against the background noise. "Grace, I apologize for asking this—you've faced so many questions already—but I heard something about you that might be relevant to Luther Dunlap's death. Someone told me you were one of a group of white girls watching him—admiring him, my source thought—just before he ran in that big track meet against Wyndham. Is—that true?"

The tears stopped as suddenly as they had started. Moist-eyed, Grace stared past Juanita to the next table, where two women examined a needlepoint pillow.

"Were you interested in Luther Dunlap, Gracie?"

The older woman still didn't speak. A muscle in her cheek

twitched.

"I understand Hattie Stevens and Phyllida Campbell were part of the group that day too. Do you recall anything any of those girls said? About Dunlap?"

"I gotta get home," Grace muttered. "Awful tired." She wheeled, made her way quickly through the crowded aisle and out the door.

I pushed too hard, Juanita thought, stricken with guilt. Grace was a friend, and increasing her stress level when she was already under immense pressure wasn't exactly a friendly act.

As she watched the retreating form, Juanita recalled something Leona Brown had told her. One of the white girls she'd seen at Dunlap's home had been tall, with long blonde hair. Grace was tallish for a woman. And her 1959 yearbook photo had shown her with a light pageboy.

Was Grace Hendershot the mysterious woman over whom Luther Dunlap had been murdered? If so, did that long-ago horror and resulting remorse help explain Grace's precarious mental state now? If anything, she had seemed worse since Davis's death. Was she carrying even more guilt now, because it was her bread that had killed Dunlap's friend?

Juanita decided against pursuing Grace. She'd try to catch her later, in more private circumstances, and raise the subject more carefully. Juanita rejoined Wayne, and they left the building by the back door, turning left into a noisy, brightly lit midway.

"Let's see those passes, babe," Wayne said. "I suppose the freebies are on something nobody'd want to ride."

Juanita drew the tickets from a pocket and examined them. "They're only good on something called the Spinner, whatever that is. Look, someone's doodled overlapping triangles on the backs. I tend to draw stars or flowers, myself."

"Want to ride the roller coaster first?" he suggested. "Before we eat?"

"Let's do the Ferris wheel instead."

"Wimp. At least let's try that Spinner thing. That's it over there. Looks like it might be fun."

Juanita eyed the high wheel with four large, enclosed, bullet-shaped cars mounted around the rim. As she watched, the ride spun at breakneck speed, the cars tumbling over and over, their human cargo mouthing screams unheard over the engine's roar. A tremor of apprehension ran down her spine. She looked back at Wayne's challenging grin.

"You're on." Juanita tried not to notice how the passengers staggered as they got off, how green their complexions were, how one teenager bolted to a trash bin and vomited. She and Wayne climbed the ramp and handed the balding, snaggle-toothed operator their passes. He eyed them keenly, as if estimating their weights for positioning on the ride, then motioned for Wayne to crawl into the open car first.

At the man's direction, Wayne took a seat midway along the last row of seats. Juanita saw him wince as a metal bar clamped shut across him. Indicating a place two rows ahead of Wayne, the attendant helped Juanita in and fastened her restraint. The door clanged shut, leaving them alone in the cubicle. She wondered why the operator had not waited to admit more riders, but decided he must need to balance the cars' weight by partially filling each. She felt theirs move back and up.

When they reached the top and slowed to a crawl, their car suddenly flipped over. She found herself dangling upside down, looking out through a heavy plastic ceiling—or floor, at the moment—a few feet below her head.

"What a view-ew-ew—," she said as the car swung to an abrupt halt.

"Yeah, of the ground," Wayne growled somewhere above and behind her.

"It's a different way to see Wyndham, that's for sure. Look, I think that's the library over there."

"Nope. It would be that way, if you could see it for all the trees."

"Well, at least I'm sure the college is over here." She pointed to a collection of brick buildings taller than nearby structures.

"Yep, that's the campus. There's the lake, and the park. That must be downtown, what I can see of it. How long we going to have to hang up here, anyway?"

"The operator's probably waiting for people to put in another car."

She strained to see directly below, but the curve of the metal cabin hid both ramp and operator. At the entrance to the ride, several people now stood in line. A man, unrecognizable from above, strode from the Spinner over to them and said something. The couple at the head of the queue nodded and walked off hand in hand. Others stood uncertainly, then left too. The man returned to the Spinner. Still, the ride didn't start.

"This rod's cutting off the circulation in my thighs," Wayne groused. "And all my blood's now in my head."

"I'm beginning to feel a little sick myself," Juanita said. "Good thing we haven't eaten yet." The shaft across her lap dug into her flesh.

"Not much of a thrill so far," he snorted. "Sitting upside down till you pass out isn't my idea of fun. You suppose that attendant went to supper and forgot about us?"

Juanita twisted around, craning her neck to see the rest of the sizeable enclosure. A few feet from their heads, reinforcing metal strips crisscrossed a clear dome, which was attached to a metal shell encasing the passenger area. A narrow aisle around the car wall allowed passage to and from the seats, which were in three rows of three each. Wayne was in the back row, she in the front.

"You'd think they'd put a telephone in these things," she said. "Some way to call for help. What if someone had a heart attack up here?"

"I *would* leave my cell phone in the car," Wayne said. "Of all times . . ."

"And I didn't even bring a purse—thought it'd be in the way when I went on rides."

As she spoke, the bar across her lap gave way. Juanita felt herself falling.

Nineteen

Instinctively, Juanita raised her hands to her face. And none too soon. Her head and hunched shoulder slammed down on the hard plastic canopy. Her shoulder took the brunt, but the fingers shielding her eyes and nose smarted from the blow. The impact left her stunned.

What had happened? Where was she?

"You okay, babe? How the hell does this clamp open?" A voice somewhere above her, disembodied, worried.

Not her mother's—deeper than Mom's. Besides, that proper woman had refused to say the "H" word, even when alive. Wayne's voice, Juanita realized through her confusion. Grunts and creaking noises sounded overhead.

The world lurched to the left. Juanita slid along. It tilted back right, sending her flying again. What was going on? An earthquake? She blinked several times, trying to clear her head.

The ground under her rocked harder, Juanita lurching first one way, then the other. Adrenaline poured through her, and at last her fog lifted.

"Lord," she moaned, suddenly aware of her situation, "I'm not fastened in—what if this thing starts whirling—?" Fear seized her like a grappling hook.

"Help!" Wayne roared, struggling to free himself. "Get us down! The bar came loose!"

His words sounded loud to Juanita, but against the din from the midway below, she doubted anyone could hear.

The car swayed faster, farther, nearly tipped over. Juanita scrabbled for a hand-hold. But her fingers found no purchase, no knob or handle to grip. She slithered around the hard plastic surface, hands, elbows and knees burning from friction. She *would* be wearing shorts and a sleeveless shirt, she thought.

"You sonofabitch!" Wayne shouted. "Stop this thing! Get us down!"

But their suspended prison picked up speed, made a full revolution, then another. Juanita bounced from one unyielding wall to another, banging her arms, hips, shoulders on the empty seats.

"I'm the police!" Wayne cried. "I'll run you in!"

Juanita saw him tug at his restraint, but the rolling of the cylinder shook his hands loose. She fell against a seatback, jarring her spine.

I'm going to die up here, she thought. *What a ludicrous way to go.* She giggled hysterically.

Each time she dropped near Wayne, his long arms reached for her—and missed. She managed to grab the edge of a seat once but couldn't hold on. Wayne's screams grew frantic, more profane, her own shrieks panicky.

She fell again, body half curled, forearms protecting her head. She felt a hand close on her right foot. It stopped her progress, shaking her to her teeth. The ankle twisted. Pain shot along her calf.

Momentarily she hung suspended, hands brushing the car ceiling below her head. As the car spun again, she crumpled towards Wayne. Releasing the ankle, he caught her in a bear hug.

On they whirled, Juanita praying he could hang on and that the rod anchoring him would support her added weight.

At last the tumbling slowed. Juanita released the breath she had been holding. Abruptly the motion halted. Her head wrenched to one side.

With an effort, she pulled it back, sat in a more upright position. In Wayne's hazel eyes, she saw relief and the remnants of fear.

"Wayne, oh, Wayne," she sobbed, trembling head to foot. She felt his heart pound beneath her palm.

"Get us down!" he called again, his voice husky now from yelling.

Miraculously, the car began to creep downward.

"Thank God," he croaked.

They descended slowly, Wayne clutching Juanita, kissing her over and over. Finally, they reached the platform. A different man, younger and more muscular than the original attendant, opened the door and helped Juanita out. Her legs wobbled, and her ankle collapsed under her weight. She caught herself on a railing.

"You okay, ma'am?" the man said, grasping her shoulder, fortunately not the painful one.

"If she is, it's a miracle," Wayne said hoarsely.

Their rescuer unclasped the metal pole across Wayne, who climbed out, slid an arm around Juanita, and snarled, "Where's the other guy? The one who put us in this deathtrap?"

"Dunno," the young man said with a frown. "I run one of the other rides. Was on my break when I saw this one actin' kinda outa control. Didn't see nobody around, so I come over and stopped it."

"Thanks a million," Wayne said, pumping his hand. "You may've saved our lives."

"Grateful," Juanita managed to murmur. "So grateful . . . "

"You're shivering, babe," Wayne said, hugging her close. "Probably in shock. You got a coat we could borrow, mister?"

"Sure. Be right back."

He returned shortly with a heavy blue jacket. Wayne folded Juanita in it and said, "Got to get her some medical attention. I'll be back, though. When the other guy shows up—a bald, gap-toothed fellow if you don't recall—don't let him stir one inch till I've talked to him. Okay?"

"Got it. I'm real sorry about this, folks. Don't know what happened. We pride ourselves on our safety record. Wait a sec, I'll get a wheelchair for the lady."

From somewhere he brought the promised chair, and Wayne pushed her to the parking lot across grass and fine gravel. She barely noticed the bumps in the path. Her head, neck and shoulder were one huge ache, her lower back throbbed, pain radiated from her ankle, and skinned spots all over her body set her aflame.

To the accompanying wail of Wayne's siren, they drove quickly into Wyndham, to Rochester Memorial Hospital. Fortunately, it was a slack night in Emergency, and Juanita's police escort helped expedite matters. Soon she lay huddled under blankets on a table in an examining room, a young bearded doctor gently probing and assessing her injuries.

"You're pretty beat up, Miss Wills," he said when he had finished the examination. "We'll get some x-rays and a CAT scan, as well as treating all these abrasions. If you'd planned on running any marathons in the next few days, I'd cancel."

Juanita felt too whipped even to glare at him.

Some time later, she lay in bed in a medication-induced floatiness. Hearing soft steps, she cut half-closed eyes towards the door. Wayne tiptoed in.

"How you doing, babe?" He planted a solicitous kiss on her partly-exposed cheek and drew a chair close.

"O—kay," she said woozily. "You?"

"Not bad, but I'm not the one encased in plaster and gauze. Want me to leave you in peace and come back tomorrow?"

Struggling against the druggy lethargy, she said, “Ice.”

Obligingly, Wayne spooned ice chips from a container on her bedside table into her open mouth. She sucked, turned the cold bits with her tongue, and gradually came alert.

“What happened to me?”

“You don’t remember your wild ride? They say concussion can make you block out all memory of an accident, including events just before and after. Probably a good thing in this case.” He briefly recounted their Spinner experience.

“Will I live? Not that I especially want to right now.”

“You apparently lucked out on a lot of things. That shoulder’s badly bruised, but there’s no fracture or rotator cuff injury. You’ll just need to be careful using the arm for a while. Your spleen’s leaking blood—they’re hoping it’ll seal itself. You’ve got a strained back, a sprained ankle and wrist, and one finger’s broken. Let’s see, whiplash, slight concussion, lacerations and contusions on top of each other. I think that’s the whole list.”

Juanita let out a moan.

“But here’s something to take your mind off your injuries. That Spinner operator seems to’ve skipped. I had the other carnival folks looking, but no luck.”

“Really?” She tried to take a deep breath. “Ouch. That hurts.”

“Oh, yeah, you have a fractured rib. Something else interesting. That bar that was across you? The fastener’d been doctored, filed off. You close it, firmly, but it gradually works its way open under pressure.”

“You’re saying I was meant to fall?”

“That’s a real possibility.”

“But why? Who’s responsible?”

“I don’t know yet, Juanita. I questioned the carnival owner and several midway workers. Owner denied his equipment was at fault, swore it had been gone over earlier today and everything was fine, closings and all. Whatever was done to that clamp, it must’ve happened after the inspection.

"Nobody seems to've known that particular operator well. He hired on a couple days ago, after the regular guy failed to show up for a shift."

Juanita closed her eyes, reluctant to deal with the questions raised. A vague recollection stirred, of something she was supposed to do. What was it?

"I also tried to find Vince Arnold at the fairgrounds," Wayne went on.

"Vince—Arnold?"

"You don't recall you and he had made a date for 8:45?"

"Sounds familiar. Yeah, I think that's what I was trying to remember."

"I was going to explain what happened and arrange for you to meet him somewhere later on. It was around 8:30 I went looking for him. But he'd high-tailed it. The gate attendant told me Arnold usually leaves around 8:15, and he left even earlier tonight. Now I think about it, I didn't see him when we got back to the cruiser right after your 'accident.'"

Juanita lifted her head, groaning as her sore neck protested. "Crap. So his promise to meet me at 8:45 was a big fat lie."

"Bingo."

"Shoot me now, Wayne. There's not enough narcotics in this hospital to ease all the pains I've got."

He grinned. "Tomorrow's another day, Scarlett. Don't worry—Wyndham's finest is on the case."

"Cruelty jokes," she groaned. "That's all I get, cruelty jokes."

Twenty

The next day—when she wasn't getting a blood test, vital-signs check, CAT scan, or other necessary interruption—Juanita slept a lot due to pain medication. That afternoon, someone gently shook her awake. From the corner of one heavy-lidded eye, she saw Wayne sitting in a chair at her bedside.

"Hey, babe, feeling any better?"

"I-ice. Ple-ease."

In a repeat of the evening before, Wayne spooned ice chips into her mouth, and she let them melt, growing little by little conscious of her surroundings and her injuries.

"I hur-r-t," she wailed. "But I'm—glad to see you, Wayne."

He hugged her, carefully avoiding the sorest parts. "I went by your house last night after I left here, planning to tell Martha about your 'accident' and say you wouldn't be home for a while. Only I couldn't raise anyone. Didn't see a light on, so if she was there, she was either hiding or sleeping like the dead."

Surprised into greater awareness, Juanita cautiously turned her upper body to look directly at him. "She wouldn't have been expecting anyone but me, and I wouldn't have rung the bell. Late at night, she might've been afraid to open the door." The neck brace chafed, and Juanita eased her head into a more comfortable position.

"Caution's a good thing for a woman alone. Wish another female I know could get that through her head. I did notice Rip was in the back yard and had water in his dish, so someone was at least looking out for him."

She began to feel drowsy again. "Don't worry, Wayne. I'll phone Martha, tell her—what happened."

"You probably won't get anyone. I went by again today and still didn't get a response, so I talked to a couple of your neighbors. One couldn't tell me anything, but Mr. Nguyen said Martha brought a half-full bag of dog food to his house this morning and asked him to look after Rip. Said she had to be gone a few days."

"Gone? Really?" Juanita struggled to stay alert. "I wonder why?"

"Maybe I should check inside your house and see if she stole you blind."

"Wayne!" Shocked awake again, she said indignantly, "How can you think that? If Martha left, she had a good reason."

"We'll see. I also stopped in at Gilroy's office and asked about those Spinner tickets. He wasn't there, but his secretary said an advance guy for the carnival had come by and handed her a bunch of passes, all for the Spinner, to give to whoever they wanted. A 'good-will' gesture, he said, to promote the show.

"I checked with offices of other local politicians, and they confirm they got freebies too, only for different rides and on different nights. As for the triangles on the backs of our tickets, Gilroy's secretary couldn't recall if they'd been there when she received the tickets."

"Why'd you ask about them?"

"It may mean nothing, but those doodles could've been a signal to the ride operator that we were the people scheduled for the 'special' trip."

"Hm-m," Juanita said, once more holding her eyes open with

an effort. "Meador and his friends . . . planned to go to the carnival last night, too. I hope they . . . didn't get the same treatment."

"They didn't. He said they rode the Spinner twice—with no problems—plus a few other rides, and had a great time. Unfortunately, he didn't notice if their tickets had marks on the backs. And there were no other injuries at the fair last night. You're a member of an elite club, babe."

"Lucky me."

After Wayne left, Juanita dozed, woke long enough for dinner and more medication, then slept again. When she awoke the next time, she thought of trying to phone Martha, but it was too early in the morning to call anyone.

After more tests, breakfast, and a nap Saturday morning, she dialed her home number. No answer. She hung up, pushing away uneasy thoughts.

Wayne called later that day to say he'd been by her house again. Still no Martha.

"When you talked to Tien Nguyen yesterday," Juanita asked, "did he say anything about how she seemed when he saw her? Eager to leave, for instance?"

"Nothing out of the way, apparently. He seemed to think she'd already let you know her plans."

Wayne left, and Juanita was drifting back to sleep when someone entered the room and stood by her bed.

"Hey, kid," a raspy but muted voice said. "You awake?"

"He-e-ey, Vi-v," Juanita mumbled, forcing her eyes open.

"Good, you're awake. I came by a couple of times before, but you were zonked out and I figured talking to you could wait. But I was about to despair of ever getting an interview."

"In-ner-view?"

"Still not yourself, eh? Should I come back later?"

Juanita licked dry lips. "No, I'd like . . . company. Water. Please."

Vivian poured a glassful and handed it to her, then raised the head of the bed and adjusted the pillow. Juanita drank the cold liquid and felt awake.

"That's better. Now, what's this about an interview?"

"You know what vultures we reporters are. An ordeal for you means copy for me. We ran an article yesterday about the carnival incident, but I'd like to get your version." Vivian pulled up a chair and patted Juanita's bandaged hand. "Seriously, how're you doing, kid?"

"Not bad, considering the shape I'm in. People help me in and out of bed, wheel me around, tap me for blood, and keep me chained to a catheter and an IV. It's one long, merry vacation."

"Great, I was afraid you might not be enjoying yourself." Vivian coughed, then continued in her cigarette-roughened voice. "You recall much about being in the Spinner?"

"Not really. I gather the ride operator hasn't been found yet."

"Disappeared off the earth, apparently. Wayne seems to think that was no accident. Who do you think was behind it, and why?"

"I don't know, and I don't want to speculate in print. If we can go off the record, I'll tell you my suspicions."

"Okay, for now. But remember, the story's mine to break as soon as there's anything concrete."

"Deal. You know the history of Wyndham I'm doing?"

"Sure. Last time we talked about it, you were starting to look into the old Dunlap murder, and I told you what little I remembered. I was thirteen then, and adults wouldn't discuss it around me. Rumors were abundant at school—one said the whole Wyndham senior class had taken turns cutting little pieces off Dunlap—but even we kids knew those were mostly wrong."

"Real information was scarce, you said."

"The secrecy around that killing helped me decide to be a reporter. I believe hiding awful facts usually does more damage than revealing them. What's that murder got to do with your wild ride?"

"Maybe nothing. But several odd things've happened since I started asking about it." Juanita mentioned the timing of Davis's death and the possibility that someone had shot at either her or Martha.

"Martha? Mavis's sister?"

Juanita explained that Martha had been staying with her since the fire.

"Hm-mm," Vivian said. "You're right, nothing provable in all that, but it makes you wonder. Your questions been zeroing in on someone in particular?"

"No one I'd call a definite suspect. Tell me, Viv, did you know Phyllida Campbell, Hattie Stevens, or Grace Hendershot during those days?"

"Phyllida and Hattie, not real well. Phyllida seemed nice enough, but she was several grades ahead and our paths didn't cross much. Hattie didn't make much of an impression either, apart from having a mother who worked in the school cafeteria—dreadful woman. Grace I do recall clearly. I wanted to be just like her, so pretty, with such an air about her. Sophisticated, I thought."

"Would you say she was a little wild—fast?"

Vivian stroked her chin thoughtfully. "I don't know that she was, really. I do think she felt hemmed in by her folks' restrictions. My mother and hers were in the same sewing circle, and Mom sometimes mentioned things Mrs. Hendershot told at their meetings. Mom thought the Hendershots were overprotective, demanding to know where Grace was and what she was doing every minute. Setting themselves up for disappointment, Mom said."

"Did Grace rebel? Openly, I mean."

"Not that I knew of. But, remember, I was much younger. And Mom would've shielded me from knowing about anything too 'naughty.'"

"How about Vince Arnold and Lonnie Tubbs? Did you know either of them then?"

"Arnold, no. At least I don't think so. Tubbs went to our church, when his mother could drag him there. He sat behind me once during the sermon and tied my braid to a pillar. When I tried to stand to sing the closing hymn, I nearly broke my neck."

"Sounds like a fun guy. You ever hear him make derogatory remarks about black people?"

"Not that I recall. He was several years older, and not at all cute, so I didn't pay him much attention."

"How about Simon Simms? You remember him from those days?"

"Stickler Simon? Surely you don't suspect him of killing Dunlap."

"Not really. Did you know him then?"

"Matter of fact, his family lived next door to us. He hadn't much time for me—last thing a high-school senior wants is to hang out with a junior-high kid—but he'd always speak and be polite. Oh, wait a sec! I asked Simon once what he knew about Dunlap's murder. I was dying to learn anything I could pass on to my schoolmates, and I figured since he was older he'd have the scuttlebutt.

"Simon denied knowing anything and said I shouldn't be asking about such awful things. You know, now I think of it, he began staying home more about that time, not going out evenings like before."

"Interesting."

"Funny, I'd forgotten that. You know how self-involved adolescents are."

A nurse came in to change the IV bag. When she had done so and left, Juanita said, "Vivian, you obviously knew Martha from when she lived here before. Did you know Mavis when she was a kid?"

Vivian rubbed an age-spotted hand. "I did. The three of us

would sometimes walk to school together, for the last part of my walk, that is. I lived four blocks away, and they were right next to the high school. Martha'd escort Mavis and me to the elementary and junior-high side of campus before heading back to the senior high for her classes. Mavis was the apple of her big sister's eye, and she adored Martha."

"I guess Mavis wasn't happy when big sis left Wyndham."

"That's putting it mildly. It was like the sunlight had been shut off in her little life. Their folks didn't help. The Haneys weren't warm people anyway, and after Martha left, they clamped down hard on Mavis. As if she didn't already have enough to deal with, her idol leaving and all."

"So you think the parents took out their anger at Martha on the one kid they could still control?"

"I do. Mavis once showed me bruises from a whipping her dad had given her. Today he'd be locked up for child abuse."

"Hm. I'm beginning to understand why Mavis is so bitter at the world."

Juanita shifted her weight, mindful of her many sore spots. "Sounds like the Haneys and Hendershots were less-than-ideal parents."

"Bringing up kids is a tough job. So I've heard, at least. I was lucky, though. My own parents were great."

"Tell me, Viv, why do you think Martha left Wyndham so suddenly after high school?"

"I don't know. I do recall her saying she couldn't wait to get out of this town, but plenty of teenagers say that. Didn't think much of it at the time."

"Was there talk about her leaving?"

"Just the usual, how young people can't be satisfied at home and have to go looking for greener pastures. Several moved to Tulsa for jobs. Grace and Phyllida were among those who left—I never heard where either went—but both were back a few months later. I don't remember if Phyllida was at all changed, but Grace seemed older and sadder. Like wherever she'd been, the adventure hadn't turned out happily.

"Listen, Juanita, you look like you're getting tired, and I've got things to do. Sure there's nothing more you can tell me about your carnival ride?"

"You got the basic information from Wayne, and I can't add to it. My memory's awfully hazy."

"Anything I can do for you before I leave? Get more ice or anything?"

"No—oh, wait—you could do me a favor if you have time. Could you run by my house and get my hairbrush and a few other things? I've been meaning to ask Wayne, but I keep forgetting—"

"I'd better do it, anyway. Men can be pretty useless when it comes to packing women's stuff."

Vivian brought Juanita her purse from the closet, and Juanita took her house key from a ring and handed it over. She then listed items she wanted.

"Oh, and if Martha's there, ask her to call me. Also, would you see if Rip seems okay?"

"Sure. Be back later. Get some rest. Oh—and be careful."

"*Now* you tell me."

Twenty-One

When Vivian brought Juanita's things later that day, she reported that Martha wasn't anywhere about but had left the house neat. Rip was fine, Vivian said, glad to see her and have her scratch his neck.

"Martha didn't leave me a note at my house?"

"Didn't see one. But I didn't really search. I don't like to prowl through other people's things when they're not there."

"And you call yourself a reporter," Juanita said, grinning. "Did . . . it look like everything was there? Wayne has this crazy idea she stole from me."

"I didn't take inventory, but everything looked as usual."

"Great. Thanks, Viv."

During the next week, Juanita tried several times to reach Martha by phone. Wayne regularly picked up Juanita's mail and newspapers but saw no sign of her. Juanita told herself Martha was fine and would contact her, that she wouldn't leave town without saying goodbye, no matter how discouraged Mavis's continued coolness made her. Juanita wasn't sure she believed her own assurances.

The spleen did seal itself, and Juanita began walking with crutches. The "bootie" cast on her foot and ankle and the neck brace threw her balance off, and her shoulder, back, and rib-cage injuries required care in moving, but being rid of the catheter and IV cheered her. Her many bruises turned yellow, green and purple, and she avoided glancing into the bathroom mirror.

A series of roommates came and went, mercifully all short-termers. One played the television constantly, mostly soaps and the shopping channel. Another's numerous visitors overflowed into Juanita's space. A hypochondriac gave a running commentary on ailments and symptoms endured or imagined. One night a patient across the hall, apparently averse to using a call button, yelled often and loudly for a nurse.

A few friends dropped by, including Katherine Greer. Meador stopped in a couple of times, bringing mail from the library Mavis thought Juanita should see. He didn't stay long, leaving both times with the same observation: "I don't know how people ever get well in hospitals—they're so depressing."

Five days into Juanita's hospital stay, Mavis appeared. Juanita was sitting on the side of the bed, catching her breath after the exertion of a walk to the bathroom.

"You're a mess," Mavis greeted without preamble. "All colors of the rainbow, like Meador said. How you doing?"

"Better. Stiff and sore, but definitely on the mend. How're things at the library?"

"Busy without you there. We're managing, though. I brought some bills that need paying." Mavis handed her a few envelopes and the library checkbook. Then she drew up a chair and perched on the edge, hands folded atop a cracked leather pocketbook in her lap.

Juanita checked the bills, signed checks Mavis had written, and handed everything back to her assistant.

"How's work on your house coming?" Juanita asked.

"The carpenter's finished, and the electrician finally got over there. He has a little more rewiring to do, but we should be moving back soon."

"Listen, Mavis, have you talked to Martha at all?"

"No. Haven't you?"

Juanita told about her own efforts to reach her, plus Wayne's and Vivian's.

Mavis frowned. "Meador said you told him she'd gone somewhere. I called your house yesterday to tell her about the electrical work but got no answer." Mavis seemed to steady her voice with an effort. "Went by just now, but she wasn't there."

"It seems so strange. She'd been sticking to my house like it was her home cell block." Juanita swung her body into the bed and drew a sheet over herself. "At least she made sure Rip's looked after."

"Yeah, your hound's still there. He growled at me—can't stand him either—but I got near enough to see he had water and food." Mavis drew a long sigh. "Martha'll turn up."

"Maybe she decided to visit someone here. Who'd she run around with, growing up?"

Mavis shot her boss a glare. "You can't resist snooping, even when you're banged up. Some people never learn."

Juanita counted to ten while visualizing herself feeding Mavis into a giant paper-shredder, its razor-sharp blades slicing the scrawny body into long, gory strips.

"It would be nice to know who to contact," she said calmly. "Had Martha mentioned wanting to look up any old pals?"

Mavis sniffed. "No."

"If you *had* to find her in a hurry, where would you start looking? Who'd you call?"

The long face settled into its perpetual frown. "My sister didn't 'run around' with anybody, didn't have slumber parties or anything. Our parents wouldn't permit such."

"She must've had friends, though. Everyone has a bud or two."

Mavis turned and gazed out the window. Finally, she murmured a single word. "Me."

Juanita barely heard the soft syllable. Immediately, Mavis scowled as if worried she'd revealed something of herself.

"Did Martha use to phone anyone to talk about school assignments?" Juanita persisted. "Or did anybody call her?"

"No. The telephone was for important business. Father said we children weren't to play with it."

"Your dad sounds strict."

"The world'd be a better place if more parents were."

"Did Martha ever mention Grace Hendershot? Or Phyllida Campbell? Or Hattie Stevens? Did she eat lunch with one of them, maybe?"

A young uniformed male came in with a tiny medicine cup. Mavis hastily said, "I'd better be going. Hope you're better soon."

Juanita held up a hand. "Wait, Mavis—"

But the older woman was already out the door.

"Shoot," Juanita said gloomily as the nurse handed her a cup of water. Mavis had clearly been worried about her sister. Would Juanita ever again find the assistant librarian so forthcoming?

Twenty-Two

A week after Juanita's accident, Wayne came by her hospital room, laid a stack of mail and a folded newspaper on her bedside table, and wedged his bulk into a chair. He glanced over at the other bed, currently made up and empty.

"Hey, no roommate—great! How you doing, babe?"

She filled him in on her progress, then asked what he thought about Martha's continuing absence.

"Looks like she's skipped," he said grimly. "Vivian may've thought things were fine at your place, babe, but you better check your jewelry and the silverware when you get home."

"Cops. Always assuming the worst about people."

"And we're usually right. I was afraid you were being too trusting, letting her move in right after you met her."

"Martha's not a thief, I'd bet you anything."

"You're on. If we find out she stole from you, you have to make me one of your special pecan pies."

"Fair enough. But if nothing's missing, you'll owe me . . . let's see . . ." She pretended to consider. " . . . a look at your file on the Luther Dunlap case."

His eyes narrowed. "No reflection on your cooking, babe, but that's not exactly an equivalent bet."

"I won't copy any papers, Wayne. I just want to look through the folder to see who-all was interviewed. Deal?" Juanita felt slightly guilty, vowing not to do what she had already done. Still, her cause was just. And if Wayne would show her the file himself, she could then ask why the investigation had been so sketchy, both in 1959 and since.

He sighed heavily. "Juanita—oh, all right. Not that it'll help you much."

"Great." Now to shift the subject before he could reconsider, Juanita thought. "You know, Wayne, Martha apparently left voluntarily, but maybe the reason she hasn't surfaced yet is that something's happened to her."

"You think she was the shooter's target that night? Not you?"

"I've been wondering. Are you admitting there really was a shot?"

For a long minute, Wayne eyed the sheet-covered mound that was Juanita's feet. Finally, he said, "I found a bullet lodged in a tree near where you said the shooting happened."

"You did? When?"

"Afternoon of the day you reported it."

Juanita sat upright, grimacing as the movement jarred her sore shoulder. "You've known this long that someone actually shot at us, and you didn't tell me?"

Wayne's frown held exasperation. "I'm the detective, Juanita. I don't have to pass on everything I learn, even about a case that involves you."

"So why're you telling me now?"

Wayne rose and slipped an arm around her shoulders, being careful of the left one. He kissed her, his lips warm and gentle, his scent citrusy-clean.

"That was great," she said when he'd resumed his seat, "but I'm not so easily distracted. Answer my question."

He shrugged. "I didn't tell you earlier because I hoped I

could get a line on that old pickup, that it'd lead me to the rifle and the shooter, and I'd make a quick arrest before telling you. Unfortunately, beat-up tan pickups are common as rocks around here.

"I'm only telling you now to make you see what a dangerous game you're playing." He gave her a long, tender look. "Let me do the job I'm paid to do, babe. Stop poking into matters that don't concern you."

Juanita pounded the pillow on her lap with her unbandaged fist. "That kiss was to soften me up so I'd listen to you nag me on this same old subject."

Wayne leaned towards her, his hazel eyes looking directly into hers. "Don't insist on taking everything the wrong way, babe. I'm crazy about you. It drives me nuts that I can't protect you every minute."

"I love you, too, Wayne. And I appreciate your wanting to look after me. I do. But you can't wrap me in tissue like a wax doll that might melt. I want to be treated like an adult, one capable of making her own decisions."

Wayne stiffened. "Tissue? I ought to wrap you in a strait-jac-" He took a deep breath. "Why don't I walk down the hall while you look over your mail?"

"Good idea."

He left, and Juanita glanced through the envelopes: a couple of bills, appeals from two charities, nothing personal. She unfolded the *Wyndham Daily News*, glanced at the headlines, and paused at an item below the fold on the front page. The previous evening outside a local teenage hangout, Wyndham Police had broken up a brawl between two groups of young people from Buffalo Flats, one white, the other black.

The incident had begun when either Todd Granger or Martin Moseley—spectators' accounts differed—spilled a drink on the other. The spillee had responded with a racial epithet, and a free-for-all had ensued.

Todd and Martin, the volleyball stars. Both gifted athletically, both leaders among their peers, yet enemies. Juanita felt tears moisten her eyes. Much had changed since 1959, and yet . . .

This quarrel, Juanita wondered—could there be more to it than skin pigment? Some old enmity, or a rivalry besides volleyball?

Wayne soon returned, made sure Juanita didn't need anything, and kissed her good night. She lay lost in thought several minutes, then picked up her phone and dialed Vivian's home number. When the reporter answered, Juanita asked if she knew anything more about the two young men mentioned in the article.

"I'm not on the police beat any more," Vivian said. "Why? You know those two guys?"

"Not really." Juanita described the volleyball game and the altercation afterwards. "I don't know, Viv, it's just a feeling I have, that there's more here than meets the eye. Could you try to learn more about them?"

"Mm, maybe. Your hunches have led to good stories in the past. I'll go out to Buffalo Flats when I get a chance and snoop around. May be a while before I can, but yeah, I'll see what I can find out."

"You're the best, Viv."

"That's what I keep telling the young cubs."

Dr. Sweeney saw Juanita early the next morning. "How're you feeling today? Think you could stand going home?"

"That blurry streak you see is me dashing for the exit."

"You may want to wait about running, but you should be able to put weight on that ankle now. Give up the crutches, but wear that bootie cast a few more weeks. Two weeks bed rest at home before going back to work. Even then, no strenuous activity, no contact sports."

"So I guess the touch football game tomorrow is off?"

"For you, it is. Your vitals are good, but remember to keep checking your blood pressure like the nurse showed you. It can drop even after the spleen seals itself."

"But you said my blood pressure was getting too high."

Dr. Sweeney frowned. "Generally, yes, but that's not the concern with a leaking spleen. Your injuries are healing well. Just be careful with the shoulder and neck. The collar you can use as needed, probably mostly at night."

"How about the hand splint? Can I get rid of that?"

"Not for another week. And call my office for a follow-up appointment."

"What about the cracked rib? Will I ever be able to breathe again?"

"Without pain? It takes a while. But you need to take a deep breath about once an hour, pain or not."

"But deep breathing makes it really hurt."

"I know. But otherwise, there's a possibility of pneumonia. Now, get dressed and get out of here."

"Great! No offense, but a week of hospital hospitality is way too long."

"You think the staff won't throw a party to celebrate seeing the last of you? Besides, we need the bed. Don't forget to watch your diet. You'd lost a couple pounds when you came in, but the four-star cuisine here has put some back on."

"Can't I even pig out while I'm sick? I have to keep up my strength, remember, to get well faster."

"Good nutrition doesn't mean stuffing yourself. Eat a balanced diet, just less of everything than you're tempted to have—especially of sweets and fats."

Juanita saluted, muttering darkly, "Whatever you say, *mein Fuhrer*."

When the wide hospital door slid open later that morning and let her wheelchair through, Juanita flung her arms wide and inhaled deeply.

"Free at last—oh! Oh, that hurts!" She clutched her side,

berating herself for forgetting the rib injury. Her enthusiastic movements hadn't helped the sore shoulder either.

Wayne stowed her plants and other paraphernalia in his trunk and helped her stand and swing her body into the passenger seat. He climbed in beside her.

"Let's run by your house first, babe, make sure everything's okay and you pick up whatever you need," he said. "Then I'll take you over to Eva's. She's right, you need to stay with them a while."

"Nope. Rip's probably ready to send out a search party as it is. I get around pretty well now, you know."

"You do. But no sense pushing yourself while you're still convalescing."

"Home, Wayne, and don't spare the horses. I will let you and Eva take care of most of the meals the next two weeks, though."

"Babe, if we're right, someone's tried to kill you twice already. At least while you were in the hospital, the nurses and aides kept an eye on you for me."

"You asked them to baby-sit me?"

"You haven't made it easy lately, wandering the halls day and night. I'd put a police guard on you now if we could spare the manpower."

"No, thanks, I just got out of one prison. Wayne, don't worry about me. I won't go on any more carnival rides or evening walks for a while."

"You think whoever's after you can't come up with a new method? Using the Spinner shows the guy has imagination."

"Chauvinist. A woman could've fired a rifle and bribed a carnival worker as easily as a man."

"Too true. But I'm serious about this, babe. I want you to stay with Eva the next few weeks. Please. For me."

"Oh, Wayne, I wish you wouldn't ask that way. Tell you what. I won't leave my house—even for a short stroll around my neighborhood—without you or Eva or somebody with me."

"And you'll keep your doors locked? Every minute you're home?"

"Zheesh! Yes."

"Eva or I will drive you back and forth to work. And once you're at the library, you won't leave except with someone else?"

"Now I have to have Meador for a sitter?"

"That's the deal, or I take you to Eva's right now, without even going by your place first."

"You're a tough negotiator, Cleary. Okay."

They rode in silence for a time, Juanita surreptitiously studying Wayne's genial broad face, the vexed frown creasing his brow, his broad shoulders, the deft way he maneuvered the car. Acknowledging the way she depended on his strength, his calmness, his sense of humor, even the way he worried about her, she felt her pique evaporating.

"Thanks for caring so much, Wayne. My house will now be so secure, even flies won't get in without a password."

He grinned. "Perfect that system, and I'll buy stock in your company. We'll leave Bill Gates in the dust."

She leaned over and planted a kiss on his cheek.

Twenty-Three

Contrary to Wayne's dire prediction, Juanita found no valuables missing when they roamed through her house. The guest room and its closet appeared as neat—and as empty—as before Martha had moved in.

"Oh, Wayne!" Juanita exclaimed. "All her clothes are gone. It looks like she's left permanently."

Wayne slid open a bureau drawer. "Hm. Empty. Except for this." He handed Juanita an envelope addressed to her.

The note inside thanked Juanita for her hospitality and said Martha had found she needed to leave Wyndham sooner than planned.

"Gone! Oh, no, Wayne."

He put an arm around Juanita's good shoulder and pulled her to him. "Maybe it's for the best, babe."

She twisted away and limped to the living room, where she sank into a chair and rested her splinted hand on a table. He followed and perched on the nearby couch. She sulked a couple of minutes, then spoke plaintively.

"What if something's happened to Martha? I know next to nothing about her friends and associates. Wayne, haven't you been the least bit bothered that she disappeared so suddenly?"

"Actually, I put out word for law enforcement agencies around the country to keep an eye out for her. But nobody's reported sighting her."

"Hmph. So you *were* concerned."

He shrugged. "Seems like she could've at least come by the hospital and told you her plans in person. After all you did for her."

"She must've had her reasons. Anyway, you owe me a look at the Dunlap file."

Wayne let out a long sigh. "I guess."

He insisted on making sure all her doors and windows were locked, including the garage door, before going back to work. Juanita slept a while, then spent time spoiling Rip and enjoying being otherwise alone. Just as she was beginning to feel hungry, Eva Brompton showed up with a picnic basket full of food.

"Ooh, nice," Juanita said as she watched Eva take containers from the basket and set them on the kitchen table in front of her.

Eva opened the dishes to reveal huge amounts of paprika chicken, noodles, homemade rolls, broccoli spears, and Bavarian cheese pie.

"This looks wonderful, Eva," Juanita said. "Get yourself a plate. There's plenty here for both of us."

"Oh, I ate with Cyril. This is for you."

"I'm not sure I can eat it all. I *am* sure I shouldn't."

Eva took a chair beside Juanita, short legs dangling, mop of graying blonde curls framing plump cheeks.

"Then put the rest in the fridge. It'll be just as good later tonight or tomorrow."

"That's what I'm afraid of. But thanks a million, Eva. Can you stay and talk to me while I eat?"

"Sure. How're you feeling?"

"Much better for being home, but thanks for offering to let

me stay with you."

"The offer stands any time. Sorry I couldn't get by the hospital. I didn't know you were there till last night when we got home from visiting Cyril's uncle and went through the newspapers our paper boy had held."

"Good of you to call me there this morning."

Juanita answered questions about her injuries, the carnival 'accident,' and visitors she'd had. She also told Eva about the fire at Mavis's home and Martha's staying with her, then leaving suddenly.

"Mavis's sister," Eva said slowly, a frown clouding her comely features. "There was a Martha Haney in my older sister's class. I've heard Phyllie speak of her."

Phyllie. Of course. Juanita's brain went into overdrive. "You were a Campbell, weren't you?" she said excitedly. "Phyllida Campbell is your sister?"

Eva nodded. Juanita had never made the connection because Eva was physically the opposite of her sister.

"Was she a good friend of Martha's? Enough that they'd have kept in touch after Martha left Wyndham?"

"I shouldn't think so. My impression is, Martha was a very proper young lady, and Phyllie—well, she evidently was a . . . free spirit."

"Wild, you mean?"

"For those days," Eva said with a smile.

"Out of curiosity, who were some of your sister's high-school friends? Anyone I might know?"

Eva mentioned a few girls' names, mostly ones Juanita didn't recognize. But one stood out: Grace Hendershot.

"Gracie, eh? Did she and your sister hang out a lot together?"

"Not the way kids do nowadays, but they'd sometimes go to movies together. Grace always had to go straight home afterwards, though."

"I've heard Grace's parents were very strict."

"I really don't know, except for the movies. What's all this about, Juanita? Why're you so interested in Phyllie? And Grace?"

Juanita mentioned her history project. "I'm trying to find people who were around in 1959 and might know something. Actually, I spoke with your sister a little one day—not realizing she *was* your sister—but we got interrupted. You must not've been very old yourself when Luther Dunlap got killed."

"I was about six. Of course, I've heard about it since."

"From your sister?"

"From Mama. The topic seems to make Phyllie uncomfortable. I had met Luther Dunlap, though. Phyllie took me along once when she went out to Bryson's Corner to buy fresh vegetables."

"Really. Tell me about him."

"He was tall and lean, had a pleasant laugh. I remember he teased me about my freckles, but in a nice way. I liked him."

"And did your sister? Like him?"

"I guess she must've. They kidded around a lot that day."

"Flirted, you mean?"

Eva frowned thoughtfully. "Perhaps. I didn't understand some of what they said. Looking back, I suppose there might've been double entendres that went right over my young head."

"Do you know if he ever gave her flowers?"

"He did that day. Picked a few roses off a bush in his folks' yard and presented them with a kind of grand manner. That pleased her—till she found out later he gave flowers to lots of girls." Eva chewed a curvaceous lower lip. "I'm afraid Phyllie was what people used to call 'boy-crazy.' She worried Mama terribly, sneaking out at night to meet guys."

"Any particular fellow?"

Eva hesitated. "I shouldn't be talking like this. I love Phillie, and I don't want to be disloyal."

"Of course you don't. But this could be important, Eva. I just have a hunch she has information—maybe doesn't even realize she has—that could help bring Dunlap's killers to justice. At last."

"Well . . . okay . . . Mama often didn't know who the boy was. But she did catch Phyllie once with Lonnie Tubbs, sitting in his car parked a block from our house. He had a terrible reputation then. Mama lit into Phyllie, so hard Sis didn't sneak out again for a week. I'm sure that cost Mama dearly—she's such a sweet, gentle woman—but it shows how worried she was."

"You think your sister spent a lot of time with Tubbs? If he was involved in Dunlap's murder, would she likely know it?"

"I . . . doubt he was anything special to her. He never came to our house. No guys did, because Phyllie wasn't supposed to date till she was eighteen—our folks were firm on that, though they later relaxed the age to sixteen for me—and Phyllie never mentioned him."

"What's the best time to catch your sister at the office without Simon Simms around?"

"Do you have to bother her again?"

"I'll respect her privacy as far as I can, Eva. And I won't tell her you've told me any of this."

"I'd appreciate that. Early afternoon, I guess. Simon often lunches late, around one or after. You don't think *he* killed Luther, do you?"

Juanita hesitated. "Probably not. But your sister may talk more freely if no one else is there. It'll be a while before I can get downtown again, though." She spread her arms to indicate her casts and sleeping attire. "Just one more question, Eva. It was rumored that Luther Dunlap and a Wyndham guy were rivals in love. I don't want to take advantage of our friendship—and I don't know any delicate way to ask this—but could the girl have been Phillida?"

Eva didn't speak for a while, one finger tracing the edge of a pocket on her denim wraparound. "I . . . hope not. Oh, I don't mean because Luther Dunlap was African-American. It's just that—there's a deep sadness in Phyllie. I hope she's not carrying guilt over his death."

"But you think it's possible?"

"I don't know. She . . . went away awhile after high school. The few letters she wrote home were postmarked Kansas City, Missouri. The folks went there once to try to find her but had no luck—I caught bits and pieces of conversations when they didn't know I was around. I've asked Mama since whether she ever learned what Phyllie did during that time, but Mama won't say much about it. I think—" Eva looked away a moment.

"—I think she suspects Phyllie had a baby out of wedlock." Her eyes teared. "This is hard to talk about, Juanita. I feel like I'm betraying my sister. But that murder seems to've marked people in Phyllie's class, her included. Juanita, you're smart. Find out the truth about this." She enclosed both Juanita's hands in hers. "Please?"

"You may be giving me too much credit. But I'll do my best."

Twenty-Four

Juanita's days settled into a routine of eating, sleeping, reading, and watching TV. She was a "good patient" for the most part, checking her blood pressure as directed, letting Eva chauffeur her to a follow-up appointment with Dr. Sweeney, who tsked-tsked about her weight gain, and keeping her doors locked except when she had visitors. Those included Wayne, Eva, Doug, and Meador, who brought library mail that couldn't wait till her return. The Nguyens from next door checked on her often, and Tien made it his mission to keep an eye on her house, whether she was there or not. Bach brought her lunches of Vietnamese delicacies such as spring rolls, beef and rice sticks, and lemon-grass chicken. The visitors helped relieve Juanita's boredom. Even so, cabin fever nearly drove her mad at times.

One early afternoon during her second week of confinement, Vivian called. She had been out to Bryson's Corner and had news.

"Martin Moseley and Todd Granger are both good students, college-bound," she said. "It seems to be a toss-up whether they'll go on athletic or academic scholarships.

"Martin's folks split when he was young. His dad moved back

east somewhere. Martin lives with his mom, Ethel Moseley, who manages a Dairy Queen in Buffalo Flats. They moved there from Checotah two years ago. Martin delivers papers to help out. Squeaky-clean kid, except for a running feud with Todd. Nobody seems to know what that's about."

"You're good, Viv," Juanita said as she jotted details in a notebook. "Any more on Todd?"

"His parents are both alive and have lived in Buffalo Flats many years. His mom's Olivia Granger, a dental assistant for a dentist in Claremore. The father, Corinthian Granger, works at Tractor Supply in Broken Arrow. Todd gets along with his white peers but has no time for blacks, Latinos, or Indians.

"That's all my source knew about either boy. Does any of that help?"

"Maybe. It's way more than I knew before. Thanks, Viv."

Juanita sat up in bed brooding a while. Two upstanding young men, both from good families. Yet something in Vivian's report nagged at Juanita. She looked back over her notes, analyzing each detail the reporter had told her.

Corinthian. Unusual name. Corinthian *Granger.* The combination seemed familiar. Had someone once mentioned a Corinthian Granger to her?

Corinthian. Corinthian. That was the real name of the Del-Viking "Kripp" Johnson. Samuel Davis had been a fan of Kripp Johnson.

Corinthian Granger. Robert Norwood had spoken of a child that Samuel Davis had befriended years ago in Bryson's Corner. He had been a Granger, had been called Cory.

Cory. Short for Corinthian, perhaps?

Could it be? Surely not. And yet—

Juanita phoned the high school and luckily caught Robert Norwood between classes and football practice.

"Hey, Juanita!" he said cheerfully. "How's the sleuth? Gone on any more carnival rides?"

"No, thank heaven. And don't let Wayne Cleary hear you call me that. I'm doing fairly well, considering."

Robert evidently hadn't connected the carnival incident to Juanita's Bryson's Corner research. Vivian's newspaper articles had told of her injuries and mentioned the disappearance of the ride's operator, but they hadn't emphasized the possibility of deliberate sabotage. A reader might think the operator had simply been negligent.

Just as well, Juanita thought. No need to worry Robert more than necessary.

"I called to check something with you, Robert. You said Samuel Davis used to carve little boats and trains for a neighborhood kid named Cory Granger? The child that moved away and never came back to visit?"

"Yeah. Samuel apparently took a real special liking to the boy. What hurt him most was that Cory didn't move far away, but still wouldn't come see him."

"Would you happen to know where Cory's folks moved to?"

"Some town around here. Can't recall which one. Actually, now I think about it, Samuel said the boy went to live with someone other than his own family."

"Really? Wonder why."

"Let's see, what'd Samuel say about that? Had the parents died, or what?" Robert seemed to ponder a moment, then went on, "Sorry, Juanita, I'm hazy on the details. Why're you so interested in Cory Granger?"

"Just a hunch, probably a dumb one. Do you happen to know if Cory was short for anything? Corinthian, perhaps?"

"Don't really know. Seems like Samuel did once refer to him by a longer name, but he usually called him Cory. Why? Is it important?"

"Probably not. This is such a far-fetched idea, I don't even want to go into it."

"Come on, now you've got me curious."

"One of these days I'll probably tell you about it and we'll have a good laugh together at my stupidity."

"I'll look forward to that. But, even if you could find Cory, Juanita, he'd be too young to be a source about Dunlap's death. I doubt he was even born yet when that happened."

"You're probably right. Well, thanks, Robert."

"Call any time you've got a question. Even a dumb one."

"Music to a researcher's ears. Will do. "

Juanita next phoned Katherine Greer and asked if, around the time of the Dunlap killing, there had been talk that a girl in the Wyndham senior class was pregnant. Katherine waited briefly before replying.

"I don't recall such rumors, Juanita. But I was so focused on my own career as a young teacher—there may well have been gossip that just didn't register."

"Okay. Thanks, anyway."

Juanita next dialed Grace Hendershot's number. The phone rang and rang, but no one answered.

She then called Vivian to ask if she could find out anything more about Todd's father, specifically where he had grown up.

"I'll try. But I'd better get a story out of this."

"It's too early to say yet, Viv. It's just a feeling I have—"

"Right. I'll get back to you."

Juanita sat for several minutes thinking about Bryson's Corner and its residents. What would life have been like growing up there for Samuel Davis, Garvin McCoy, and Luther Dunlap?

Deciding to research the subject of all-black towns, she fastened the lightweight cast onto her injured foot. The cast no longer seemed irksome as it had initially. It wasn't hot or bulky but consisted of gel-filled panels placed around the calf and held together by fabric bands fastened with Velcro. Another band around her instep anchored it. She could wear a regular shoe with it and could remove the cast as needed.

Seated at her computer, Juanita typed the phrase "all-black

towns, Oklahoma" into a search engine and visited several of the 42,000+ sites that popped up.

Oklahoma's experience with such settlements, she was reminded, had begun in Indian Territory even before the Civil War. Some slaves and free blacks marched with members of what had been called the Five Civilized Tribes—Cherokees, Chickasaws, Choctaws, Creeks and Seminoles—on the infamous "Trail of Tears" from the southeastern states to the Territory. More African-Americans came later, especially during the Land Run of 1889, searching for land and escape from abuse and discrimination suffered in the South and elsewhere.

Historically, Juanita learned, Oklahoma had had the most all-black towns of any state, numbering more than 50 at their peak.

A leader in establishing all-black towns and in campaigning for making Oklahoma an all-black state, Edward P. McCabe, had even tried to prevent white ownership of land in the town of Langston he established, by using restrictive covenants in land titles similar to those often used, before and since, to exclude blacks.

The black-state idea had failed, and rigid "Jim Crow" laws passed by the new state of Oklahoma in 1907 made life in the locale less appealing to African-Americans. After 1910, a combination of social and economic factors caused most all-black towns to dwindle. Many had ceased to exist.

But in their heyday, such towns had been places of safety and equality for their residents, largely self-sufficient municipalities where black entrepreneurs owned thriving businesses of all types and former slaves governed themselves free of white dominance.

Even in the 1950s, Bryson's Corner would have represented more than a familiar place to be for Davis, McCoy, and Dunlap, Juanita thought. In Dunlap's case, it had literally meant life itself. His forced removal to nearby, hostile Wyndham had led to his death.

That wouldn't have been a foregone conclusion in Wyndham,

though, Juanita thought as she exited the software. Even in those days, most whites wouldn't have participated in killing Dunlap. They'd have been horrified at the thought.

But they had allowed the system of treating blacks as less than human to continue, she conceded sadly. Most hadn't actively tried to change it.

That was the point: If Dunlap knew members of his race weren't welcome in Wyndham after sundown, how could he have trusted any Wyndhamite not to do him harm?

The two weeks' bed rest ended at last, and Juanita's doctor pronounced her fit to return to work the following Monday. Eva picked her up and drove her there. Juanita agreed, though she felt certain she could have walked—or hobbled.

Entering the library Monday morning, Juanita breathed a happy sigh at the sight of the beloved full bookshelves. Meador greeted her as if she'd just returned from a war. Mavis didn't quite smile but didn't glower.

In her office, Juanita saw new slips of paper dotting the Quote-War wall, evidence of a non-fisticuffs squabble between her assistants during her absence. It had begun with a quotation copied in Meador's sprawling cursive:

> What mighty ills have not been done by Woman! . . .
> Destructive, damnable, deceitful woman!
> —Thomas Otway, *The Orphan,* act III, sc. 1

Mavis's tight printing responded, one word pointedly underlined:

> The silliest woman can manage a clever man; but
> it needs a very clever woman to manage a *fool!*
> —Rudyard Kipling, *Plain Tales from the Hills.*
> *Three and—an Extra*

Meador replied:

Woman's at best a contradiction still.

—Alexander Pope, *Eloisa to Abelard,* l. 270

Then Mavis:

The usual masculine disillusionment in discovering that a woman has a brain.

—Margaret Mitchell, *Gone With the Wind,* pt. IV, ch. 36

Meador:

. . .she is not yet so old
But she may learn.

—William Shakespeare, *The Merchant of Venice,* III, ii, 160

Mavis:

Age in a virtuous person, of either sex, carries in it an authority which makes it preferable to all the pleasures of youth.

—Sir Richard Steele, *The Spectator,* no. 153, August 25, 1711

Meador:

Nature abhors the old . . . .

—Ralph Waldo Emerson, *Essays: First Series. Circles*

Mavis had posted the last of the new quotations:

The old know what they want; the young are sad and bewildered.

—Logan Pearsall Smith, *Last Words*

So they had again gotten around to the age-youth thing. Juanita scanned the quotes for the fourth time later that day and decided it was time for a third party to get involved. Grabbing a tattered copy of *Bartlett's Familiar Quotations,* kept on her desk after a new edition replaced it in the reference room, she found a suitable comment:

> The minds of different generations are…
> impenetrable one by the other….
> —Andre Maurois, *Ariel,* [translated by
> Ella D'Arcy], ch. 12

Juanita copied it on a fragment of paper and taped it below the others.

She hadn't long to wait for a reaction. Meador came into the office while she was catching up on accumulated paperwork, and leaned over her desk. While telling about the large crowd at a Gilroy speech the previous evening, his eyes strayed to the quote wall.

"They donated a lot of—" He broke off and practically ran to the new slip, stood gazing at it, then wheeled and left the office.

He must have reported the development to Mavis, for she immediately came in, read Juanita's entry, and left without a word. Later that afternoon, Juanita noticed the two at a table in the reference room, poring over the newest Bartlett. It never boded well to have sworn enemies collaborating. She should have remembered that they'd been known to unite against her.

Sure enough, just before closing time, she returned from a trip to the stacks to find a new quote below her own, typed this time.

> History is more or less bunk.
> —Henry Ford, interview with Charles N. Wheeler,
> *Chicago Tribune,* May 25, 1916

A low blow, Juanita thought, criticizing her through her new avocation. She quickly replied:

> Histories make men wise….
> —Francis Bacon, *Essays. Of Studies*

After the others had gone that evening and Juanita finished her locking-up chores, Eva Brompton drove her the five blocks home.

"This is such a short distance, Eva," Juanita said, "I hate for you to go to so much trouble."

"Remember your promise to Wayne. Besides, you shouldn't lug that heavy purse five blocks, not with that cracked rib."

"Okay, that makes sense. And I do appreciate it."

Entering her front door and re-locking it, Juanita felt a pang of loneliness for Martha, for her good company and her excellent meals. Bach and Eva were wonderful cooks, but Juanita felt guilty letting them do so much. She had told them yesterday she'd handle her cooking from then on. Reluctantly, they'd acquiesced.

As she stared into her refrigerator today, however, she had second thoughts. Sighing, she pulled cheese, bread, and butter from the fridge and got a can of mushroom soup from the pantry.

"I like to cook, Rip, but not so much for just one," she told the dog as he lay watching her heat soup and grill a sandwich. "And not when I'm tired. I better figure out some better meals, though. I've regained all the weight I'd lost, plus some."

His placid doggy smile suggested his only concern about food was whether it kept appearing in his own dish.

Twenty-Five

The next day started badly when Juanita was awakened around 4:30 A.M. by a nightmare in which wild dogs were trying to tear her apart. She arrived at the library tired and hoping for an easy few hours. Unfortunately, on returning from her first trip to the restroom that morning, she saw a new volley had been fired in the Quote War. The typed quotation below her last posting said:

> History . . . is a nightmare . . . .
> —James Joyce, *Ulysses*

She sighed, considered leaving it unanswered. But her mind wouldn't leave it alone. Finally she looked up a quote and responded, adding a couple of words of her own in brackets:

> Anybody can make history. Only a great man [or woman] can write it.
> —Oscar Wilde, *Aphorisms*

The conflict continued through the day, Meador and Mavis placing their entries when Juanita wasn't in the office. Their next said:

> America was discovered accidentally by a great seaman who was looking for something else . . . History is like that, very chancy.
>
> —Samuel Eliot Morison, *The Oxford History of the American People,* ch. 2

Then came Juanita's:

> The whole history of the progress of human liberty shows that all concessions yet made to her august claims have been born of earnest struggle . . . . If there is no struggle, there is no progress. Those who profess to favor freedom, and yet deprecate agitation, are men who want crops without plowing up the ground, they want rain without thunder and lightning. They want the ocean without the awful roar of its many waters.
>
> —Frederick Douglass. *Speech at Canandaigue, New York, August 3, 1857*

The reference said more about freedom than about history, but Juanita liked being able to quote a black man, since her history project had to do with the clear denial of basic rights to an African-American male.

Her opponents replied:

> Faithfulness to the truth of history involves far more than a research, however patient and scrupulous, into special facts . . . . The narrator must seek to imbue himself with the life and spirit of the time . . . . He must himself be, as it were, a sharer or a spectator of the action he describes.
>
> —Francis Parkman, *Pioneers of France in the New World,* Introduction

Juanita figured the quotation was meant as a comment on her inadequacy as a historian, but she chose to view it as a serious suggestion. In fact, it recalled an idea she had had during long hours of boredom at home, a way to get a fresh perspective on the Dunlap case. First she phoned Katherine and asked a few questions, then called Wayne at the police station. She might be able to manage the logistics of her plan alone, but having company sounded better. And there was that annoying promise she'd made not to go anywhere by herself.

"How'd you like to take me out this evening, big boy?"

"Out where?"

She imagined him narrowing his hazel eyes and bracing his huge shoulders in preparation for an argument.

"Wrong response. You should've said, 'Anywhere, you divine creature.' But to answer your question, to the high-school athletic field."

"That's a destination I could not have predicted. Why there?"

"Atmosphere. I need to see what Luther Dunlap saw the night he was killed, hear what he heard . . ."

"Get real, Juanita. Nearly a half century has passed."

"If I didn't already know that, people keep reminding me. Some things've changed there, sure, but the track's still in the same location."

"Maybe so. But as for what Dunlap heard, traffic noise must've increased by leaps and bounds since then."

"Okay, so I can't reconstruct the scene exactly. I still want to go." Juanita heard a pleading note creep into her voice. "I need to, Wayne. But if you don't want to take me, forget it. I'll go over there tonight on my own."

"You will not! Aside from the fact you're recently recovered after that 'accident,' there's the danger. Someone has apparently tried to kill you twice. You seem to've forgotten that. And you promised me you'd be careful."

"I remember. That's why I called you."

Silence.

Then, "Okay. Though I'll probably regret it at some point."

That evening after a quick supper at a downtown café, Wayne drove Juanita to the complex in southwest Wyndham where most of the town's schools were clustered. In 1959, four buildings had occupied a roomy campus: one for high school, one for elementary, one for junior high, and one for Wyndham Junior College. Since then, the town's growth was reflected in its educational facilities.

The name and location of the college had changed, with Wyndham Community College expanding into several structures on a roomy site farther from downtown. A new, much larger high school was being built near WCC, and until its completion those upper grades occupied their original building and part of the old WJC one. The middle and intermediate schools used the rest of that, in addition to the former junior-high structure. Three additions had been made to the elementary school since 1959, and two temporary buildings were in use. Once the new high school was complete, its current quarters would be renovated for elementary-school use.

Wayne parked on South Sixth beside the athletic field, and they got out. Juanita could see the track and the nearby stadium through a line of redbud trees, their limbs nearly bare of leaves as winter approached. The weather had been warming up, then getting cooler, for several weeks. Tonight's temperature was mild, but an occasional chilly gust stung Juanita's cheeks.

"Eva told me her family—and Phyllida's—lived across the street and two blocks up from the high school," she said to Wayne. "The Campbell girls passed here each day, Eva said. Phyllida walked her to the elementary school over there before coming back to the high school for her own classes."

"Mm-hm."

"Those redbuds wouldn't have been here then, according to Katherine. She said the field was surrounded by tall, dense pines that hid the track from the street. So on the night Dunlap was killed, people in the neighborhood might not've guessed anything was wrong over here."

Again, he made assenting sounds.

"Until later, that is. And how did the neighbors react when they *did* learn about that murder?"

"Angry calls for better police protection," Wayne offered. "Demands that the guilty be brought to justice."

"Not according to what I've heard. Hushed conversations. Denial that something so horrible could happen so near. A pretense of life going on as usual."

"You don't know that. You say you realize it happened long ago, but I'm not sure you do. People forget, Juanita. Their minds change facts, without their being aware of it. Plus, you may not have even talked to the people who really know. Your information's sketchy at best, babe."

They were standing under a pole light in front of a gate in the high chain-link fence that separated the redbuds from the oval track they enclosed. Juanita turned to look him full in the face.

"I know I don't have all the facts, Wayne. Why do you think I want so much to see the police file on Dunlap?"

"I'm going to show it to you. It's against policy, but you might just pick up on something in it that we've missed."

"That's the spirit." Juanita turned back to the field. "The fence around the track then was made of wood, Katherine said."

Wayne opened the broad gate, which typically was unlocked to allow community members access to the track for exercising. She had suggested to Martha once that they drive over one evening and walk there, but Martha had declined, saying she didn't like to go out of her home neighborhood at night.

Juanita walked ahead of Wayne into the enclosure, a sudden breeze whipping dry leaves against her cast. She noted with surprise that no walkers paced the brightly lit path on this relatively pleasant evening.

"Would there have been lights around the track then?" Juanita had asked Katherine that afternoon.

"You're really taking me back, Juanita," the reedy voice on the phone had said. "Oh, yes, I remember now. There were two lights, high on poles at the ends of the oval. We didn't have night events in those days, but Coach Jackson encouraged his boys to train individually during the evenings, especially before a big meet."

"Two bulbs, then? Would they've been lit even if nobody was out there?"

Katherine chuckled softly. "Oh, yes. Coach Jackson wouldn't give his players the excuse of a dark track in case they tried to avoid practice."

On their ride home, Juanita had asked Eva if she recalled any details about the athletic field in 1959. But Eva had been the young daughter of adults with no interest in sports and little in activities at their older offspring's school. Eva had never attended an event here as a child.

"I need to walk around the track by myself a while, Wayne," Juanita said, "so I can imagine myself back in the fifties. "If you come with me, you'll take me out of the past and back to now."

"Good to know my presence is so powerful. Sure you'll be okay walking so far? You're not long out of bed, remember."

"I'm a little tired, but I'm doing okay."

"Suit yourself. I'll wait here."

She left him leaning against the gate and limped along the paved oval, trying to imagine the place as it had been then, with two garish points of brilliance at the ends. Garvin McCoy had said it was bright moonlight the night Dunlap was kidnapped. It had been spring then, not autumn as now. The fitness craze had not yet hit, bringing out multiple joggers and walkers. The track would probably have been bare of people till Dunlap's captors dragged him onto it.

But *had* it been empty? A witness, McCoy had said. A white one. Maybe a conscientious young track star had been here honing his racing skills?

Juanita realized she had been thinking in stereotypes herself, assuming the whole Wyndham track team had so hated being defeated by Bryson's Corner that they would have welcomed Dunlap's murder. But what if one boy had been here, taking a break from running, resting in a secluded area where Dunlap's tormentors hadn't seen him? The witness might have sympathized with the victim but been afraid to try to help. If Dunlap's torturers had been surprised by one of their own race, they might have hesitated about killing him too, but chances were they'd have done it anyway.

At least a scared watcher could have thought so.

Juanita stumped slowly along the path, trying to put herself in Luther Dunlap's place. The track would have been well-packed earth then, not asphalt as now. His hands had been tied to posts, part of the wooden fence. The line of uprights would have come closest to the track just there, near the curve of the loop farthest from the gate. According to the account in the old newspaper, tire tracks of a vehicle had bitten into the hard soil at that end, suggesting it had pulled some burden.

Had he been gagged to prevent his crying out? If not, shouldn't someone in a neighboring house have heard him? Too, an automobile had been used. Surely it would have been heard in nearby residences, especially as it strained to accelerate with his legs tied to it.

Juanita shuddered. Adolescents weren't necessarily the most empathetic of creatures, but how could mere boys have deliberately done such an awful thing?

She recalled her dream of that morning, in which she herself had been torn apart by ravening dogs. Not unlike what had happened to Dunlap. Horrid, horrid.

People *had* lived nearby; she kept coming back to that. But if anyone had heard Luther scream, even in that supposedly more neighborly time, it could have seemed easier, safer, not to notice.

Juanita had reached the end of the oval and started around the curve when she glanced up and saw part of a house through the redbuds. An upper-story window, curtains open, overhead light on, looked down on her.

Had Luther Dunlap seen this same view through the tall pines of yesteryear? Had his frightened eyes turned to that house seeking help? Assistance that hadn't come?

She tried to feel the terror he must have felt, conjuring memories of horrifying experiences real and imagined: a rock-climbing incident in college, facing a murderer a few months ago, the terrifying carnival ride, this morning's dream—the hounds' evil eyes, her panic, the rending of flesh—

But even her worst frights couldn't compare.

What would Dunlap have felt besides raw fear? Anger at his unfair treatment, undoubtedly. Resentment at being hated over mere skin color, surely. But Juanita was like a civilian trying to imagine being in combat, unable to fathom the full range and intensity of emotions involved.

Despondently, she trudged back to Wayne, thinking how easy, even pleasant, this evening at the track was for her—and how terrifying a young African-American man's last moments here had been for him.

Twenty-Six

The rest of that evening after Wayne left, Juanita brooded about Luther Dunlap and his killers. Those boys—men now—had never paid for their unspeakable act. But that would not be true forever, she resolved. She *would* see his killers brought to justice.

Only how could she, when she kept running into walls?

Her incomplete conversation with Phyllida Campbell a few weeks ago weighed on her mind. Had Eva's sister been about to confide important information before Simon Simms's inopportune entrance stopped her?

It seemed worth another effort to find out.

Just before one o'clock the next day, Juanita asked Meador to drive her to Simon Simms's accounting office, making up a story about needing to discuss library business with him. Mavis gave her an odd look but said nothing. Never averse to leaving work, Meador gladly got his car from the small lot behind the library and dropped her downtown.

When Juanita entered Simms's outer office, Phyllida sat at her desk typing, her rigid shoulders and severe glasses at odds with her perky nose and freckle-dusted cheeks. She glanced up, saw

Juanita near the door, and jumped.

"Oh, goodness—Miss Wills. I'm afraid Mr. Simms is out to lunch. Can I help you with anything?"

"Actually, you're the one I came to see."

Phyllida's eyes flickered. "Really?"

"When I was here before, you and I were talking about Luther Dunlap's death, but we got interrupted before you finished something you were going to say."

"I'm afraid I'm quite busy today, Miss Wills. And I have to leave early for a meeting at the nursing home where my elderly aunt stays. Besides, I'd rather not relive those days any more."

"I understand. But this could be important. I'll not stay long. May I sit down?"

Phyllida hesitated. "I suppose, for a few minutes."

Juanita pulled an armchair close and sat. "You and I don't know each other well, Miss Campbell, but your sister Eva and I are friends."

"She's spoken of you. How're your injuries healing after that strange accident?"

"I'm still sore and have to watch how I move, but my doctor says I'm progressing well, thanks. Miss Campbell, what I'm going to ask will seem intrusive, but I assure you I've a good reason for asking. I understand one possible motive for Dunlap's killing was that he and a Wyndham boy liked the same young woman. Do you remember hearing that rumor?"

Eyes wary, Phyllida nodded.

"I'd originally understood the girl in question lived in Bryson's Corner, but now I wonder if she wasn't a Wyndham girl." Juanita watched the secretary rearrange papers on her desk. "Could it have been you, perhaps?"

Phyllida stiffened. "You . . . think I . . . Why?"

"I've heard you had a reputation then of being . . . a little wild."

"People are terrible gossips."

"They can be. But I'm asking because I want to see justice done about that old murder, and to help Wyndham come to terms with its past. This town's far from perfect, but I love it."

The secretary closed her eyes as if consulting an inner oracle. When she opened them again, she nodded. "Eva thinks a lot of you, Miss Wills, and she has good instincts about people. So I'll answer. I was not Luther Dunlap's girlfriend. I never went out with him."

"But you did know him, used to buy produce from him?"

"Yes. We kidded around, nothing more."

"Did he ever give you roses?"

Phyllida's eyes widened. "How did— Oh, you've heard that was his trademark, presenting flowers to girls." She sighed. "It's true. I thought it meant more than it did, at first, then learned it was almost a reflex with him."

"Do you have any idea, then, who the young woman was?"

"I—that's not my secret to tell."

Juanita felt her mouth go dry. "You *know* who she was?"

"Yes."

"Someone in your class at Wyndham High?"

"I won't give you any details about her."

"May I ask how you know? Did she tell you herself?"

"I've—said enough."

Juanita searched for a less pointed question to try to get Phyllida talking again. "Did you ever buy things from anyone else in Bryson's Corner? Other than Dunlap?"

"Some," the secretary said cautiously.

"Did you know Leona Brown, perhaps?"

"No." A quick, definite answer.

"Samuel Davis?"

"Ye-es." A more reluctant reply.

"Did you know Mr. Davis well?" Inspiration struck Juanita. "Is he the one who told you who Dunlap was seeing?"

Phyllida's eyes grew larger again. "Why do you think it was

him?"

"He seems to've been in Dunlap's confidence. If anyone knew the other party in the affair, it must've been Davis."

The secretary ran a trembling finger along her thin throat. "I—Miss Wills, I haven't talked about this before . . . with anyone . . . but I think I want to tell someone. If you'll *swear* not to reveal who told you."

"Unless the police need to know, okay."

"You're right about Samuel. I did know him. When I'd be in Bryson's Corner buying eggs and chickens from his folks, he used to flirt with me. Rather awkwardly. I think now he was practicing his technique, trying to imitate Luther's smoothness with women. I liked playing the coquette myself and flirted right back. Then one afternoon when I went out there, Samuel's folks weren't home. He asked me to come inside for a Coke. I went."

"Oh. I see." It sounded as if Mrs. Campbell's suspicion about her daughter's pregnancy had been true, Juanita thought.

"No, you don't. We weren't intimate. We just talked and laughed—Samuel could be very witty—and he took a daisy from a glass on the table and pinned it in my hair. A gallant gesture, though less practiced than Luther when he handed me roses. Sweeter, somehow." As if in memory, Phyllida touched her honey-gold hair, now shot through with silver.

"It's true, I was considered fast in high school. I was so thrilled with life—and boys—that I often acted impetuously. But I was smart enough to realize the risks of spending time alone with Samuel. So when he asked me to go picnicking with him the next week, I said no."

"Was that when he told you who Dunlap was seeing?"

"Yes. He said others were breaking the rules of racial separation and getting away with it, using the two of them as an example." Phyllida brushed a hand across her eyes. "But Luther's killing proved the opposite."

"I suppose that could've been Samuel on the track that evening, if you had dated him," Juanita said softly.

"Maybe, maybe not. None of the Wyndham boys would've been particularly jealous over me. But I guess any black-white dating could've set someone off." Phyllida studied the back of her bony hand. "I think now Samuel wasn't really interested in me, that he asked me out as a trial run. He actually cared for someone else."

"A girl in Wyndham?"

"I . . . can't say." Phyllida's eyes took on a faraway look.

Fearing Simms's return, Juanita broke into the secretary's reverie. "Miss Campbell, I've heard you dated Lonnie Tubbs. Is that correct?"

Phyllida started. "Lonnie? Not much. He wasn't handsome and had awful manners. I only went with him for kicks, to be able to say I'd dated one of the bad boys. I liked a hint of danger—though not on the life-threatening scale I sensed that dating Samuel could be."

"When you were with Tubbs, did you ever hear him say anything to suggest he did, or would, take part in Dunlap's murder?"

"No."

"But he did use racial epithets?"

"Yes, but many did. Sad to say, such talk wasn't out of the ordinary then."

"When we spoke before, you mentioned rumors circulating at the high school about who'd killed Dunlap. Who did the kids think was involved?"

"I'm not sure I—" Phyllida's eyes shifted towards her employer's office, then back to Juanita. "Reputations of others are involved here, Miss Wills. Perhaps I've said enough."

Inwardly sighing with frustration, Juanita tried to form another question to unlock Phyllida's inner sanctum of memories. But just then, the front door opened. Simms entered, eyebrows rising at the sight of Juanita. He looked at Phyllida, and a slight smile passed between them. The secretary flushed.

"Miss Wills," he said. "Another problem at the library?"

"Oh, no. I just dropped in to visit with your secretary. We share mutual friends. I'll be going now, let her get back to work."

The accountant glanced from one to the other, shrugged, and headed for his own office. Juanita said goodbye to Phyllida, who mouthed the word "thanks" in reply.

Outside again, Juanita called Meador on her cell phone and then waited for him on one of the benches recently installed at intervals along the sidewalk in a town beautification effort. As she sat, she pondered what she had learned. And what she hadn't. Phyllida Campbell obviously knew more than she'd told Juanita, and perhaps suspected even more.

Was Phyllida Campbell protecting a man she *knew* had participated in that long-ago crime?

Twenty-Seven

Soon after Juanita returned from downtown, she heard the main library door open. Moments later, Wayne's bulk filled her office doorway.

"I'm ready to pay off on our bet," he said in a resigned tone. "Can you take off a few minutes?"

"To see the Dunlap file? Sure. Let's go."

During the drive to the police station, Juanita asked if Wayne had been able to locate Vince Arnold yet.

"He wasn't at the shelter Gospel Tabernacle runs," he said. "I did find street people who know him, but the leads they gave didn't pan out. One guy said the last he knew, Arnold was living in an abandoned building in east Wyndham. He's not there now, of course. According to the street guy, Arnold moves on when and where the spirit takes him."

"You're still looking for him, though?"

"For all the good it's doing."

"Suppose he went out of town?"

"If so, he must've latched onto some cash somehow."

They reached the police station and went in. Juanita answered Louise's and Ruth's questions about her midway mishap. Then

Wayne ushered Juanita into an interview room off the detectives' room, set a cup of coffee for her on the table, and handed her the same file she had copied earlier. She sat across the table from him, scanning pages critically as if seeing them for the first time. Wayne leaned his chin on his hand, watching her. Finally she closed the folder.

"It's pretty skimpy, isn't it?"

"Some cases, you find more evidence than others."

"But not many people have even been interviewed. Those who have aren't always identified by name. And some leads don't seem to've been followed up on." Juanita spoke calmly, fighting an urge to grab Wayne's shirt and yell into his face. "I'm no legal eagle, Wayne, but even I can see the Wyndham Police haven't made solving this murder a priority."

His wry look contained both defiance and amusement. "In the 1950s, babe, it wasn't unusual for a black person's death to get less attention than a white's. It wasn't right, but it was a fact of life. We can't change that now."

"But your efforts since then haven't exactly been exhaustive."

"Time to time, people in both Wyndham and Bryson's Corner have been questioned. Nobody's been all that helpful." He leaned forward, his chair creaking. "And you know what a work load this department carries, babe. How chronically short on manpower we are."

"Well . . . I'm only one person, Wayne, and I've already turned up more on Dunlap's death than is in your records."

"Oh? You been holding out on me?"

Too late, Juanita realized her mistake. "I've told you most of what I've learned," she hedged.

"Most? As in, not all? Juanita, you've no business even looking into a police matter, let alone withholding information you stumble onto."

"Stumble? *Stumble?*"

He was the one in the wrong. Suppose she chose to make

an issue of this matter? Get it splashed all over the media? The investigation had been botched, and he was making excuses. It wasn't like him at all, not like the Wayne she had thought she knew so well. She couldn't have been that wrong about him all this time, could she? She must be missing something . . . .

But the nagging doubt, plus her own guilty conscience, increased her sense of frustration and came out as anger. "If *I* had been derelict in my duty the way certain people have, Wayne Cleary, I wouldn't cast stones."

"Derelict? Now, just a minute—"

She stood erect and attempted a grand exit. But with her cast and injured rib, she couldn't manage a decent flounce. And having no wheels of her own outside further lessened the impact of her getaway. Reaching the squad car, she sat inside it, fuming, until Wayne joined her five minutes later. His cheery chatter about the weather—as if nothing had happened—added to her ire. On the ride back, she gave him the silent treatment, and at the library bid him a frosty farewell.

She retired to her office to bury her exasperation in paperwork. But she couldn't concentrate, her mind still worrying at the Dunlap matter. Nothing in Wayne's previous behavior had suggested he was a racist—even now, she didn't believe that—but his lack of concern over the inadequate inquiry troubled her. Would he be satisfied with such shoddiness in any other case?

Bigotry's ingrained in all of us from childhood, a small voice inside her said. *Even Wayne.*

"No," she muttered. "Not Wayne."

Even you.

No way! Juanita wrenched a paper clip into a straight line.

And yet—why was Althea so cool in spite of Juanita's overtures? Was the legal secretary picking up on some prejudiced "vibe" from her?

Juanita had to admit she'd felt uncomfortable at times in Bryson's Corner. But that was because the place was unfamiliar, many people there reluctant to talk to her.

Wasn't it?

Or had the interviewees' race been a factor?

No, that couldn't be. She'd had black friends in high school. And her best friend in college had been bright, hysterically funny Arbetha Washington. Arbetha had died in an airplane crash two years ago, and Juanita still missed her common-sense wit and droll, dead-on impressions of people they knew.

Besides, hadn't Juanita chosen to sit at an integrated table at the Buffalo Flats potluck?

Superficial, the skeptical voice inside said.

Didn't she and Robert Norwood talk easily together?

Norwood's a teacher, in a white-collar career. Maybe it's class, not race, that bothers you. The Bryson's Corner folk you know are all blue collar.

That wasn't true either, she insisted, twisting the wire into a circle. Althea was a secretary, a future lawyer, and Juanita definitely felt awkward with her.

So it is race.

No!

But something was wrong between the two of them, Juanita had to admit. And why did she care so much whether Althea liked her or not? Could it be *because* she was African-American that Juanita wanted them to be buddies, as proof she herself wasn't prejudiced? Wasn't that racist thinking in itself?

She somberly considered the question.

No, Juanita felt certain of her motives. She liked and admired Althea for her own qualities. But she could only offer friendship; she couldn't force Althea to accept it.

As for Wayne, there must be some circumstance about the Dunlap case he wasn't leveling with her about. She could *not* have been so wrong about him. But the dual worries left her out of sorts.

She flung the ruined clip into a wastebasket and stalked out to the circulation desk. At her approach, Meador turned from talking to a scrawny teenaged girl.

"This is Becky Zuba, Juanita," he said. "She's got an English assignment you might be able to help with."

Her pimply face animated, with brown eyes snapping behind granny glasses, Becky explained she had to research and write about the Wyndham of 1920.

"Interesting assignment," Juanita said, her mood improving with the challenge. She'd be needing to delve into that same time period herself one of these days, and she'd need the same sources Becky would.

"Most of the kids're planning to go to that little museum near downtown," Becky said, retying the loose knot that caught back her frizzy hair. "But then their papers'll all be about the same. I heard you got this real old diary—a Miss Corbett's—and thought it'd be neat to see what's in it."

"I'm afraid Jane Corbett died long before 1920," Juanita said. "But hers was a journaling family, and others carried on the tradition. Let's go see what we can find. You're an enterprising young woman to think of this."

Beaming at the compliment, Becky followed Juanita upstairs to the room housing the Maizie Stevens Collection. Juanita limped among the cartons, opening a couple and examining their contents. Finally she gave a satisfied sigh.

"We need to label all these boxes better, at least note the years covered on the outsides. But here's Anson Parker's diary, which goes from 1901 till some time in the forties. That should help you."

"Cool. These sure look old. Where's the 1920 one?"

Juanita checked through the carton and handed her a faded blue hardback. "If I were you, I'd examine several years before and after 1920, too. Small-town life doesn't change all that much from one year to the next."

"Good idea." Becky picked out a few other volumes. "Can I

check all these out at once?"

"I'm afraid you can't take them out at all. Anything in the Stevens Collection has to be used here in the library. But I'll keep the ones you need in my office till you finish your research. You can get them from me each time you come in."

"Neat. Thanks, Miss Wills. Could I just see one of Miss Corbett's while we're up here? I've heard hers are pretty interesting."

"Sure. They're right over there." Juanita closed the Parker box and opened one labeled "Corbett." She pulled out slender red-backed books and examined the dates written in pen on the fronts. "Here's the 1842 one. I want to show you something in it." She flipped through and found the account of Charles Dickens's visit to Cincinnati. "Here, read this."

Becky read the portion indicated. "Dickens—cool. We read *A Tale of Two Cities* in school. I expected to hate it, but when I got into it, it was pretty exciting. Is there much stuff about famous people in these?"

"I doubt it." Juanita chose another from the box. "Let's see what Mrs. Corbett found to write about in . . . 1851." Opening the book at random, she ran her eyes over a few pages of faded writing. "Sick baby, new bonnet, visit by a circuit-riding clergyman. Typical stuff. Oh, wait, here's another reference to Dickens." Silently, she read a lengthy section, then looked up with a grin.

"This is interesting. The traveling minister—who sounds pretty full of himself—had dinner at the Corbetts' one Sunday, and the conversation got around to *Martin Chuzzlewit.* That's the novel Dickens wrote after his first trip to America. In it, he portrays many Americans as uncouth and uncivilized. The preacher commented, '. . . them foreigners come here expectin' the worst and never say nothin' good about this country.'

"However, Mrs. Corbett had a reply ready."

"What'd she say?"

"That she'd seen Dickens in person in Cincinnati and he'd

been very gracious. She also showed the minister a passage in *American Notes,* published just before Dickens began *Chuzzlewit,* in which he said very nice things about Cincinnati."

"Did that shut the guy up?"

"Evidently. Let's take these downstairs, Becky—I think I'll take this 1851 Corbett one, too—and you can get started on your research."

"Cool."

That evening, Juanita telephoned Althea, wondering what sort of reception she would get. "Hello, Miss McCoy?" she said when a feminine voice answered. "This is Juanita Wills."

"My daddy's already told you what he knows, Miss Wills," Althea said distantly. "Please don't bother him any more."

Juanita pictured the other woman's dark eyes narrowed in suspicion, the softly rounded chin jutting stubbornly. "Oh, I'm not calling about the Dunlap case," she said hastily. She told about finding the later reference to Dickens in the diary. "I thought the conversation between Mrs. Corbett and the preacher might be an interesting footnote for your paper. Contemporary reaction to his visit, you know. I can scan this passage and e-mail it to you if you like."

"O-okay, thanks," said Althea, her voice warming. She gave Juanita her e-mail address.

"You might like to look through other volumes after 1842 as well. There may be more usable references. What do you think?"

"I wish we weren't so busy at the office—I've had to work late some evenings—but . . . I'll think about it."

"Fine. Just in case—you remember our hours? We close at eight on Thursdays, two on Saturdays, other days at 5:30. Or . . . if you . . ."

She'd started to offer a look at the journals after library hours but hesitated. If Althea wanted nothing more to do with her, she should respect her wishes.

Forget the complexities of the race issue, she decided. Think of Althea as a fellow readaholic.

"If you can't make it during regular hours, I could open up for you another time."

A pause at the other end, then, "Thanks, but I can't ask you to go to so much trouble."

"I wouldn't mind. I'm interested in your project. Besides, your dad helped me with mine."

"How's . . . that going?"

"So-so. I sometimes think I'm getting near the truth, then I seem to run into a wall. I'm determined, though."

"That's what it takes, I guess." Another pause. "Why do you care so much?"

"I . . . guess because . . . someone *has* to?"

Althea chuckled sadly. "People *had* to in 'fifty-nine, and ever since. Sure hasn't caught those killers."

She made a good point, Juanita thought. Talk was indeed cheap.

Twenty-Eight

Juanita spent much of Friday evening wondering about the inadequate investigation and Wayne's cavalier response to questions about it. After her initial reading of the Dunlap file, she'd reassured herself that, once she confronted Wayne, he'd offer a logical explanation for its brevity. She still thought there must be one, which for some reason he couldn't share with her, but hadn't a clue what it could be.

Though she pestered him from time to time to take her advice on a case (and secretly didn't much blame him for not doing so), she'd always admired Wayne's devotion to his work and to the truth. Their relationship, though occasionally stormy, seemed to be what both wanted. She loved her time with him but also her life apart, and he apparently felt the same. Both had been married, she widowed, he divorced. Neither had pushed for remarriage.

But a real breakup would be painful. She didn't think their differences over the case would lead to one. Still, she had to admit feeling somewhat distanced from him at the moment.

They'd planned earlier in the week to take in a film Saturday evening in Tulsa, a comedy-mystery she particularly wanted to see. Juanita didn't want to phone during the day Saturday to ask if the plan had changed, and he didn't call her. She got ready in case, deliberately "dressing down" in a sweatshirt and pants that accommodated her cast, to show she hadn't gone to special trouble.

Promptly at 6:45, her doorbell rang. She opened the door, her pulse fluttering at the sight of Wayne standing uncertainly on her porch, wearing khakis and a red University of Oklahoma sweatshirt.

"We still on for the flicks?" he said without smiling.

"Guess so," she said, matching his casual tone. "Let me get a wrap." She collected her jacket and purse, and he helped her into his car.

On the drive to Tulsa and while waiting for the movie to begin, they made polite conversation like teenagers on a first date. She didn't enjoy the film as much as she'd expected, because her mind wouldn't focus enough to follow its complex plot. When they reached her home afterwards, she said, "Mind if I don't ask you in, Wayne? I'm fairly tired."

"No problem," he said, sounding relieved. "I'm beat, myself." He walked her to the door, opened it with her key, and gave her a perfunctory kiss. "Get a good rest."

"You too." When he'd gone, Juanita locked the front door, let Rip in from the back yard, made cocoa, and collapsed onto a kitchen chair. He nuzzled her hand, lips drawn back in his doggy grin. She hugged him.

"Still love me, boy? Good. Nobody else does, including me. Wayne and I are barely being civil, and other people whose help I need won't talk to me. Guess I'll eat worms."

At her disgusted tone, Rip cocked his head, looking so bewildered she had to laugh.

"You're right. In the grand scheme of things, what've I got to complain about? Oh, Rip, I wish I could figure out who that witness was."

He rested his chin on her lap.

"I wonder if it was someone who lived near the school. Let's see, Eva's family was a couple of blocks away, probably too far to've heard—" She lolled against the table, absently scratching the dog's ears.

"Oh!" she said, sitting upright. "Of course."

She jumped up, threw on a jacket, and grabbed her purse. Then she recalled her promise to Wayne. She mustn't drive by herself. Oh, bother, she thought, one little trip couldn't hurt.

But she'd be livid if he broke a vow to her. She plopped onto the chair again, fuming.

The phone rang—Eva saying she'd tried a new recipe and the resulting cake was much larger than she'd expected.

"I've decided to freeze some, but it's nut cake and I'm sure you'd love it. How about I bring you a hunk tonight?"

"I don't—" Juanita started to beg off, pleading her need to diet, but then had a thought. "Actually, that sounds wonderful, Eva. And if you'll have time, could you do me another little favor? Run me over to the library and let me check on something?"

"Sure. See you in a few minutes?"

Eva arrived, bringing a huge, plastic-wrapped piece of cake, which Juanita placed in her refrigerator. She'd have to slice that into several small pieces later and try to ration herself, else she'd eat the entire thing in one sitting.

Soon, they were parallel-parked under a street light near the west end of the gray-stone library. They would enter by that door, since Juanita's reminders to Meador over the past several days to fix the sticking lock on the front door had so far only served to remind *her* how he excelled at procrastination. She could do the chore herself, of course, but wasn't about to. It had now become the principle of the thing.

As she got out, a shiver of apprehension went through her. Silly, she thought. She wasn't usually afraid when outside at night in Wyndham, even when alone. Anyway, she wasn't alone.

Of course, Eva wasn't the most fearsome bodyguard. But still.

Juanita had been at the library lots of times at night by herself.

She joined Eva on the sidewalk, her eyes searching the shadows for phantoms. Somewhere a cat yowled. Otherwise, all appeared serene. A light-colored auto slowed, sped up, and passed. They crossed the narrow lawn to the side door, and Juanita used her key by light of a partly hidden moon.

They stepped inside, and Juanita took a deep breath. Her own library, of all places, should hold no dangers. However, her nervousness and the low-wattage night light turned bookcases into blocky, threatening giants. She found the light panel and flicked the overhead fixture on.

The brighter light revealed the "monsters" for what they were. Ah, she thought, much better. But she resented having been made to feel afraid even in her cherished library.

"Now, what is it you're looking for?" Eva said cheerily, showing no trace of jitters herself.

Juanita explained she needed to consult old phone directories in connection with her Wyndham history.

"Then would you mind if I look up something in your big dictionary while we're here? Cyril and I were wondering over supper how old the phrase "hither and yon" is. Silly, isn't it?"

"Not at all. I like finding out when words and expressions came into use, myself."

Juanita turned on the reading-room overhead light, and Eva settled herself with the *Oxford English Dictionary* at a table in an alcove. Juanita returned to the west-wing stacks.

In the area where old telephone books were shelved, she gathered directories for 1958 to 1960, carried them to a carrel, and opened the slim 1959 volume.

Fewer phones had been in service then, of course. Paging through slowly, Juanita found no listings for Arnold or Nutchell. Perhaps the families of young Vince and Ward had had unlisted numbers? Or no phones at all? The latter seemed more likely, given what she knew of life in 1959. A less-than-affluent family might have chosen to economize by doing without a phone.

She found five Simmses, one next door to a Mathiesen, but as Vivian had said the families had lived several blocks from the school compound. One Hendershot, three Tubbses and two Gilroys turned up, none in the right section of town. A dozen or so Stevens families had had phones, the closest address about seven blocks from the high school.

Six Campbells included a Henry S. that Juanita thought must be Eva and Phyllida's father, living, in 1959, two blocks from the high school. Checking the current directory, Juanita saw he wasn't listed and thought she recalled Eva's saying her parents were both deceased. Some time, not tonight, she would casually ask Eva about her parents.

Then she remembered Eva's saying that the Haneys had also lived near the high school. Checking 1959 listings, Juanita found a Roscoe Haney on Birch Street, a number that should be next to the athletic field.

Juanita sat back, her mind whirling. Her hunch had been correct.

Could Martha be that witness? Had she, from that upstairs window, seen Dunlap tortured and killed? Was that the real reason she'd left town right after high school?

Excitedly, Juanita glanced at her watch but saw it was too late to call Mavis. This particular query should probably be made in person anyway—although distance between herself and Mavis had usually proven to be a good thing. She dreaded the interview, especially given Mavis's aversion to answering questions she saw as intrusive.

And one couldn't get much more personal than asking, "Did your sister happen to witness a murder during her senior year at Wyndham High?"

The interview with Mavis the next Monday proved to be as much fun as Juanita had expected.

"Can you come into the office a minute, Mavis?" Juanita said about mid-morning. "I need to ask you something."

Mavis sighed audibly but motioned for a part-timer to take her place at the desk. In the office, she declined a chair and stood with a resigned air, watching her supervisor.

"It's about the night Luther Dunlap was killed," Juanita said.

"I've already told you I don't know anything about that. I was just a kid."

"I know, but—Mavis, I'll level with you—I've just realized your family lived next to the high school then. In that big white two-story?"

"So?"

"Did Martha's bedroom overlook the high school athletic field?"

"That's a pretty nosy question. What if it did?"

Juanita felt a thrill of triumph. "Do you suppose Martha could've seen and heard something that night? Maybe even saw the murder committed?"

"No! 'Course not!"

"Did she ever say anything that might suggest she did?"

Mavis gave her a disgusted look.

"Did she act nervous when anyone mentioned Dunlap's death?"

"Not that I remember. Now, if that's it, I've got work to do. It doesn't get done by itself, you know."

"Mavis, I'm not just being a snoop. I've learned that there was a witness to Dunlap's torture and killing. A white person. And since you lived right next door—"

"We weren't even home that night." Mavis's eyes widened, as if her words had surprised even her.

"I thought you didn't recall anything about that evening."

Mavis glowered. "I didn't . . . till now. I don't know why that detail stuck in my head. Maybe because the killing did happen nearby, and as a kid I wondered what I could've heard or seen if we'd been . . ."

"Are you absolutely certain nothing in Martha's behavior ever implied she knew something? This is important, Mavis."

"Oh, my goodness, why didn't you *say* so? Usually it makes *no* difference who could've witnessed a murder or not."

"Cute. Where'd your family go that evening?"

"I—do—not—remember." Mavis clipped each word. "But I'm sure Martha couldn't have seen anything. I'm going back to work." She turned on her heel and stomped back to the checkout desk.

Juanita sat leaning on her computer and considering murder strategies. Maybe this time she'd borrow a javelin from the high school's track equipment, run Mavis through, and pin her to the circulation desk like a mounted insect.

Better not. Might get blood all over the returned books.

So Martha couldn't have been the witness. Yet Garvin McCoy had seemed positive there was one. Juanita went to the stacks and flipped through the old phone books again, hoping an address might jump out at her to suggest a lead. More slowly, she paged through several volumes, but nothing came to her. She was sitting in a carrel, gloomily pondering the row of directories, when her eye fell on the high-school yearbooks a shelf below.

Well, why not look through those again? Maybe a face or name would trigger an idea. In the 1959 book, she examined black-and-white individual class photos. Again, nothing. She leafed through the rest of the book, pausing at a picture of the track team.

Several familiar names and/or faces in that group: Lonnie Tubbs. Vince Arnold. Simon Simms. Ward Nutchell. Cyril Brompton, Eva's husband.

Cyril wasn't that old, was he?

Looking more closely, she saw that the name was Cecil Brompton. This must be the older brother Cyril had mentioned, who looked much as Cyril would have at sixteen, with a mop of light hair and a skinny frame.

Juanita's spirits lifted. She'd never met Cecil Brompton, but if he was anywhere close by, he might prove to be another source. At least, it would be worth asking Cyril.

Twenty-Nine

That evening Juanita phoned the Brompton residence. Cyril answered.

"'Lo, Cyril," she said. "How're you doing?"

"Fine. Yourself?"

"My injuries are healing well. Cyril, you have an older brother, don't you? Does he live around here?"

"In Muskogee. Matter of fact, Cecil's coming over tonight. Why?"

Juanita explained. "Do you think he might be willing to talk to me about events in 1959?"

"Cecil isn't much for rehashing old times, but I'll ask him."

"Terrific. Thanks, Cyril."

Less than an hour later, Juanita's phone rang. It was Cyril.

"Cecil says as a favor to me he'll talk to you. Would it be convenient if we come over now?"

"That would be great."

Juanita put on a fresh pot of decaf and took a loaf of homemade banana-nut bread from the freezer. Soon Cyril arrived with an older version of himself, both men small and gnomish, with nearly identical facial features and green eyes. Juanita served them coffee and toasted slices of the sweet bread. They ate sitting in her large living room. Light from the chandelier shimmered on the brothers' similarly balding crowns. Cecil Brompton eyed her uncomfortably as she explained she had seen him pictured with the track team in the old yearbook.

"I'm hoping you can help me visualize events at the 1959 interscholastic track meet, Mr. Brompton," she said with a smile she hoped would put him at ease. "For a town history I'm working on."

He looked at his brother, then back at her.

"It seems from my research so far that the match between Wyndham and Bryson's Corner may have led to Luther Dunlap's death. And since you were on the team, you might have insights others wouldn't. What can you tell me about that day?"

The older Brompton harrumphed. "Lots of excitement in the air. Yeah, everyone was . . . excited."

Great, Juanita thought, *I could've guessed that much.* Maybe she needed to ask more specific questions.

"What events did you participate in that day?"

He pulled his shirt straight out from his chest, as if it was binding him. "Just one, the relay."

"And how'd that go?"

"It was my first time to run it. I was scared I'd fall down or drop the baton."

"But you didn't?"

"No. And we won."

"I understand Wyndham didn't do so well in other events."

Cecil nodded, scrunching one side of his mouth thoughtfully. "We won more over all, but Bryson's Corner took several events."

He seemed to be relaxing a bit, Juanita thought. She risked another general question.

"Other than the excitement, what was the atmosphere like between the two schools?"

"Tense. Strained."

"Were there any fights?"

"None I knew about. Hostile looks, though."

"Between Dunlap and the Wyndham boys?"

"Some." Cecil tugged at his shirt front again, a nervous habit, Juanita decided. "Dunlap got kinda cocky after he'd trounced us a couple times. Our guys, waiting on the sidelines, said some pretty rash things."

"Such as?"

Cecil stared at the mushroom-colored carpet at his feet. "You can probably guess. 'Uppity niggers' who didn't 'know their place,' how they were 'asking for it.' You know."

Juanita set her empty cup on an end table. "I hope you'll forgive my asking this, Mr. Brompton, but did you participate at all in that talk?"

"Juanita!" Cyril said. "My brother's no racist!"

"Sorry. I didn't mean to suggest that, Mr. Brompton. It's just that the more details I can learn about that day, the better prepared I'll feel to write the story. I apologize if my question was out of line."

Cecil scrunched a corner of his mouth again. "I hate to admit it, but I used the 'n' word a couple times. That's burned into my memory by what happened to Dunlap." He yanked at his shirt. "I was small for my age, younger than most of the team, unsure of myself, and trying to be accepted. It sounds horrible now, but then . . ."

Cyril eyed him with a mixture of surprise and compassion. "I've never heard you talk about any of this before, Cecil."

His brother frowned. "It's not something I'm proud of."

"Is that all?" Juanita asked gently. "You didn't . . . help teach Dunlap 'his place'?"

"Juanita!" said Cyril. Both brothers looked dismayed

Then Cecil's shoulders slumped. "It's okay, Cyril. I guess I do feel . . . partly responsible for his death. Maybe if I'd spoken up for him . . ." He passed a trembling hand over his shiny pate. "No.

Nobody'd have paid *me* any mind . . . ."

"I didn't think you'd been involved, Mr. Brompton," Juanita said softly, "but I felt I had to ask." She cleared her throat. "I like to think I'd have behaved differently from the crowd if I'd been around then. But I wonder if I really would have."

"I should've been man enough to speak up for Dunlap, anyway," Cecil went on, his expression forlorn. "Shoot, Miss Wills, why do we sometimes go against all our best impulses?"

"With my dismal record on that, I'm not the one to ask. Could I throw some names at you, Mr. Brompton? If you recall these guys, would you tell me how each behaved towards Luther Dunlap that day?"

His slight nod gave assent.

"Lonnie Tubbs."

"He was one of the angriest. Couldn't stand getting beat by anyone, especially a black fellow."

"Think carefully—did Tubbs actually threaten physical harm to Dunlap?"

"Yes."

Now we're getting somewhere, Juanita thought with grim satisfaction. "D'you recall exactly what he said? Anything about *how* he'd hurt Dunlap? Or when? Or where?"

Again, Cecil did the shirt tug. "I don't think he gave specifics. I think it was something like, 'Just wait, nigger, you'll never run another foot race.'"

"What about Vince Arnold?"

"Arnold . . . he was going along, agreeing with the crowd. Tubbs was his idol, so anything Lonnie did, Vince pretty much followed."

"Simon Simms."

"I don't remember him saying anything. Simon was a low-key guy. Always hard to tell what he was thinking."

"Ward Nutchell."

Cecil was silent a moment. "Nutchell. I don't recall him

being—wait, I do, too. He lost the 100-yard dash to Dunlap. Didn't say a word afterwards, just stared at Dunlap as if he'd like to kill him."

"Really. So—you didn't hear any guys making actual plans that day to harm Dunlap?"

"Not that I heard. Just letting off steam, far as I knew."

"Did the Wyndham Police question you following the murder, Mr. Brompton? Ask who'd said what and so on?"

"No."

"How about later? Have you *ever* been interviewed by the police about that incident?"

"Oh, yes. A detective has gone into it with me more than once."

"Really?" Juanita and Cyril asked in unison.

"Yes. We talked again just a couple of weeks ago. Mr. Cleary seems to be very professional and thorough."

"Cleary," Juanita said. "Wayne Cleary."

"That's right," Cecil said. "You know him?"

"Not as well as I thought I did."

"This amazes me," Cyril said, shaking his head at his brother. "All these years, you've never told me any of this."

"Like I said," his brother replied, "my part in it was nothing to be proud of. Guess I still wanted my little brother to look up to me. And I kept hoping the Dunlap case would get solved, or people would forget—one or the other—but it's just drug on."

"Mr. Brompton, I've been told the track coach encouraged his boys to practice at the school on their own time. Did you ever go to the track in the evenings?"

"No. A few guys did, but not me. I hated the idea of being there at night by myself."

"Do you recall which boys did go there evenings?"

"Hm, that was a long time ago. I sure can't remember after all this time."

They talked a while longer, but Juanita learned nothing more.

Finally, she thanked both men for coming over and Cecil for his helpful information.

As they prepared to leave, he smiled sadly and said, "I'm glad you asked me all this, Miss Wills. I haven't even told my wife most of it. Good to finally get it out."

After they left, Juanita pondered what Cecil had said. She was certain his name didn't appear in the papers she had copied from the police file. Yet, he'd said Wayne had interviewed him multiple times. What was going on? Wayne must be questioning people but for some reason not placing the resulting information in the official file.

The thought eased her worry. She had never truly suspected Wayne of dereliction of duty, Juanita told herself. Still, she felt better.

But why would he do that? Did he suspect someone in his own department wasn't on the up-and-up? Or—maybe he was trying to guard against more leaks, as had happened with the Davis autopsy story?

That must be it. The autopsy leak must explain Wayne's keeping the Dunlap interviews to himself for now.

"Oh, what a relief, Rip," Juanita said aloud. "Wayne hasn't swept the Dunlap case under the rug, after all. Not that I ever thought he had, of course."

The dog eyed her sleepily from his rug under the bay window.

Juanita then dialed Yvonne Cousins' number and asked to speak to Leona Brown. Mrs. Cousins greeted Juanita not as an old friend but as someone she had decided to tolerate. Her mother had just waked from a nap, she said. Soon Mrs. Brown herself spoke into the telephone. The amenities out of the way, Juanita asked if Mrs. Brown had known a boy named Cory Granger, possibly short for Corinthian.

"Oh, yes. Corinthian lived for a time in Bryson's Corner. A handsome little boy."

"You said he lived there 'for a time.' Where'd he go then? And why?"

"May I ask why you are interested in young Mr. Granger?"

"I'm not sure, but I think he's somehow connected to the Luther Dunlap case. Probably not—it's most likely a wild hare—but there seems to be some secret concerning the boy's parentage. Tell me, was Corinthian Granger . . . a black child?"

"Of course. Fairly light-skinned but certainly African-American. Bryson's Corner was still all black in those days, as I'm sure you're aware. I . . . don't believe I ever heard who his parents were. The Grangers weren't, I know. Nor were they his grandparents, though he called them Grandpa and Grandma."

"Do you know how he happened to be living with them?"

"I don't. But they were a kind-hearted family who often took in children whose own parents couldn't care for them. All the same, I believe they weren't sorry when those white folks offered to give the boy a home. The Grangers had several other children to look after at the time. They're both deceased now. Wonderful people."

"Cory Granger was adopted by a white family?"

Silence, for a moment. Then Mrs. Brown said thoughtfully, "I doubt an adoption occurred. But the couple seemed taken with the boy. Corinthian had nice manners for such a young child, and a pleasant way about him. Mr. Granger used to take him along to his job at the service station that those folks owned, and they made rather a pet of the boy."

"Do you recall where this couple lived? Or their last name?"

"No. It was some distance away, though, because Mr. Granger's old truck broke down sometimes, driving back and forth so much. But he kept it running. He was an excellent mechanic. Everyone for miles around knew to take their ailing vehicles to that station to have them fixed. Unfortunately, Mr. Granger had a serious accident and couldn't do that work any more. I believe that may've been soon after Corinthian went to live with the white employer."

"Would the station have been in Buffalo Flats, perhaps?"

"Buffalo . . . hm-m-m . . . that might have been the town."

"So Corinthian ended up living with Mr. Granger's white boss?"

"At first, it was for a weekend, then for longer periods. Finally, the boy pleaded to stay there all the time, and the white couple agreed. They had no children of their own, I believe."

"And Corinthian never came back to Bryson's Corner to live?"

"I—actually, I have to say I lost track of him. I was . . . having difficulty with my daughter at that point, and—I can't tell you anything more about Corinthian Granger, Miss Wills. Now, if you'll excuse me . . . I'm tiring easily today."

"Of course. Thanks very much for your help, Mrs. Brown."

After she hung up, Juanita sat thinking about young Corinthian Granger. Had he been a mixed-race child? Raised among whites from childhood, had he learned to hate the non-Caucasian part of his lineage? And had he passed both African-American blood and self-loathing on to his son Todd? Could that explain Todd's antipathy towards people of color?

The next day Juanita phoned Simon Simms at his office. She was placed on hold for a few minutes, then the accountant came on the line. After opening pleasantries, she said she needed to ask him something about the Dunlap murder case.

"I've told you all I can about that, Miss Wills."

"And I appreciate all your help, Simon. But I've learned more since you and I talked about it, and now I need to run something else by you."

He was silent a second or two, then said, "All right."

"I was looking through old high-school yearbooks and noticed you were on the track team in 1959."

"'On it' is accurate. I wasn't much good."

"I understand the coach encouraged his team members to practice at the track on their own time. Did you ever practice there in the evening?"

"I . . . may have done so. A few times."

Juanita felt a tingle of excitement but willed herself to stay calm. How should she phrase the next part?

"Were you the only one at the track on those occasions? Or did others come sometimes?"

"I suppose . . . I'd have been there alone. What's this about, Miss Wills? What are you getting at?"

"I found a source who insists there was a witness to Dunlap's murder. A white witness. I thought it might be someone who came to the track to practice and saw the incident from hiding. Could that have been you, maybe?"

Juanita heard a quick intake of breath.

"Absolutely not! Do you really think I'd have kept such a secret all these years? You have quite a nerve accusing me of that, Miss Wills."

"I didn't mean it as an accusation, Simon. If it had happened, you'd have been scared to tell anyone, I'm sure."

"Well, it didn't."

"Okay, then. Thanks."

After work that day, having recalled other details from a conversation weeks ago, Juanita asked Eva to run her by Grace Hendershot's home, pleading her desire to see how Grace was faring these days.

When they pulled to a stop at the curb, Grace was kneeling by a rosebush near the front porch, pulling weeds. Grace looked up, saw Juanita opening the car door, and glanced furtively towards the house.

"Juanita," she called. "How . . . nice to see you."

"Likewise," Juanita replied. She turned to speak to her driver. "I'll probably just be a minute, Eva, but you're welcome to come, too, if you like."

Eva waved a hand. "I'll just wait for you here."

Juanita crawled from the car and crossed the lawn. "It's been a while since we've seen each other, Grace. How're you doing?"

"Oh, fine. And . . . how are you? I heard you'd been in the hospital."

Juanita briefly told about her injuries. "Except for aches and pains, and this clumsy cast—" she indicated the offending item—"I'm fine."

Grace's eyes strayed again towards the curtained picture window. "I'd . . . ask you in, but . . . the house is a mess."

"No problem. I can't stay, anyway. Just got to wondering how you were doing."

"I'm okay." Grace studied her soiled hands.

"So I see. There was something I wanted to ask you, Grace. I know you deliver your baked goods and preserves to other towns sometimes. Did I once hear you mention going to a town called Buffalo Flats?"

Grace's fingers went to her unrouged cheek, which looked white as paper compared to their grime. "Buffalo—can't say I know the place."

"Careful, you're getting dirt on your face. Are you okay? You look upset."

The older woman swallowed hard and nodded. "I'm okay."

"Buffalo Flats is small," Juanita said, "and a bit of a drive from here. I just thought you might know people there."

Grace shook her head, eyes on the ground.

"You sure keep your rosebushes looking healthy. I'm not much of a gardener, myself. Too hit-or-miss about weeding and watering."

She got no reply.

"About your roses, Grace. Did you say a high school beau used to give you flowers?"

Grace's eyes flew wide. She still didn't speak.

"Would that boy have been Luther Dunlap, by any chance?"

"No!" Grace thrust out a hand, steadied herself against a pillar. "No!"

Juanita put an arm around the thin shoulders. "You really don't look good, Grace. Maybe you've worked in the sun too long. Let me help you inside and pour something cold for you, and you can lie down."

"No! I . . . just lost my balance a second. "

The pale eyes left Juanita's face and stared into the distance, the faraway look Juanita had come to think of as "Gracie's gone-again gaze." She tried to bring her back with more talk of the rosebushes but got no response.

"Okay," Juanita finally said, "thanks, Grace. Sure I can't help you into the house?"

Grace didn't answer. Juanita hugged her, said a gentle goodbye, and left. On the rest of the drive home, Juanita pondered why the Todd-Martin conflict fascinated her so. Surely it was just one of many indications the races hadn't fully made peace—no news there. And it was distracting her from the Dunlap case.

Still, Corinthian Granger seemed to be a link between Bryson's Corner and Buffalo Flats. She couldn't let it go just yet.

Nor could she let go the idea that Grace Hendershot was somehow a part of the story.

Thirty

Wednesday morning, Juanita was at her desk, checking information to present to a Wyndham City Council committee that was drawing up a five-year plan for the library, when the phone rang. She answered.

"Wyndham Public Library, Juanita Wills speaking."

"Uh, Miss Wills," said a feminine voice, "this is Althea McCoy. I've been thinking—is your offer to let me see the Corbett diaries again still open?"

"Oh, hello, Althea! Yes, it is. When would you want to come?"

"You said the library's open till eight tomorrow? I'm afraid I couldn't get there till about seven-thirty. At that, I'll be cutting my evening class. And chances are I'll need more than half an hour."

"Tomorrow evening? Sure, I—oh, wait, let me think about that." Thursday Juanita was scheduled to work late at the library anyway, but Eva was going to a party that night and wouldn't be able to drive her home if she stayed later than eight. Meador, who also worked tomorrow evening, was afoot himself while his car was in the shop.

If she were back to driving herself, alone . . . .

In fact, the driving shouldn't be difficult. The problem was that dratted promise to Wayne not to go outside alone. She'd have to find a bodyguard, or at least an escort, someone who could call for help if needed. Wayne would be in Tulsa tomorrow settling details from an uncle's estate, then would be working an evening shift.

She had it. Rather than ride with Eva tomorrow morning, she'd have Eve caravan with her from home to library. That way she'd have her own car here. Then in the evening . . .

"Sorry to hesitate, Althea," Juanita said, "I just had to figure out how to work this. I feel silly saying it, but I promised my boyfriend I wouldn't go out alone at night. Could you possibly follow me home in your car after we finish here tomorrow evening?"

"Oh . . . okay. Yeah, I could do that. Thanks. This is really helpful."

"We researchers have to stick together."

As Juanita hung up, she remembered how spooky the library could sometimes seem at night, especially lately, and an involuntary shudder went through her.

Get a grip, Juanita, she told herself.

She'd be careful, but wouldn't become a prisoner of her own fear. As Shakespeare had written in *Julius Caesar:*

> Cowards die many times before their deaths;
> The valiant never taste of death but once . . . .

The next day proved to be a full one. As planned, Juanita drove her car to the library, Eva following in hers. Not having driven for weeks, Juanita felt elated but a bit strange as she slid behind the wheel and turned the ignition. Backing out, she relied more on the side and rearview mirrors than usual because her neck—

though much improved since its injury—didn't turn as easily and comfortably as before.

She met with the Five-Year-Plan Committee most of the morning. In late afternoon, school children crowded the reading room and stacks. Becky Zuba collected the Parker journals from Juanita and took them upstairs to study. Soon afterwards, five other high-schoolers swarmed the circulation desk.

"Got any books on the history of Wyndham?" asked a gangly buzz-cut boy. "Something that tells what it was like here more'n eighty years ago?" From his rhinestone-studded lips, the words "eighty years ago" sounded as distant as the Pleistocene Age.

"Not really," said Juanita. "I'm researching a town history myself, but it's nowhere near ready to publish. And I'm not back to the 1920s yet."

His hopeful expression fell. "Got the local newspaper back that far?"

"Afraid not, not even on microfilm or microfiche. But you might be able to find copies at the newspaper office."

The teens held a low-voiced conference.

"Me and Kenny went down there yesterday," Juanita heard a girl with spiky green hair say. "Got zilch. It's hot and dusty where they keep the real old papers, and there ain't no place to set. Anyway, all the twenties ones was missing."

Juanita considered suggesting the Parker diaries, but it seemed unfair to Becky to offer others a source the girl had found through her own initiative.

"What about family histories or autobiographies of local citizens?" she suggested. "Sometimes people write their memoirs or stories they've collected about their ancestors, give or sell copies to relatives, and put one copy in the library. We have quite a few volumes like that."

The youngsters exchanged doubtful glances.

"We don't need stuff on somebody's relatives," said their lanky leader.

"Suit yourself. But those books often contain details about how the authors or their family members lived long ago. I think they might help."

He shrugged a thin shoulder. "Guess it's worth a try."

Juanita led the students to the reference room and showed them the genealogy section, two long shelves of which were filled with donated family histories of every size, some professionally printed and bound, others amateurish in appearance. Spying one she knew well, a squat volume with typed pages and a homemade cover of blue denim, she skimmed it till she found a remembered passage. It told how, in 1921, the author had rubbed her hands raw while scrubbing the hems of her older sisters' long dresses, after they'd dragged in mud on Wyndham's then-unpaved Main Street. Juanita showed it to the spokesman. His eyes moved over the page, and his attitude changed from doubt to pleased surprise.

"Yeah," he said. "We can use this."

The teenagers conferred again. From words drifting her way, Juanita gathered they were all vying for first chance to use the book she had shown them. The rhinestone-lipped leader, voice raised above the rest, convinced the others to split up the available material, each examine a few books, share any useful passages found, and take their actual notes individually.

"We can't have the papers all sounding alike," he said. "'Ol' Lady Hawkins'd nail us for cheating."

"Excellent thinking," Juanita said. "Remember to footnote any information you use and put quote marks around specific wording you've copied, even if it's just a phrase. Many scholars can use the same material but put their own interpretations or emphases on it."

Half-glazed, half-amused looks told her she sounded like their teacher.

"Okay, it's your project," she said. "Let me know if I can help."

Meador took his supper break at 4:30, slouching back at 5:35, five minutes late. Mavis, whose turn it was to leave before closing time Thursday, left reluctantly at 5:45, fifteen minutes after her scheduled getting-off time.

"Mrs. Workaholic and Mr. Work-Resistant," Juanita muttered as she ate a brown-bag supper at her desk during a lull.

Thursday evenings always brought out people who worked or attended school during the day, and tonight a large number of patrons populated the reading room, reference room, and stacks. Juanita mostly stayed at the circulation desk checking out materials, including a tome on gardening for Cyril Brompton and a Dean Koontz novel for Simon Simms. Katherine Greer, her failing eyesight more and more pushing her towards large-print or audio books, took out a bestseller on tape.

During a lull, Juanita sat at her desk thinking about Althea and wondering what might be buried in her subconscious from childhood. Juanita's eyes fell on a small recording device on a shelf over her desk. She hadn't used it when interviewing Garvin McCoy and others, for fear it would make her interviewees nervous and less talkative. But she thought she might try it tonight. Popping a new cassette into the recorder, she slid the device into one of two large pockets on her skirt.

Althea arrived at 7:25 P.M., breathless in a navy sweatshirt, jeans, and tennis shoes, and carrying a laptop computer. "I changed before I left the office and got here as soon as I could."

"Did you have any trouble finding a parking spot?"

"Yes. I had to park up the street a couple of blocks."

"I should've warned you. The quilters are having their monthly meeting across the street. They usually stay till eight-thirty or so, and their cars fill this whole block."

They both sounded polite but formal, Juanita thought, as if some invisible barrier existed between them.

"Let me set your laptop in my office till you're ready for it," she said.

"Okay. Thanks."

Althea handed over the small computer, Juanita stowed it by her desk, and they went upstairs. Becky waved to them from a row of carrels. Juanita unlocked the collections room, and she and Althea stepped inside. They opened cartons containing the Corbett journals, examined dates on the fronts, and chose the volumes from 1843 to 1854. Juanita showed Althea the passage she had found earlier.

"I don't recall why Jane's story stopped with 1854, whether she suddenly died or what," Juanita said, flipping to the back of that volume. She read the last entry to herself, then aloud: "'The arthritis that now afflicts my hands makes writing a painful task. Reluctantly, I must cease this record. I shall miss the pleasant hours spent setting down, and reflecting on, the events of my days. Farewell, Dear Diary, Farewell.'"

"I almost feel I knew her," Juanita said sadly. She closed the boxes and was about to re-lock the door when a thought occurred. "Why don't you go on down and get started, Althea. I want to look for something else up here."

Althea left, and Juanita prowled among the cartons, finally finding one labeled "Maizie Stevens's Journal." She opened it and lifted out several tan spiral notebooks, the author's name and a year printed boldly in green ink on each. Juanita located one marked "1959" and others for the years just before and just after, closed the lid, and was locking the room when Becky hailed her.

"Somebody else using those old journals?"

Juanita explained Althea's mission.

"Cool. I didn't know diaries could help so many people. Maybe I'll start one."

"I've begun several over the years but always gave up after a few days," Juanita admitted. "Journaling must take a kind of discipline I don't have."

She took the notebooks downstairs, where one elderly man dozed over a *Reader's Digest* in the periodicals section. In an alcove,

Althea was typing on her laptop, a diary open beside her. Finding the reference room empty, Juanita locked the east door, returned to the checkout desk, and told the remaining part-time employee she could go. Then Juanita stood at the desk smearing hand lotion on her dry hands and forearms, trying to decide whether to ask Althea what was wrong between them. Becky came downstairs, handed the Parker books to Juanita, said thanks, and left.

"I've finished my closing chores," Meador said. "Okay if I leave?"

His query, delivered in a loud stage-whisper, woke the old man, who rose, returned the magazine to its shelf, and sauntered out. Juanita glanced at her wrist.

"Let's review the finer points of telling time, Meador. Eight o'clock is when the little hand's on the eight and the big hand's *on* the twelve, not midway between the ten and eleven."

"Like we're going to have a huge rush in the next seven minutes."

She sighed heavily. "Go ahead. But some day I'll total up all your late-comings and early-goings. You must owe the library a couple of weeks, at least." Absentmindedly, Juanita stuck the hand lotion bottle into her pocket beside the recorder. "Be sure to clear that mess of empty cartons out of the back hallway tomorrow. It's impossible to walk through there. Oh, and work on that front-door lock—first thing in the morning!"

"Thanks, Juanita. You're the best."

He got a tan windbreaker from the office closet, strode through the west wing, and opened the side exit. Juanita heard the lock lever snap, then a soft soughing as the door closed.

She finished tidying the circulation desk and jotted notes to herself about tomorrow's duties. The wall clock said 8:05. She took a key ring from her desk and worked at the lock of the front entry. It was getting more recalcitrant all the time.

The key finally turned. Juanita dropped the ring into her empty skirt pocket, took the Stevens books to Althea's table, and sat at the other end.

"Finding anything?" she asked.

"Just what you showed me, so far. It's interesting, though."

"Jane Corbett was a good writer."

"I get involved in her stories and forget to watch for Dickens's name."

Juanita smiled. "That's the toughest part of research to me. Staying on-subject and not 'chasing rabbits.'"

Althea nodded and returned to the diary she was studying. Juanita blew dust from a spiral-bound cover, opened the tablet, and began to read Maizie's faded inky flourishes.

But after a few minutes, unable to keep her mind on her reading, she laid down the notebook. Taking a deep breath, she plunged.

"Althea, I need to ask—have I done something to offend you? I'd like us to be friends."

Althea shrugged, eyes still on the journal. "We are."

"Are we? It seems to me there's a coolness between us."

Althea looked up without expression. "Why do you think that is?"

"I don't know."

"Don't you?" Althea's tone held a challenge.

"Is it—because we're of different races? People of all backgrounds are friends these days."

Althea studied her a long moment. "You think it's that easy, don't you?"

"I—easy?"

"Have you really thought about why Bryson's Corner exists at all?" Althea folded her hands and shook her head. "Because it was necessary. Till a few years ago, people of my color weren't allowed to live next door to people of yours."

"I know. I can't defend slavery or segregation, and won't try. A lot of what happened in the past was horrid. I'm deeply sorry."

"Sorry. Miz McCoy, I regret my great-granddaddy kidnapped

your great-granddaddy and made him work all his life for free. I regret my daddy wouldn't let you go to school with me and get a decent education. But that's all over now, so let's let bygones be bygones.

"You seem like a nice woman, Miss Wills. And you've been very helpful to me. But history's history. We can't ignore it."

Juanita was silent a moment. "We shouldn't try. We need to remember what outrages people can commit when self-interest overcomes simple decency—so that such things'll never happen again."

"That's a pretty speech."

"I mean it. I realize you can't know that. But would you help me learn what happened in 1959? I promise to write the truth as best I can. That's all I know to do."

Thirty-One

Althea's eyes searched Juanita's face. Finally, she nodded. "Ask your questions. But I wasn't around then, so I doubt I can help."

"Okay if I tape—?" Juanita reached into her pocket for the recorder and grabbed the bottle neck instead. "What in the— oh, would you like some hand lotion? Can't imagine why I'm carrying this around." She held the bottle out to Althea, who shook her head no. Juanita set it on the table and plunged her hand into the pocket again, this time bringing out the recording device. "Okay if I tape our conversation?"

Althea shrugged assent.

Juanita clicked the recorder on. "You said you used to hang around Samuel Davis when you were a kid. Did he ever mention Dunlap's murder? Maybe in a veiled reference you didn't fully understand at the time?"

Althea looked away several moments, her eyes on the low bookshelf wall surrounding their table.

"When he'd had a few beers," she finally said, "he'd get to crying. Not loud, blubbering sobs, just quiet weeping, like something gnawed at him but he couldn't express his grief aloud."

She moved the shiny bracelet up and down her arm, still staring into space. "A couple times he muttered something like, 'Why'd he meet her?' or 'She shoulda left him be.'"

"Really. You think he might've meant Dunlap and some girl?"

Althea looked at Juanita. "I do think so, now. Mom didn't want me around Uncle Sam when he drank, so I didn't often hear such things. But it set me wondering who the 'she' and 'he' were. He never mentioned a girl's name. I'd have remembered."

"Your dad and mom ever talk about the killing?"

"No. Mom wouldn't have thought it proper for me to know about. Wait, something else . . . I'd forgotten this. Once, I went over to give Uncle Sam a message from my dad, and I found him listening to an old record and holding onto a photograph."

"A photo. Of whom?"

"June Allyson, the movie star. It wasn't a real glamour shot; she just looked girlish and sweet. She wore her blonde hair turned under, and Uncle Sam said that hair and smile reminded him of someone. Funny I hadn't recalled that till just now."

"You mentioned he was listening to a record. Do you remember which one?"

Althea considered. "It was real scratchy, like it had been played a lot. Don't recall the tune, but it was by the Del-Vikings. I remember because I'd been studying the Vikings in school."

"The Del-Vikings and June Allyson. Wonder what that was about?"

"I haven't a clue. And that's really all I can tell you."

"Thanks, Althea. Thanks a lot." Juanita switched off the recording device and set it on the table.

"What are you reading?" Althea asked.

"A woman's diary from 1959. I don't know why I didn't think of it sooner. There might just be something helpful in here."

"Good luck, then." Althea turned back to her own book.

Juanita opened the notebook again, read a few entries, and

soon formed an unflattering opinion of its author. Whereas the Corbett journal focused on events in Jane's own life, Stevens's mostly discussed what she heard or surmised about other people and their activities. An entire page derided a new minister's wife's taste in hats. Other entries detailed comings and goings at all hours by the diarist's neighbors. Another criticized the high school principal's behavior when his wife left town. The author had worked in the school cafeteria, a job that had let her observe and overhear much, and she seemed to have taken full advantage of the fact.

Maizie Stevens had been a gossip. A particularly mean-spirited one, who had not only relished learning other people's secrets but also exposing them. Her diary had been an ammunition-filled arsenal.

What was it Martha or someone had said about Hattie Stevens's mother, Maizie? "Dreadful woman."

Juanita had to concur.

A barely audible sound, as of air entering an open door or window, came from the west wing. Juanita held her breath, listening. Althea glanced up, also.

Had Meador come back for something? Swiveling gradually, Juanita looked towards the arch leading from the reading room into the wing. No one there, of course. She shook herself, trying to dispel the nameless fear tensing her spine.

"Old buildings," she muttered, smiling at Althea in what she hoped was a reassuring way. "This one creaks and groans like a plowhorse with sciatica."

She turned her attention back to the journal, letting her eyes run quickly over paragraphs, looking for names she recognized. She found nothing until March 10, when the words "Simon Simms" leapt out at her.

The Simms family had attended the same church as the Stevenses, and Maizie had picked Simon out as a match for Hattie. Simon would be a good provider, Maizie noted, a "steady" young man who would take his saucy wife "in hand" when necessary. The fact that the two young people apparently disliked each other had not deterred the would-be mother-in-law. Accolades about Simon alternated with Maizie's criticism of other teens, including Phyllida Campbell, Lonnie Tubbs, Claude Gilroy, and Ward Nutchell. Phyllida was a bad influence on Hattie. Lonnie, Claude, and Ward were too high-spirited, "bad boys" who might get young Miss Stevens pregnant. Maizie had seemed to live in fear that her rebellious daughter would disgrace her.

Ward Nutchell was the boy said to have had a dispute with Luther Dunlap over a deer, Juanita recalled. But Althea's dad had pooh-poohed the idea that Dunlap would steal an animal shot by anyone else. And Garvin McCoy was as close to the situation as anyone still alive.

So far as Juanita knew.

Anyway, the mysterious "she" that Davis had spoken of to Althea seemed to offer a stronger motive for his murder than a dispute over a hunting trophy.

Maizie Stevens's diary also denigrated Cecil Brompton, whom Hattie had once flirted with in the cafeteria. A weakling and a "mama's boy," according to the diarist.

Juanita continued to scan pages until she found two other names she recognized: Grace Hendershot and Martha Haney. Maizie had apparently suspected each young woman at various times of being Hattie's rival for Simon's affections.

Of Grace, she had written: "That Hendershot hussy's stuck on herself, thinks she's too good to walk the earth. Other kids tell her so, flat-out, but she don't say nothing back. The men sure fall for that above-it-all act, young ones especially. I hear boys talking to each other like they can't stand little Gracie, but then one of them will make an excuse to talk to her. They don't fool me a bit."

About Martha, Maizie had said: "The Haney tramp's such a sneak. Left her notebook in the cafeteria the other day, and when I cleaned off the table, I looked in it. She'd drawed lacy hearts all over that notebook paper, put her name inside. Somebody else's, too, but she'd inked through it—heavy, so you couldn't read it. I bet anything she's seeing some guy her folks wouldn't like. Wish I knew who. I'd send them a unsigned letter about Martha and him."

"Lovely person, Mrs. Stevens," Juanita murmured.

Althea glanced up, eyebrows raised.

"Maizie had lots to say about people, little of it good," Juanita explained.

"She tell anything about Luther Dunlap's murder?"

"Not yet. Anyway, I'm not sure I'd fully trust her version of the facts."

Several pages later, Juanita stopped at an entry a week before the interscholastic track meet. Maizie had been scandalized by the idea that the "cream of Wyndham's young men" would have to share a field with "them filthy niggers." She went on in great detail, repeating comments she had heard at school and elsewhere.

"Nobody but that pitiful excuse for a superintendent wants this match to happen," she wrote.

Juanita paused in her reading, gripped by a sudden feeling she was being watched. They were locked in, she reminded herself, and no one could have entered without her knowledge. The diarist's meanness must be affecting her nerves.

Later in the journal, after the visiting team's respectable showing at the meet, Maizie theorized that the superintendent had rigged some events to favor Bryson's Corner. How he had managed that—whether by bribing or threatening Wyndham boys to make them lose those events, or what—she didn't explain.

After Dunlap's death, Maizie pronounced the torture-murder to have been "better than that uppity nigger deserved." She recounted rumors about boys said to have been involved—the entire male contingent of the senior class, it seemed—among them Lonnie Tubbs, Simon Simms and Vince Arnold. She also mentioned juniors Claude Gilroy and Ward Nutchell and sophomore Cecil Brompton, but discounted Claude and Cecil as suspects, Cecil because he had "no guts," Claude because such behavior didn't seem "his style."

The culprits, whoever they were, had clearly ranked high in Maizie's estimation.

On the basis of such suspicions, she had even changed her view of Lonnie Tubbs. If he wanted to take Hattie out again, maybe marry her, Maizie wouldn't stand in his way.

Juanita shivered. "After reading this, I'll need a long, hot shower."

"What's in that book that's got you so bugged?"

Juanita hesitated, embarrassed to tell what someone of her own race and locale had written. Finally she handed over the book, pointing out several offending passages. Althea read them with a somber expression, then shoved the notebook back with a cynical smile.

"This is news to you, that white folks would think that way?"

"No, some did—and do. It's just that this woman sounds so —smug—when she justifies the horrid way Dunlap was treated. Imagine encouraging your daughter to date, marry, and have your grandchildren with, somebody you believe could be a vicious killer."

"Racists breed, like everyone else. It's one way they keep their numbers up."

"Sick." Turning a page, Juanita read about a fight in the cafeteria in which Nutchell, Arnold, Simms, Tubbs and Gilroy had heaved various foods at each other, dodging and laughing the while. Fried okra, pickle slices, crackers, even condiments, had become missiles. Maizie's descriptive powers reached new heights as she told how the young men had looked with mustard dripping off their chins and splotching their shirts, how dollops of catsup had clashed with one boy's carroty hair.

Juanita felt her mouth go dry. According to Garvin McCoy, one of Luther Dunlap's kidnappers had had red hair.

The hue hadn't shown up in the black-and-white photos in the yearbook, of course. And people's tresses would look different in person now than in 1959. But knowing this lad's original hair color made many things fall into place. She saw now who must've been the ringleader among Dunlap's killers.

Althea seemed engrossed in a page of the Corbett journal. Juanita closed the Stevens notebook, her mind busy with implications of the new information.

One question that had bothered her was why Samuel Davis had been killed only recently, when he'd lived well over four decades with knowledge about Dunlap's death. Something must have happened in the recent past to change the dynamics, something important. Now Juanita thought she knew part of the answer. But how had her own investigation affected events, if it had?

She got up, left the alcove, and began to pace—a bit awkwardly with the cast—back and forth between the half-wall and a long, freestanding bookcase.

Had her research helped trigger Davis's murder, on the very day he would have talked to her? Had one or more of Dunlap's killers feared he'd tell her what he knew? If so, it seemed tragically ironic, since, according to Robert Norwood, Davis might not have told her anything useful anyway.

A footfall sounded behind Juanita. She froze, a sudden realization enveloping her.

God, he's here. The former redhead. He's come to kill me.

Thirty-Two

Claude Gilroy, pistol in hand, strode through the arch from the west wing, cowboy boots clomping on the wood floor now that their wearer wasn't trying to be quiet. The sight of his confident smile sickened Juanita, and she clutched at a shelf for support. Gilroy's prominent eyes narrowed as they looked around the reading room, resting first on Juanita, then widening as they reached Althea. Juanita felt as if a heavy weight had fallen on her.

"So—you're not alone after all, Wills," he said, as if struggling to process the information.

"What's going on?" Althea asked apprehensively.

"No need for . . . violence, Mr. Gilroy," Juanita said, forcing the words through her tight throat.

"I'll be the judge of that," he said smoothly, as if now adjusted to the new situation. "You haven't made this easy, Wills, sticking close to other people or to your own place. I decided I'd have to get at you here, if I could ever catch you alone. When I saw only your car out front tonight, I decided now was the time. Fooled me again, did you? But you won't live to enjoy it."

Althea's puzzled gaze moved from one to the other. Juanita

took two deep breaths, wincing at the pain from her cracked rib, and felt slightly more calm. She eased her right foot backwards and over, partly behind a bookcase.

"Bet you're Garvin McCoy's kid, aren't you?" Gilroy asked, turning more towards Althea.

She nodded slowly, understanding dawning in her eyes.

"What're you doing here so late?" he demanded. "Where's *your* car?" He rubbed at an eye, and for a moment his hand obscured his view of Juanita.

Impulsively, Juanita slipped behind the bookshelf. Pulse racing, she cowered there. Okay, what now?

Her heart thudded hard. She had acted rashly, with no plan. She had the library keys in her pocket, but even if she could make it to the front door, with its sticking lock she wouldn't be able to get it open quickly enough.

Anyway, she mustn't leave Althea alone with him, at his mercy.

"I'm doing . . . research," Althea quavered. "My car's . . . up the block a ways."

Juanita knew she had no choice. Slowly, reluctantly, she edged from behind the bookshelf. This time Gilroy noticed her movement.

"Oho, Wills, trying to be cute, are we?" Eyes narrowed and menacing, he walked towards her, his gun trained directly on her now.

Panic seized her again. Would he shoot her immediately, out of pique? Maybe kill both of them? Her legs rubbery, she grabbed a shelf for support.

Don't give up, Juanita, she told herself. *You're still alive, and so is Althea. Don't give him the satisfaction of giving up.*

If she could just remain calm enough to think straight—Taking another painful deep breath, she forced herself to stand upright and face Gilroy without flinching.

He grinned. "Now you get it, Wills—escape's not in the cards for you. Go join your friend there at the table."

Avoiding Gilroy's eyes, striving for dignity despite her anxiety, Juanita walked past him and along the alcove half-wall to the entry point. Inside it, she resumed her seat. A glance at Althea's face showed a mixture of fear, bewilderment, and suspicion. Did she think Juanita had tried to run out on her? Leave her to face Gilroy alone?

Uncomfortably, Juanita realized she'd considered doing just that.

"You're in bad company, Miss McCoy," Gilroy said. "Wills can't keep her nose out of other people's business." He rested his gun arm on the half-wall.

"I'm so sorry, Althea," Juanita said in a hushed voice. "I've . . . gotten myself into a mess . . . and you with me."

"Speak up," Gilroy said, cupping his left ear.

As Juanita repeated herself, her brain went into overdrive. Maybe she could take advantage of his hearing limitation. She had to keep him talking, buy time to plot strategy.

"How'd you . . . know . . . I'd be staying late tonight?" she quavered.

Gilroy chuckled grimly. "Gullible young Meador has been a great help. He's quite talkative."

Of course, Juanita thought. All that time the two men had spent together in the campaign had given Gilroy ample opportunity to pump Meador for information about library schedules and procedures, the staff's habits, her investigation. Her insides ached, as if her stomach and spine had knotted together. She took another deep breath—which hurt but helped calm her—and let it out slowly, mentally measuring the distance to the telephone on the circulation desk.

Too far. And her cell phone was in her handbag in an office desk drawer. If she could reach the fire alarm—set it off—but that was even farther away than the phone at the checkout counter.

"Let us go, Mr. Gilroy," she said. "We haven't . . . done anything to you."

"Not yet. But you would."

Just then, Juanita spied the recorder on the table near her right hand. Gilroy apparently hadn't seen it, since a stack of diaries blocked his view. The cassette was new, a long-playing one, and the interview with Althea wouldn't have used much space. If she could turn the device on without his noticing, she might at least leave a record of his conversation for the police.

"How'd you . . . get in here? Meador flipped the lock—on that side door when he left," she said, head-gesturing towards the west wing. "I heard him. "

Gilroy glanced towards the west exit, following her motion. In that instant, Juanita let both her hands slide forward on the table. Her right index finger found the recorder's control and activated it. There.

The tiny victory helped steady her nerves.

"Meador's very careless with his library keys," Gilroy said, looking back at her. "He left them on my secretary's desk once, and I volunteered to return them to him when we drove to a campaign event that evening."

"You made duplicates of them. And you killed Luther Dunlap," Juanita said, statements rather than questions. "You and Lonnie Tubbs and Vince Arnold."

Gilroy's eyebrows rose in surprise. "Meador hinted you were getting close, but he didn't seem to realize you'd figured it all out."

"I hadn't, till just before you walked in here tonight. You had red hair as a teenager, didn't you?"

He frowned. "What're you talking about, woman? Not that it matters now. Yes, it was the three of us, but I'm the one left with the chore of taking care of you. Vince never could be depended on for much. And going 'respectable' has made Lonnie cautious. Ironic, isn't it? He was the one driving that night, the one who actually killed Dunlap."

Gilroy with a gun in his hand looked unbeatable, Juanita thought. But she thought of another question to at least delay the inevitable. "Where's Vince Arnold gone? Did you kill him, too, to keep him from talking?"

Gilroy smiled. "Didn't have to. All it took was money and a bus ticket to Chicago. He hadn't squealed in over forty years, but I couldn't take the risk any longer. Not now."

"Because of your Senate campaign?"

"Exactly." Gilroy leaned heavily against the bookcase and was silent a few moments. "We didn't plan to kill Dunlap that night, you know," he finally went on. "Just humiliate the nigger."

"So what happened?"

"Lonnie was supposed to ease the car forward, give Dunlap a final scare before we cut him loose." Gilroy shook his head. "But Lonnie got caught up in the excitement and floorboarded it instead.

"I know you won't believe this, but I tried to make Lonnie stop. Vince was giggling like a maniac, though, and Lonnie just kept gunning the motor."

"And you three kept it quiet all these years." Juanita glanced at Althea, saw her eyes—anger now added to their mix of emotions—shift between her and Gilroy. What was she thinking? Wondering if Juanita would sacrifice her at the first opportunity? "At least let Althea go. She's no threat to you."

"Correction," he said, "she might not've known anything before, but she knows plenty now. She has to die too."

Althea's trembling hand covered her mouth. Juanita tried to smile reassuringly but knew her own worry must show in her face. Closing her eyes, she took another long breath, winced at the stab of pain, and issued a challenge.

"You don't dare kill us. Wayne would hunt you down like a chicken hawk after a fat hen."

"You put too much faith in your boyfriend, Wills. Lonnie and I have considerable influence in this part of the state. We can easily get Lieutenant Cleary fired."

Gilroy straightened and rubbed his back as if it had a crick from bending. "Now, let's go. Lonnie's old pickup's outside, same one I drove the night I shot at Martha. I have a farm outside town, with a secluded spot where no one'll ever find your bodies."

Renewed panic seized Juanita. Could she delay their leaving? As unsafe as the library now felt, it had to be better than some lonely pasture.

"Wait," she said, "you were shooting at—Martha? Not at me?"

"Too bad I missed. Where *is* she, anyway?"

"You don't know, either? Was Martha the witness? Did she see Dunlap's murder from her upstairs bedroom?"

"Nope." The query seemed to interest Gilroy, and he leaned his paunch on the half-wall again. "When we first decided to get Dunlap and take him to the track, I was hoping she'd be home. I wanted her to see him beg for his life. He wasn't such hot stuff then.

"But after things got out of hand, I was afraid she might've seen and would tell. I got her alone next day at school and asked enough questions to make sure she hadn't. Unfortunately, she guessed from them that I was involved. But I threatened her little sis, and that kept Martha quiet."

Gilroy passed a hand over his wavy white hair. "She had the gall to *mourn* that nigger. Not openly, but if you're nuts about a gal—if you watch her like I watched Martha—you can tell. Any time his death got mentioned—which was often, the rest of that school year—she'd go all quiet and inward. I finally saw her for what she was, a coon-lover, and went off her."

"Martha was Dunlap's girl? Not Grace?"

Gilroy laughed, a harsh braying sound. "Grace? She *wanted* to be his girl, but he was stuck on Martha. So Grace turned to his fellow nigger."

"Grace and . . . Samuel Davis were . . ."

"Lovers. Yeah. Story around school was, he called her his June Allyson. Ain't that just precious?"

Juanita's curiosity momentarily overcame her terror. "Then who did see the murder? Who was the white witness?"

"You haven't figured that out either? And you think you're a detective."

"If it wasn't Martha . . . or anyone in her family, it had to be . . . one of the young athletes. Someone there at the track . . . to practice. Was it Simon Simms?" A sudden thought struck Juanita. "Or Ward Nutchell?"

"You're not totally stupid, after all. Nutchell saw the whole thing from behind a bush. We paid him not to tell, for a while. But that got old. His body's buried on that same land where yours'll be. Lonnie's folks owned it then, but he got them to deed it to him. He later sold it to me—his first real-estate transaction."

"But I heard Nutchell went into the military without finishing high school."

"Lonnie and I put out that rumor. Soon it was 'common knowledge.'"

"So you weren't shooting at me that night. But what about my carnival 'accident'? You were behind that, weren't you?"

He grinned. "I bribed the regular ride operator not to show up for a shift, and my hand-picked replacement conveniently stepped in."

"And you hired someone to pose as a carnival advance man and hand Spinner tickets to your own secretary. But he must've given her many more than just the ones Meador got. That would've been too obvious."

"True. My secretary showed me the tickets he'd brought, and I instructed her to clip several bunches together for specific people—Meador included—to make sure those folks got some. Then when she was out of her office, I doodled on the backs of the stack she'd set aside for Meador. Ingenious, huh?"

Juanita frowned, pretending to work it out with difficulty.

"You told your ride operator to watch for two people of Wayne's and my descriptions, bearing tickets with triangles on the back. We'd be the ones he was to put in the 'special' car."

He chuckled. "You're fairly intelligent, Miss Wills, when someone helps you along some. I actually showed the operator your picture. Remember, I took one of you and Meador the night we went to Buffalo Flats?

"Too bad another carny noticed what was going on with the ride and rescued you." Gilroy motioned with the gun towards the west wing. "Okay, enough delay. Get up and walk that way."

Althea pushed her chair back. Juanita sat frozen, a memory flashing through her mind of a discussion she'd once had with Wayne about a convenience-store clerk's abduction and murder. He'd said that a kidnapper counted on his victim's passivity and that a smart person could turn that assumption against him. The young woman should have made a break for it before the crook got her into his car, Wayne had insisted.

"Easy to say when you're sitting cozily on my sofa drinking coffee," Juanita had objected.

Too bad Wayne wasn't here now to test his own theory, she thought.

"You too, Wills. Get up."

Juanita still hesitated, her brain pondering possible escape ploys. Maybe when they got outside she could yell and catch the attention of a quilter leaving the meeting. But Gilroy had said her car was the only one outside, so they must all have left already. Anyway, Gilroy could probably bundle his victims into the pickup and drive off before any of those middle-aged ladies reacted to a shouted appeal.

Ever so slowly, as in a dream, Althea began to rise.

Juanita thought about creating a diversion, to let her and Althea slip away into the darkness—

Darkness, that was a thought. Perhaps she could cut the lights and make a break before they went outside. The breaker box controlling electricity throughout the building was on a wall just inside the west wing. If she could get to it—

But she'd need to distract him first.

"Hurry up!" Gilroy commanded. "Both of you!"

Juanita imitated Althea's languidness in getting to her feet, mentally inventorying her pockets. A tissue or two. Her keyring. She hated to throw that, in case she'd get a chance to use a key and leave. Her eye fell on the small hand lotion bottle on the table. Hm-m, might do.

Althea was now walking towards the opening in the half-wall. During the second that her bulk blocked Gilroy's view, Juanita slid the bottle off the table and held it in the folds of her skirt. Silently, she followed Althea from the alcove. Gilroy fell in behind her.

Juanita started through the archway, paused, and turned—unhurriedly, to avoid startling him. "My car's outside," she reminded him in what she hoped was a calm voice. "Althea's, too. How'll you explain their being there all night?" As if intent on what she was saying, she stepped slowly backwards through the arch.

"Crap, Wills, nobody'll even suspect—"

Clutching the bottle by its neck, Juanita flung it at him, ducking and pushing Althea to one side almost in the same motion. The bottle struck his arm and jarred the weapon just as Gilroy squeezed off a round. The gun fell to the floor and skidded.

Juanita's hand found the light panel beside the archway and slapped its switches down. The bright overhead lights in the reading room and west wing went off, leaving only the low-wattage night light near the ceiling lit. Juanita heard, more than saw, Gilroy drop to the floor and grope for his gun. As she lurched towards the breaker box, her cast collided with a bookshelf. She caught herself mid-fall and staggered on.

She heard Gilroy scramble up and come after her as she yanked open the cover to the electrical box. She karate-chopped row after row of levers. The faint night light went out. The air-conditioner's hum ceased.

Juanita waited, listening. Gilroy seemed to have paused near the arch. A boot heel clattered as he started along the center aisle between the stacks. Then shuffling sounds—his attempts to tiptoe? Then a "clack"—his toe catching an upright? She realized he was moving towards the side door. Fortunately, his flashy boots were made for style, not stealth. He must have removed them when sneaking through the wing earlier, donning them again just before confronting her and Althea.

Speaking of Althea, where was she? Her tennis shoes would let her move quietly. Juanita eased her loafers off, pushing them with a stockinged toe under a shelf unit. Thank God for modern medical technology, she thought, for the noiseless bootie cast anchored to her injured foot with its Velcro band. An old-style metal cast would have been horribly noisy.

Whump. The sound, like a pillow hitting a wall, came from the corner nearest the arch. That must be Althea.

Silence. Then a heel clacked as Gilroy reversed course. The thumping sound must've been loud enough for him to hear.

Half-sliding on her shoeless feet, Juanita moved along the breaker-box wall and turned the corner. Slowly, spine rigid with tension, straining ears following Gilroy's movements, she progressed across the second wall. She heard no other sounds she could identify as Althea's.

Gilroy's progress stopped, then moved tentatively towards the breaker-box wall. Oh, no, Juanita thought, if he manages to turn the lights back on—

But he was unfamiliar with the building, would likely have a hard time locating the controls in the dark.

A thought flitted through Juanita's mind: Would Gilroy's shot have been heard outside, through the library's thick walls? Would any hearer have realized it was gunfire and even now be summoning help?

Iffy, she decided. Better not depend on that possibility. She wished she knew for certain whether he'd found his weapon after dropping it.

Gilroy evidently decided against pursuing his search for the breaker box. Juanita heard him turn again.

She reached the second corner and began her glide along the outside wall towards the exit. What would happen, she wondered, when Gilroy heard her open the door? If he realized one of his captives was fleeing, would he come charging after her with everything he had? The open door might let in enough light from outside to frame her silhouette.

Or—would he take out his rage on Althea? She was also unfamiliar with the library, and wouldn't easily find the side exit in the dark.

Juanita paused half a yard from the door, weighing options. Every instinct urged her to get out now, take what might be her best chance at freedom.

Yet . . . Althea . . .

Throat constricted with fright, Juanita forced herself to pass the exit, turn the third corner, and head back towards the archway, where she had last heard Althea. Could she somehow locate her in the dark—a black woman, wearing navy blue—and lead her to safety? Unlikely, Juanita thought.

But her eyes were adjusted to the darkness now, and she realized something: The blackness wasn't absolute. The wide, nearly opaque window near the ceiling let in weak rays of some luminescence—moonlight or radiance from the house next door—that picked out edges of metal shelves and showed bulky lines of bookcases. By straining her eyes, she could occasionally discern what must be Gilroy's shimmery shirt moving several yards away. She guessed he was soft-toeing towards the same corner she was bound for. Something glinted at about his waist level. A belt buckle? Or the gun?

Unsure how well her own red blouse and pale skin reflected light, Juanita eased behind a shelf unit. She peered carefully around it, still hoping to spot Althea. But that seemed impossible in such paltry light.

Juanita's searching eyes caught a glint from something on a nearby carrel, about where the beige extension phone would be. Of course! She had forgotten the seldom-used telephone, but it seemed a godsend now. Her trembling fingers found the smooth plastic and lifted the receiver from its cradle. Juanita paused, heard the clomping of Gilroy's boots two aisles away.

Shaking with haste and fear, she found the buttons by feel and pushed the "9" once and the "1" twice. If only her hearing-impaired pursuer wouldn't notice the tiny beeps. A dispatcher answered. Juanita started to whisper her need for help, but at that moment she heard a thump from the next aisle over, near the arch.

Could that be Althea? Or had Gilroy moved there now? She peered at the place where she'd heard the sound, hoping his shirt would catch the light and reveal his position. Unfortunately, she could make out nothing.

Perspiring in non-air-conditioned stuffiness, Juanita laid the receiver gently on the carrel, leaving the line open to reveal her location. She listened, heard Gilroy moving now, near where the thud had sounded. Juanita cringed. Was he about to grab Althea?

Impulsively, Juanita seized a couple of hardbacks from a shelf and heaved one in his direction. The other she tossed at the side door.

He stopped, as if unsure what was happening. Juanita looked back at where the arch would be, saw something glittery a few feet off the floor. It moved a yard or so, then disappeared. That must be Althea's bracelet.

Juanita grabbed more books and, hoping to confuse Gilroy further, threw them in all directions, some hitting shelves, others walls.

A shot rang out! Her heart skipped a beat. So he *had* found the gun.

He fired again, the bullet pinging off a bookshelf and slamming into a wall or a book. Juanita realized a wild shot could kill her or Althea. She crouched behind a shelf unit, wishing she knew how many bullets he had. But this wasn't the Old West, where a six-shooter was dependably empty after firing half a dozen times.

Eerie quiet descended. Juanita dared poke her head from behind the shelves. She no longer saw the glimmer of the bracelet, anywhere. Had Althea been shot? Was she now lying on the floor? Juanita's heart plunged at the thought. But maybe Althea had felt her way back to the reading room. Plenty of hiding places there. And beyond it lay the bathrooms, the east wing, the upstairs, lots of concealment possibilities.

No way to know. And if Althea had been hit, she might be needing medical help. Juanita decided she had to leave now. Only, where was Gilroy?

She heard his boots, then saw the reflection of his shirt a few yards away. He seemed to be moving uncertainly back towards the arch, pausing occasionally. Juanita eased towards the side exit, careful to keep shelf units between herself and him.

Moments of stealthy movement later, she found herself within a yard of the door. Just then, her injured shoulder connected hard with a metal upright.

"Umpf," she said involuntarily.

A bullet splintered the wall behind her. She lunged for the doorknob, twisted it, felt it turn. She shoved it open and flung herself through.

On the doorsill, she stumbled and fell. Something pliable and hairy, yet strong, caught her.

It felt like a human arm.

Thirty-Three

The west door shut with a sigh.

"It's okay, babe, I've got you." Wayne held Juanita and smoothed her hair with a big paw.

As she struggled to make her throat work, he continued. "What's going on? Somebody dialed 911 from here, and I was cruising in the vicinity. Didn't see any lights on, and the front and east doors're locked. But your car's out front."

"Oh, Wayne—I'm so glad—" Juanita gasped. She pointed at the door. "Gilroy—in there—with a gun. Althea's—don't know where—or if—she—"

Wayne asked a couple of quick questions, which Juanita answered with lips that trembled. Then he unhooked his cell phone from his belt. He requested backup on the potential hostage situation at the library, ended the call, and asked for more details about the scene inside

"Don't suppose you have your library keys on you?" he said.

"Actually, I do. Glad I didn't throw them at Gilroy." Feeling a bit calmer, Juanita took the keys from her pocket and handed them over.

"Great! Glad you didn't, either. Which way'd give the best chance to catch him off guard?"

Juanita considered. "The main door sticks. The rear one opens easily—from outside *or* inside—but the back hallway's full of boxes. East door. Yeah, that'd be best."

Wayne eyed the thin crescent peeking through clouds overhead. "Wimpy moon tonight." He took a flashlight from his belt. "Hope I don't have to use this. Maybe those big windows in the reference and reading rooms'll let in some light. Which key's the east door? Okay, now you stay—"

He broke off as a squad car pulled up in front and two uniformed officers got out. Wayne waved them over, and the three conferred in low tones. Then he turned to Juanita.

"Okay, Ted'll be on this door. Ron'll disable that pickup, then guard the east door after I've gone in. Just in case, I want you watching the back. Don't try to be a hero—keep out of sight, but yell if Gilroy comes out." Wayne hurried eastward along the front wall, while the other men carried out their assignments.

Juanita took up her post behind a large tree a few yards from the back door. Light streaming from next door revealed that one of its branches, broken off a bigger limb, was hanging by a few fibers. She twisted it free and brandished it like a cudgel. It wouldn't be much good against a loaded gun, but having any sort of weapon made her feel better.

Then she decided the tree was too far from the door. Clutching the branch, she crept behind a low bush nearer the stoop. Her shoulder ached from colliding with the bookcase.

Time passed at the pace of a lethargic snail. Juanita rose cautiously, stretched to relieve her back and legs, and crouched again.

Anxiety for Wayne crowded out other thoughts. She trusted his judgment, intelligence, and strength, but Gilroy was desperate and unpredictable. *Be safe, Wayne,* she silently pleaded.

How could she have been so irritated at him earlier? At the

moment, she couldn't recall what had ticked her off.

And Althea. Was she okay? She didn't deserve—

Popping noises came from the building. Shots? *Oh, God,* Juanita thought. Who's shooting? Who's hit?

The back door burst open, and boots struck the concrete stoop. Struggling for balance, boxes of all sizes surging around him, Claude Gilroy tottered out. At sight of his pistol, fear clutched Juanita again.

But she couldn't let him get away. Leaving her cover, she heaved the branch at him as hard as she could. It hit his hip and knocked him further askew. He sprawled on the ground, his weapon firing into the tree.

"Here's Gilroy! Help!" Juanita shrieked with all her might.

She threw herself onto the killer's back and pounded his right hand till his fingers released the gun.

Wayne dashed out the back door and paused to catch his breath. Juanita heard him whistle under his breath. He ambled over and picked up Gilroy's weapon.

"Okay, Officer Wills," he drawled. "You can let him up."

She got to her feet and took a painful deep breath. Gilroy reluctantly rose. The other two officers arrived, and one handcuffed the prisoner.

"Thank God you're okay, Wayne," Juanita said, throwing her arms about him.

"What about you? Did you hurt yourself?"

"I'll be okay. What about Althea? You see or hear her anywhere?"

"Nope. You guys take Gilroy in. I'll check around inside and secure the scene. Let's go look for her, babe."

Using Wayne's flashlight, Juanita and Wayne picked their way through mounds of scattered cartons in the back hall.

"I thought I knew a lot of cuss words," Wayne said. "But when Gilroy stumbled into that mess, he let fly with some new ones."

"So Meador's procrastination finally paid off," she said. "Too bad Gilroy was able to get the back door open, but that lever's easy to turn."

They went through the reading room into the west wing, where Juanita opened the breaker box and restored power throughout the building. The air-conditioner started to hum.

Shielding her eyes from the sudden blaze of light, Juanita called, "Althea! You okay? Where are you?"

No response.

"Wayne, if she's been killed, it's all my fault."

He put an arm around Juanita. "She may be fine, just hiding somewhere, scared half to death."

They looked among the stacks and carrels in the west wing. Flung books lay everywhere, but no Althea.

"I don't see any blood," Juanita said. "That's a good sign, isn't it?"

"For sure."

Juanita found her shoes under the shelf and put them on. Then they checked the reading room, restrooms, reference room, and east stacks, Juanita occasionally shouting Althea's name. All were empty.

They climbed the stairs to the second story, Juanita stopping at the top to call out again. "Althea! It's Juanita and Police Lieutenant Cleary. Please answer."

Althea appeared from behind a bookshelf. "Where's Gilroy?" she asked fearfully.

"He's in police custody," Wayne assured her.

"Thank heavens," Althea said with a sob. "When the lights came on, I was afraid—"

"—he had turned them on," Juanita said. "I know." She lightly touched Althea's arm. "And when the gunfire started downstairs, you wouldn't have known who was shooting, or at what."

"When I first heard you calling my name, I didn't know but what Gilroy was making you do it."

The women exchanged looks. Then, as with one thought, they

clasped their arms around each other—tentatively at first, then in a bear hug.

"Glad you're okay, Miss McCoy. Now, I've got things to do." Wayne turned to go.

Althea grabbed his hand and shook it. "Lieutenant Cleary. You've been out to see my dad a couple of times, haven't you? Thanks so much for your help tonight."

"You're welcome." He shook hands with her and gave Juanita a level look, as if challenging her to comment.

She decided it was a good time to keep silent.

"You'll both need to come down to the station and make a statement." Wayne started downstairs.

"Wait a sec, Wayne," Juanita called. She told him where to find the incriminating tape of her conversation with Gilroy.

"Sounds promising," he said. "Thanks, Juanita."

After he left, the women looked at each other.

"I don't know about you, Althea," Juanita said, "but I'm still shaky. How about something to drink before we go down to give our statements?"

Althea smiled. "Sounds good."

Juanita started down the steps. "There are soft drinks in the fridge, or I can make coffee."

"Water's fine," Althea said, following her. "Research can sure be tiring, can't it?"

"Yep. But then, my doctor says I'm not the fittest person alive."

"Doctors, what do they know?"

"Actually, mine's okay. Just wish she didn't give me such sage, and unwelcome, advice."

"What diet're you on? I've tried 'em all."

"Me too. Dr. Sweeney recommends not cutting out anything, though, just trimming portions, especially of fats and sweets. Even that's tough when you love food." Juanita grinned wickedly. "But frankly, when I landed on top of Gilroy tonight, I was glad of every ounce I weighed."

Althea's smile conveyed a new comradeship based on shared danger. "Wish I could've added my pounds to yours."

Juanita unlocked her office and filled plastic glasses with ice from the refrigerator under the worktable and water from the sink on the back wall. They sat at the table.

"Thanks, Juanita," Althea finally said. "And not just for the water. You probably could've gotten out earlier if it'd just been yourself to consider."

"It was my fault you were in Gilroy's clutches. You had tried to convince me to butt out."

"Good thing you didn't listen! Now maybe justice will get done, for both Luther and Samuel." Althea lifted her glass in a toast. "To your tenacity, Juanita Wills."

"Thanks. Not everyone appreciates that quality of mine. But lots of people helped, including you and your dad."

She added casually, "I'm especially grateful to Robert Norwood. He came up with useful sources and wouldn't let me quit."

A half-smile softened Althea's features. "Yeah, Robert's all right."

"He told me you'd refused to go out with him. What's the deal with that?"

"You *are* a snoop, aren't you?" Althea grinned to take the edge off. "Actually, Robert caught me at a bad time. I'd just heard from my ex that he was refusing to give me back some things I'd stored in our attic and forgotten. The house belonged to his folks before we married, and he got it in our divorce. He's since returned my stuff, but that day I was off all men, for sure.

"I've kicked myself about turning Robert down, though. And he doesn't have the gumption to ask me out again."

"You could ask him."

"I like a guy to do that part."

"Then at least give him a clue—or I will. Most men are terrible at mind-reading."

"I'll think about it." Althea got up and put her empty glass in the sink, then sat again. "Sorry if I was a hard-ass before. My ex is a white guy. I know that doesn't mean all whites are jerks, but plenty of you are."

"No argument there. But plenty of us try not to be, too. I guess we're all too inclined to make assumptions based on race. With most things, it doesn't matter."

"But racial pride's important, too."

"True. It's a hard balance to strike, isn't it?"

"You got that right."

Thirty-Four

The women drove both their cars to the station and gave statements to a detective. Then Althea hugged Juanita and left. Juanita waited in the detectives' room, drinking decaf Wayne had brewed for her, until he at last returned and plopped down in his desk chair.

"What a night." He tilted back and stretched his arms above his head.

"I'm so glad you weren't hurt, Wayne. And I've realized how lucky I was that Gilroy didn't pull out a flashlight and locate the breaker box. Who was doing the shooting just before he ran out, Wayne—you or him?"

"Both. Neither of us did any real damage. As for the light, it's also a good thing Gilroy's not a smoker, with a cigarette lighter or matches handy."

"Where were you when Gilroy spotted you?"

"Reading room. The light was dim there, but you could make out objects. He thought he'd shot you and had gone back in there to search for Althea. I was pretty quiet and managed to get halfway across the room before he saw me."

"Gilroy has a slight hearing problem, which probably

helped."

"Yeah, I noticed. Anyway, he fired at me and started running for the back door at the same time, weaving around so I couldn't get in a good shot." Wayne chuckled. "Gilroy probably had no trouble with your back door lock—even in the dark, those old levers are easy to find and twist—but he sure didn't expect the piles of boxes."

"Guess I won't bug Meador for a while about putting things off."

"It wasn't easy for me to get through there either, though—especially after Gilroy knocked the stacks all cockeyed."

"Wayne, I've been wondering something: Did Gilroy somehow know Samuel Davis was planning to talk to me that day? Is that why he killed him?"

"According to Gilroy, that was coincidental. He'd known for years from a source in the police department that Davis had tried to give evidence in '59, and Gilroy finally decided to eliminate him as a risk."

"What a relief to know I wasn't responsible for his death."

"Um—in a sense, you were. Partly. Gilroy knew you were doing that history, and he'd heard about your reputation for nosiness, so that made him more nervous." Wayne leaned forward, elbow on desk. "But the real impetus for killing Davis at that time was Gilroy's political ambition."

Juanita nodded. "With a senatorial job at stake, he could no longer take a chance Davis would keep quiet. Yet he left Arnold and Tubbs alive. They both knew."

"But they were involved themselves, of course. Tubbs also had a profitable business and a standing in the community to protect. As for Arnold, Gilroy knew money, loyalty, and wariness of the law would keep him mum. But he did take the precaution of sending Arnold away. I've alerted the Chicago authorities to be on the lookout for him. We have Tubbs in custody now."

"Good. He's the one who actually killed Dunlap, according to

Gilroy."

"Yeah. It's good you found that out and got it on record—gave us something to go at Tubbs with. Don't let this go to your head, Juanita, but you did ask some helpful questions on that tape."

Juanita smiled tiredly. "Good to hear you admit it. If I weren't so wiped out, I'd leap for joy. Did Gilroy have something against Grace, Wayne? He sure implicated her with that poisoned bread."

"He never liked her, considered her stuck-up, but mainly she was someone he could use. Her habit of distributing food randomly was ready-made for a poisoner. It wasn't too hard for him to get hold of one of her labels, as much food as she's given out over the years."

"Poor Grace. This may unhinge her even further. Especially since I suspect Davis was the father of a baby she had out of wedlock years ago."

"He was. She went to Kansas City, to a place Phyllida Campbell had heard of, where they didn't ask too many questions. After the baby was born, Phyllida and Grace brought it back to Bryson's Corner, and Davis found some neighbors to bring up the kid. He and Grace decided that, for their own safety and the boy's, they'd end their relationship and keep his parentage secret."

"It's sad what fear can do to lives, isn't it?" Juanita rubbed her tired eyes. "I recall Grace was married briefly. She said it didn't take."

"That was in the mid-sixties. She was trying to have a normal life, but the husband found out about her half-black child and skedaddled. She became more and more reclusive, then hit on the idea of delivering food around the area so she could sometimes catch glimpses of Davis and Corinthian."

"Pretty devious. So the 'crazy lady' image was one she cultivated?"

"At first. But they say you become what you pretend to be. And Grace does seem to have problems with reality. But she's not as loopy as people think. Emotionally scarred, but a canny old girl."

"Gilroy could be sure Davis would eat that poisoned bread," Juanita mused, "with Grace's name attached. So in a way she *was* responsible for her former lover's death. Gilroy must've loved that bit of irony."

Juanita finished her fourth cup of decaf and stretched. "Ouch, that wasn't good for my rib. I guess Ruth the Sleuth really solved the Davis murder for you. If not for her, you wouldn't have thought to have a test run for corn cockle, would you?"

"True. I'd suspected homicide already, of course, because of Davis's tie to that old case. And I probably should've remembered my granddad telling about losing livestock to corn-cockle poisoning one summer, but I didn't. Now that Ruth's suggestion has helped solve the Davis murder, as well as clearing the old Dunlap file, she'll be hard to live with."

"You cops probably need to be reminded occasionally that you don't know everything."

"We get reminders enough, thanks."

"Hm. You know, Phyllida seems to have been a much better friend to Grace than I realized. I wonder how Martha's doing. Wish I knew if she's okay."

"She is."

Juanita's eyes flew wide. "You know where Martha went?"

"She's at Grace Hendershot's. I went over to question Grace again yesterday, and she came out to meet me before I could knock. From her manner, it seemed there was something inside she didn't want me to see. We kept talking, and I finally got her to admit Martha was there."

"So you've spoken to Martha?"

"Yeah. Actually, she seemed relieved I'd found out she was there. Said she'd asked you about me some time back, wondering if she could safely confide in me. By the way, I was glad to hear you said yes."

"Yet it was Grace she went to. Why?"

"Couple of reasons. First, Martha knew she could trust *her.* They kept secrets for each other years ago, when both were seeing black guys—a huge no-no in those days. Second, people think Grace is half nuts and leave her alone." He leaned back in his chair. "Martha returned to Wyndham with the idea of finally getting the truth out about Dunlap's death. It's haunted her all these years.

"Immediately after it happened, she wondered if Gilroy could've been involved, since she knew he liked her and was crazy jealous of Dunlap. Then when Gilroy kept asking where she'd been that night, what time she got home, and so on, she felt pretty sure he'd helped kill Dunlap."

"You said exposing the truth was her intention when she came home. But when she was with me, she didn't seem to be trying to do that. What happened to change her mind?"

"She learned what a big man Gilroy was in state politics and lost her nerve. Incidentally, it was *her* he meant to shoot that night, not you."

"So Gilroy said. But how'd he even know she was in Wyndham? She hardly went out of the house. And Meador hadn't told him, because that shooting happened before the two of them got chummy. For that matter, how'd Martha know Gilroy was the one who fired that shot?"

"They saw each other the night of the Ralston fire. He heard about it on his police scanner and drove by to check it out, since his agency insures the house next door. She knew he'd figure out why she was back. That attempt on her life scared her even more about exposing her connection to Dunlap."

"That's why she liked staying with me. She could keep up with what I learned as I learned it."

"Partly. However, she genuinely likes you. She hadn't worried about your safety, since she knew it was her Gilroy meant to shoot—and because you seemed able to take care of yourself."

Wayne grimaced. "Doesn't seem so to me sometimes, but she thought so, at least. When news of your 'accident' hit the media, she was frightened for both of you. Part of her decision to go to Grace's when she did was thinking you'd be safer without her around.

"She called the hospital a couple times to see how you were, but someone else answered your phone and she lost her nerve. Grace tried to call there once, too, but hung up before you answered."

"Thanks for telling me that. I'd wondered, especially about Martha."

"I called tonight to tell them we've arrested both Gilroy and Tubbs. They were thrilled, of course. Martha said she's thinking of staying around a while."

"Great!" Juanita was silent a moment. "But if you learned from Martha yesterday that Gilroy was probably guilty, why didn't you arrest him then? Why was he still free tonight to come after Althea and me?"

"I didn't have everything nailed down yet. Before arresting somebody as important as Gilroy, you'd better have the i's dotted and the t's crossed. But I was closing in on him. What you found out tonight, plus testimony from you and Althea, makes the case pretty strong. Even though he did 'lawyer up' after a while and quit talking."

Juanita stifled a yawn. "Another thing I don't understand, Wayne. Several people have told me you've talked to them about that old murder. Why were you looking into it after all this time?"

"The case intrigued me when a fellow cop mentioned it shortly after I came to Wyndham. I read the file and, as I could spare time from other cases, I talked to people mentioned in it. Didn't turn up much that was new at first, so I put the file aside.

"Then a few weeks ago, an anonymous call came in to 911, saying the Wyndham Police needed to look at that old murder again. The caller mentioned people we should talk to that hadn't been named in the file, including Lonnie Tubbs, Vince Arnold, and Simon Simms."

"You figure out who the anonymous tipster was?"

"Not for sure, but it was a man. My guess is it was Simms. Guilty conscience. He seemed relieved to be questioned about that old case. I talked to Tubbs and Arnold too, but they gave me very little, as you could probably figure. It was hit-or-miss finding Arnold, much as he moved around, and I didn't have enough on him to arrest him. He's apparently been homeless quite a few years.

"I went back through old yearbooks, too—the set at the high school, so you wouldn't guess what I was doing—and questioned others who were around then. One or two mentioned having seen Gilroy with Tubbs and Arnold sometimes, so I started looking at him, too. And I got bits and pieces of information out at Bryson's Corner.

"Eventually Martha's name surfaced in the conversations."

"So why's there nothing about those recent interviews in your file on the Dunlap case? Why's the folder so thin?"

Wayne took keys from his pocket and opened the bottom right drawer of his desk. He took out a folder bulging with papers and held it aloft.

"This look skimpy to you?"

At first, Juanita didn't comprehend. "What do you—what are you saying, Wayne?"

"This is the Dunlap file. The real one. It includes interviews with several people at Bryson's Corner, including Samuel Davis and Leona Brown—plus records of my *attempts* to question Garvin McCoy—and also several folks in Wyndham and elsewhere."

"Cecil Brompton, among others?"

Wayne nodded.

"You—you—you set me up! That's a fake in your cabinet over there."

"Yep. I originally divided the file because somebody in the

department had been loose-lipped enough to leak the Davis autopsy results. For a while, I kept two files on all the more sensitive cases. We've now identified and reprimanded that person. But since you'd asked to see the Dunlap records, I figured it was just a matter of time before you finagled a way to do so. I kept the two Dunlap folders and went along with your phantom-car-noise ploy."

"You devious son of a—"

"Language, language. You are in a police station, you know." He winked and grinned. "Besides, it takes one to know one."

"Touché." Juanita leaned across the desk and smiled her most seductive smile. "Wayne, just think how much we could learn if we worked together, instead of against each other."

He crossed his arms as if defending against her come-hither approach. "Me investigate a case with you as my assistant? No way."

"That wasn't the command structure I had in mind."

Wayne lifted his eyes to the ceiling. Juanita thought she saw him shudder.

Epilogue

Martha and Mavis didn't become inseparable buddies overnight, but the realization she'd almost lost her older sister a second time seemed to diminish Mavis's lingering resentment. Martha moved into her sister's home but after a few days called Juanita to ask if she'd be interested in renting her a room. She had gotten a job as receptionist in a dental office, Martha said, and suggested a monthly rental fee. The figure was more than fair, based on what Juanita knew of room rates in Wyndham.

"Besides paying you rent," Martha said, "I'll cook as often as you'll let me. Of course, if you'd rather have your house to yourself, I'll understand."

"Are you kidding? I'll never get a better offer. But would that be okay with your sister? I'm not her favorite person."

Martha chuckled. "You haven't exactly said so, but I suspect it's mutual. Mavis'll be fine with it. I told her I'd realized that having me there makes her place too cramped, especially when her kids and grandkids come to visit, so I was thinking of asking you about renting a room. She said I can stay with them as long as I like, but I think she's secretly glad I might be moving out."

"Then, welcome, housemate. Bring your stuff over whenever

you like."

Juanita smiled to herself one day a few weeks later to see Althea and Robert walking hand in hand along a downtown street. A couple of days later, she read in the newspaper the announcement of Phyllida Campbell's marriage to Simon Simms.

Most heartening of all was a visit from Grace Hendershot one Saturday morning about two months after the arrest of Gilroy and Tubbs. Standing straighter than usual in a sprightly pink dress, Grace had a sparkle in her eyes that made her look almost pretty. The roses in her cheeks seemed due more to happiness than to rouge.

"Something's happened, Juanita, that I want to tell you about," Grace said as they took chairs in Juanita's living room. "I've been thinking a lot lately about Samuel's death, and Luther's, and Martha coming back, and you nearly getting killed, and I decided I had to make the most of what time I have left."

Juanita watched the play of emotions over her visitor's face. Grace was more lucid and engaged than she had ever seen her. Had the solving of the old murder case, at last, made this huge difference?

"I drove to Broken Arrow about a month ago, to Tractor Supply," Grace went on. "I was shaking, I was so scared. But I walked right in and went right up to Corinthian. He didn't recognize me—how could he?—but I told him my name and said I was a friend of his mother's. His real mother."

"Oh, Grace, how brave of you!"

"Well, he looked kind of worried, but also excited," Grace continued, her voice less steady now. "He said it was about his lunch time, so I must join him and tell him everything I could remember about her.

"I almost lost it right then, Juanita, thinking 'what have I gotten myself into?' I went with him, though—couldn't think of an excuse, then, not to—but the whole time we were walking down the street to a café, I kept thinking how mad he'd probably get when I told him the truth. I tried to think up a good story about how his mother had died in childbirth or something.

"But then we sat down in a booth and the waitress brought our iced tea and he looked at me with those big, trusting eyes—just like Samuel's—and I knew I couldn't tell any more lies."

A sob shook the gentle woman. She buried her head in her hands and wept. Juanita slid an arm around the frail body and patted the thin shoulder, thinking that at a time she needed comforting words to say she was, for once, speechless.

At last, Grace raised her head, eyes streaming, and smiled.

"I just blurted it all out, told Corinthian he was the son of Samuel Davis—he'd read in the papers about Samuel's . . . death . . . and how it related to Luther Dunlap's—and then I said I was his mother. His face—he looked stricken, Juanita. I was sure he'd throw me out.

"But he just kept sitting there, looking at me like he was trying to take it in. Finally, I decided he probably needed to be alone and started to leave. But he—he put out a hand and stopped me. He stopped me, Juanita." Another sob burst from Grace's throat.

Juanita held her breath, giving the fragile shoulder a supportive squeeze.

"He asked . . . asked me not to go without answering some questions. Oh, he asked so many questions, Juanita. And why wouldn't he? I answered them all, didn't try to whitewash my part in things. Told him I'd longed to raise him myself, that giving him up cut me at the heart, but I'd been so afraid—for Samuel, for myself, most of all for our dear little baby . . . ."

Grace smiled a watery smile, tears coursing unheeded down her cheeks. "Finally, Corinthian—Cory—had to get back to work. He says his full name always sounds strange to him, though he uses it on anything official, because he's always gone by Cory.

"He thanked me for telling him the truth, finally. Said it was a shock, but he'd wondered about his parentage. He was very young when he went to live with the Harrisons, and evidently they discouraged the Grangers from trying to see him, so his memory of his earlier life is shadowy. He did know he was part black, but the Harrisons encouraged him to 'pass,' and his skin and features were such that he could.

"Corinthian told me he'd have to think about our conversation—it was a lot to take in. But he wrote down my phone number in case he'd want to call some time with more questions."

"That's good, at least," Juanita said, forcing heartiness into her tone.

Grace nodded. "I thought I wouldn't hear from him again. But then he called me yesterday. He asked if I could come over to Buffalo Flats today. And I'm going." Her voice acquired a hushed, awed quality. "Juanita, Corinthian has asked me to meet his family."

"Oh, Grace. Grace, that's wonderful."

"I'm scared, real scared. As much as before I first went to see him. Corinthian—Cory—says he thought about things for a long time, and finally decided he must own up to *all* his heritage, even the part the Harrisons taught him to despise and deny. So he told his wife—Sandra, who's white—and his son, Todd. Sandra took it better than he'd expected. And the Harrisons are both gone now, so he didn't have to confront them.

"But his son, Todd, is having a hard time with the news."

From what she'd seen of the youngest Granger, Juanita could imagine how much he'd enjoyed learning his grandfather had been African-American. Still, he needed to know the truth. It might even make him question his own attitude about people of color, eventually.

If it didn't make him even more hostile.

"Seems Todd endured teasing as a kid for having curly hair and full lips," Grace went on. "He looks more like Samuel, I gather, than like me or his mother, more even than Corinthian does. And Corinthian says he realizes now they could've helped Todd more to deal with the taunting if they'd encouraged him to value people of all races. Instead, they simply assured him he had no African-American blood—Sandra because she didn't know, and Corinthian because the habit of 'passing' was by then well ingrained."

"Sounds like Todd's a troubled young man," Juanita said. "I hope they'll get counseling for him."

"He may not talk to me today, I know," Grace said, swallowing hard. "But I'll at least have met my grandson. And maybe some day, he will."

Tempered as Grace's news was with the worry over Todd, it was still the best Juanita had heard for a while. At the very least, making contact with her son had changed Grace's life for the better.

"I'm happy for you, Grace. Thanks so much for telling me."

The slender woman smiled a slow smile. "I also need to let Corinthian—Cory—know he has a half-brother in Florida. Maybe I'll even meet Samuel's other son myself some day." She stared past Juanita, her eyes moist but full of hope. "But one step at a time."

"One step at a time. Right."

That evening Juanita and Wayne went to dinner in Tulsa, then found a florist shop open late and bought a single long-stemmed red rose. They swung by the Wyndham High School athletic field, and, as before, Wayne waited at the gate while Juanita strolled around the track. She held the rose near her face, sniffing its sweet perfume, until she reached the far end of the oval. There, she stood looking up at what had been Martha Haney's bedroom window. Dark now.

Juanita turned, looked around at the athletic field. Of course, there had been changes since 1959—more lights added, for one thing—but she could visualize the scene then, when four young men, one black, three white, had become forever linked by an unspeakable act.

In the white boys' eyes, Luther Dunlap had been a threat to them because of who and what he was: strong, fast, vital, handsome, engaging. Black.

Cocky, too, she thought, as the young often are—not having yet grasped their relative unimportance among the billions populating the planet.

And yet individual lives make a difference, she amended. Dunlap's had. People in Bryson's Corner and Wyndham would remember him, some with pain, others with guilt or with anger.

But some with fondness. Juanita herself hadn't known him, yet she would now carry in her mind the picture of a brash but likable young man, gallantly bestowing a flower on a young lady.

Juanita took a final whiff of the rose, leaned over, and laid it on the track at about the spot where Luther Dunlap had breathed his last.

AUTHOR'S NOTES

I gratefully acknowledge assistance from the following:

Charles Stiefer, retired Captain of the Durant (Oklahoma) Police Force and retired Supervisor of Communications for the City of Durant and Bryan County, who made possible my portrayal of Wayne's workplace and job;

Dr. Angela Latham, Denison, TX, who advised me about Juanita's injuries and treatment;

Hannibal B. Johnson, Esq., whose book *Acres of Aspiration: The All-Black Towns in Oklahoma* helped me create Bryson's Corner;

Dr. Constance Taylor, Professor Emeritus of Biology, Southeastern Oklahoma State University, Durant, OK, who told me about corn cockle;

The staff of Morrison Drug, Durant, OK, who let me "try out" Juanita's cast.